FRANKENSTEIN IN BAGHDAD

'Ahmed Saadawi has wrenched a fable ... Romantic myth to urgent new use... In their bicentenary year, Mary Shelley's scientist and his creature will take plenty of contemporary spins. Surely, no updated journey will be more necessary than Saadawi's... A nightmarish, but horridly hilarious, tale... Sinister, satirical, ferociously comi oddly moving.'   ***Spe***

'A darkly delightful nove... Detective story and satire as gothic horror, *Frankenstein in Baghdad* provides a trag take on a society afflicted by fear, and a parable conc responsibility and justice.'   ***New Star***

'Saadawi's novel. is more than an extended metaphor interminable carnage in Iraq and the precarious na its body politic. It also intimately depicts the lives o affected by the conflict [and] offer[s] a glimpse into the day-to-day experiences of a society fractured by bloodshed.'
Economist

'In the 200 years since Mary Shelley wrote *Frankenstein*, her monster has turned up in countless variations – but few of them have been as wild or politically pointed as the monster in Ahmed Saadawi's *Frankenstein in Baghdad*.' ***New York Times***

'Helped by Jonathan Wright's elegant and witty translation, which reaches for and attains bracing pathos, Saadawi's novel mixes a range of characters and their voices to surprising, even jolting effect...a remarkable book.'   ***Observer***

'[*Frankenstein in Baghdad*] is more than just a black comedy. It's as much of a crossbreed as its ghoulish hero – part thriller, part horror, part social commentary... Saadawi, slickly translated by Jonathan Wright, captures the atmosphere of war-torn Baghdad with the swiftest of penstrokes, and picks out details that make the reader feel, and even taste, the aftermath of the explosions that pepper the book.'

Financial Times

'*Frankenstein in Baghdad* is complex but very readable and darkly humorous; it has well-observed characters, whose back stories reflect the wider context. The monster is a metaphor both for the physical horrors of Iraq, and for the development of groups within that chaos. The translation by Jonathan Wright is first-rate.' ***Times Literary Supplement***

'[Saadawi is] Baghdad's new literary star.' ***New York Times***

'A fantastical manifestation of war's cruelties... Saadawi blends the unearthly, the horrific and the mundane to terrific effect... There's a freshness to both his voice and vision... What happened in Iraq was a spiritual disaster, and this brave and ingenious novel takes that idea and uncorks all its possible meanings.' ***New York Times Book Review***

'*Frankenstein in Baghdad* gives an intimate, tragicomic look at the Iraq War through the lens of a small neighbourhood in U.S.-occupied Baghdad... Come for the fascinating plot; stay for the dark humour and devastating view of humanity.'

Washington Post

'A bold literary conceit and executed with some aplomb.'

Mail on Sunday

'One of the best novels to emerge from the catastrophe of the Iraq War... Extraordinary... Earthy and vibrant... There are striking continuities with the original Shelley novel... Saadawi's monster in *Frankenstein in Baghdad* is a hybrid creature for our times. It is a desperate marker of the brutal violence that has taken countless lives in the wars unleashed in the region... But *Frankenstein in Baghdad* is also a sign that the imagination can still survive in these conditions, literary works flowering in the cracks of the rubble.'

Los Angeles Review of Books

'This adroitly written literary fiction ingeniously blends absurdist horror with a mordantly funny satire about life in a war-torn city... Extraordinary in its scope and inventiveness.'

Irish Times

'There is no shortage of wonderful, literate *Frankenstein* reimaginings...but few so viscerally mine Shelley's story for its metaphoric riches... In graceful, economical prose, Saadawi places us in a city of ghosts, where missing people return all the time, justice is fleeting, and even good intentions rot... A haunting and startling mix of horror, mystery, and tragedy.'

Booklist

'Painful and powerful.'

Hassan Blasim, author of *The Corpse Exhibition*

'Winner of the International Prize for Arabic Fiction, this complex novel weaves the experiences of a diverse group of Iraqis during the chaos of internecine warfare. This Iraqi perspective is one that may surprise and challenge casual readers; highly recommended.' **Library Journal**

'*Frankenstein in Baghdad* is a quietly ferocious thing, a dark, imaginative dissection of the cyclical absurdity of violence. From the terrible aftermath of one of the most destructive, unnecessary wars in modern history, Ahmed Saadawi has crafted a novel that will be remembered.'

Omar El Akkad, author of *American War*

'Horrifically funny and allegorically resonant, *Frankenstein in Baghdad* captures very well the mood of macabre violence that gripped Baghdad in 2005.'

Brian Van Reet, author of *Spoils*

'Brilliant and horrifying, *Frankenstein in Baghdad* is essential reading.' **World Literature Today**

'Outrageously adroit... Saadawi's black sense of humour and grotesque imagery keep the novel grounded in its genre. Call it "Gothic Arabesque", but this haunting novel brazenly confronts the violence visited upon this country by those who did not call it home.' **Kirkus**

'A harrowing and affecting look at the day-to-day life of war-torn Iraq.' **Publishers Weekly**

'*Frankenstein in Baghdad*, Saadawi's part-fantasy, part-sci-fi war novel, is something of an exorcism of the evil spirits of an era not quite past. Saadawi's goal isn't to resolve the horror of war, but rather to thrust the reader into its midst so that they may question its senselessness... A scathing critique of the U.S. invasion by way of front-row seats to its disastrous, lingering consequences.' **LitHub**

'Gripping, darkly humorous...profound.'

Phil Klay, National Book Award– winning author of *Redeployment*

FRANKENSTEIN IN BAGHDAD

Ahmed Saadawi

Translated from the Arabic by

Jonathan Wright

ONEWORLD

A Oneworld Book

First published in Great Britain and Australia
by Oneworld Publications, 2018
This mass market paperback edition first published 2018

Originally published in Arabic by Manshurat al-Jamal in 2013

Mass market paperback ISBN 978-1-78607-397-6
eBook ISBN 978-1-78607-061-6

Printed and bound in Great Britain by Clays Ltd, Elcograf S.p.A.

Oneworld Publications
10 Bloomsbury Street
London WC1B 3SR
England

MIX
Paper from
responsible sources
FSC® C018072

LIST OF CHARACTERS

Abdullah: Mahmoud al-Sawadi's brother, who lives in Amara

Abu Anmar: the owner of the dilapidated Orouba Hotel in Bataween

Abu Jouni: the janitor at the offices of *al-Haqiqa* magazine

Abu Salim: an elderly neighbour of Elishva and Hadi; the husband of Umm Salim

Abu Zaidoun: an elderly barber and ex-Baathist, held responsible for sending Daniel off to war in the 1980s

Adnan al-Anwar: a journalist at *al-Haqiqa* magazine

Ali Baher al-Saidi: a prominent writer, and the owner and editor of *al-Haqiqa* magazine

Aziz the Egyptian: the gossipy owner of the local coffee shop

Daniel: Elishva's son, who disappeared in the Iraq–Iran war

Daniel (junior): Elishva's grandson, the son of her daughter Hilda, who lives in Melbourne

Elishva: an elderly Assyrian Christian widow living alone in Bataween

Faraj the estate agent: a small-time real estate manager who acquires properties in Bataween

Farid Shawwaf: a journalist who writes for *al-Haqiqa*

Hadi the junk dealer: creator of the Whatsitsname

Hammu: the receptionist at the Dilshad Hotel

Hasib Mohamed Jaafar: a hotel guard whose soul animates the Whatsitsname's body

Hazem Abboud: a news photographer and Mahmoud's occasional room-mate

Hilda: one of Elishva's daughters in Melbourne; the mother of Daniel junior

Father Josiah: Elishva's parish priest

Luqman: an Algerian man who lives in the Orouba Hotel

Mahmoud al-Sawadi: a young and ambitious journalist at *al-Haqiqa*

the Mantis: a gangster politician in Amara

Matilda: one of Elishva's daughters in Melbourne

Nader Shamouni: the deacon at Elishva's church

Nahem Abdaki: Hadi's late partner in the junk business

Nawal al-Wazir: a glamorous middle-aged film director

Ninous Malko: the head of an Assyrian family that stayed for a while in Elishva's house

Brigadier Sorour Mohamed Majid: the head of the mysterious Tracking and Pursuit Department

Sultan: Ali Baher al-Saidi's personal driver

Umm Raghad: the madam at a local brothel

Umm Salim: an elderly neighbour of Elishva and Hadi; the wife of Abu Salim

Veronica Munib: a middle-aged Armenian woman who cleans the Orouba Hotel

Zaid Murshid: a journalist at *al-Haqiqa*

Zeina: a prostitute with a superficial resemblance to Nawal al-Wazir

Final Report

I.

With regard to the activities of the Tracking and Pursuit Department, which is partially affiliated to the civil administration of the international coalition forces in Iraq, the special committee of inquiry set up under my chairmanship, with representatives of the Iraqi security and intelligence agencies and observers from US military intelligence, has come to the following conclusions:

a. On 25 September, 2005, under direct political pressure from the Iraqi side, the activities of the Tracking and Pursuit Department were partially suspended for the purposes of the inquiry, and the committee summoned the department director, Brigadier Sorour Mohamed Majid, and his assistants to testify. They briefed the committee on the nature of the work they had been engaged in since the formation of the Coalition Provisional Authority in April 2003 and up to the time of the inquiry. It is clear that the department had been operating outside its area of expertise, which should have been limited to such bureaucratic matters as archiving information and preserving files and documents. Under the direct management of Brigadier Majid, it had employed several astrologers and fortune-tellers, on high salaries financed by the Iraqi treasury, not by the US authorities. According to Brigadier Majid's testimony, their only purpose was to make predictions about serious security incidents that might take place in Baghdad and surrounding areas. It is not clear to the committee to what extent these predictions helped avert security incidents or whether they had any practical benefits.

b. The committee established that a number of files preserved in the department had been leaked from inside. All those working in the department were subsequently detained for questioning.

c. Through an examination of the computers used in the department, it was discovered that documents had been sent by email to someone referred to as 'the author'. Upon further investigation, this person was identified and arrested at his place of residence in the Fanar Hotel on Abu Nuwas Street. No documents related to the Tracking and Pursuit Department were found in his possession. 'The author' was found to be in possession of the text of a story he had written drawing on material contained in documents belonging to the Tracking and Pursuit Department.

d. The story is about 250 pages long, divided into seventeen chapters. Experts from the committee examined the text and concluded that it does not violate any provisions of the law, but for precautionary reasons they recommended that the information in it should not be published under any circumstances and that the story should not be rewritten.

II. Recommendations

a. The committee recommends that Brigadier Sorour Mohamed Majid and his assistants be transferred from the Tracking and Pursuit Department and that the department revert to its original work of archiving and documentation. Those employed as astrologers and fortune-tellers should be laid off. The question of the mistakes the department has made over the past few years must remain under review, and the documents relevant to the department's activities must be preserved.

b. The committee discovered that the personal information in the identity papers of 'the author' is incorrect. It therefore recommends that 'the author' be rearrested and questioned in order to learn his real identity and any other information relevant to the work of the Tracking and Pursuit Department, and also to identify the people in the department who cooperated with him to assess the extent to which this matter poses a threat to national security.

Signed: Committee Chairman

CHAPTER ONE

The Madwoman

1

The explosion took place two minutes after Elishva, the old woman known as Umm Daniel, or Daniel's mother, boarded the bus. Everyone on the bus turned round to see what had happened. They watched in shock as a ball of smoke rose above the crowds, huge and black, from the car park near Tayaran Square in the centre of Baghdad. Young people raced to the scene of the explosion, and cars collided into each other or into the central reservation. The drivers were frightened and confused: they were assaulted by a cacophony of car horns and of people screaming and shouting.

Elishva's neighbours in Lane 7 said later that she had left the Bataween district to pray in the Church of Saint Odisho, near the University of Technology, as she did every Sunday, and that's why the explosion happened – some of the locals believed that, with her spiritual powers, Elishva prevented bad things from happening when she was among them.

Sitting on the bus, minding her own business, as if she were deaf or not even there, Elishva didn't hear the massive explosion about two hundred yards behind her. Her frail body was curled up by the window, and she looked out without seeing anything, thinking about the bitter taste in her mouth and the sense of gloom that she had been unable to shake off for the past few days.

The bitter taste might disappear after she took Holy Communion. Hearing the voices of her daughters and their children on the phone, she would have a little respite from her melancholy, and the light would shine again in her cloudy eyes. Father Josiah would usually wait for his mobile phone to ring and then tell Elishva that Matilda was on the line, or if Matilda didn't call on time, Elishva might wait another hour and then ask the priest to call Matilda. This had been repeated every Sunday for at least two years. Before that, Elishva's daughters had called irregularly on the landline at church. But when the Americans invaded Baghdad, their missiles destroyed the telephone exchange, and the phones were cut off for many months. Death stalked the city like the plague, and Elishva's daughters felt the need to check every week that the old woman was okay. At first, after a few difficult months, they spoke on the Thuraya satellite phone that a Japanese charity had given to the young Assyrian priest at the church. When the wireless networks were introduced, Father Josiah bought a mobile phone, and Elishva spoke to her daughters on that. Members of the congregation would stand in line after Mass to hear the voices of their sons and daughters dispersed around the world. Often people from the surrounding Karaj al-Amana neighbourhood – Christians of other denominations and Muslims too – would come to the church to make free calls to their relatives abroad. As mobile phones spread, the demand for Father Josiah's phone declined, but Elishva was content to maintain the ritual of her Sunday phone call from church.

With her veined and wrinkled hand, Elishva would put the Nokia phone to her ear. Once she heard her daughters' voices, the darkness would lift and she would feel at peace. If she had gone straight back to Tayaran Square, she would have found that everything was calm, just as she had left it in the morning. The pavements would be clean and the cars that had caught fire would have been towed away. The dead would have been taken to the forensics department and the injured to the Kindi Hospital. There would be some shattered glass here and there, a pole blackened with smoke, and a hole in the asphalt, though she wouldn't have been able to make out how big it was because of her blurred vision.

When the Mass was over she lingered for an extra hour. She sat down in the hall adjacent to the church, and after the women had laid out the food they had brought with them, she went ahead and ate with everyone, just to have something to do. Father Josiah made a desperate last attempt to call Matilda, but her phone was out of service. Matilda had probably lost her phone, or it had been stolen from her on the street or at some market in Melbourne, where she lived. Maybe she had forgotten to write down Father Josiah's number or had some other excuse. The priest couldn't make sense of it, but kept trying to console Elishva, and when everyone started leaving, the deacon, Nader Shamouni, offered Elishva a ride home in his old Volga. This was the second week without a phone call. Elishva didn't actually need to hear her daughters' voices. It was partly just habit, but maybe it was something more important: that with her daughters she could talk about Daniel. Nobody really listened to her when she spoke about the son she had lost twenty years ago, except for her daughters and Saint George the Martyr, whose soul she often prayed for and whom she regarded as her patron saint. You might add her old cat, Nabu, whose hair was falling out and who slept most of the time. Even the women at church grew distant when she began to talk about her son – because she just said the same things over and over. It was the same with the old women who were her neighbours. Some of them couldn't remember what Daniel looked like. Besides, he was just one of so many who'd died over the years. Elishva was gradually losing people who had once supported her strange conviction that her son was still alive, even though he had a grave with an empty coffin in the cemetery of the Assyrian Church of the East.

Elishva no longer shared her belief that Daniel was still alive with anyone. She just waited to hear the voice of Matilda or Hilda because they would put up with her, however strange this idea of hers. Her daughters knew their mother clung to the memory of her late son in order to go on living. There was no harm in humouring her.

Nader Shamouni, the deacon, dropped Elishva off in Lane 7 in Bataween, just a few steps from her door. The street was quiet. The slaughter had ended several hours ago, but some of the destruction was still clearly visible. It might have been the neighbourhood's biggest explosion. The old deacon was depressed; he didn't say a word to Elishva as he parked his car next to an electricity pole. There was blood and hair on the pole, mere inches from his nose and his thick white moustache. He felt a tremor of fear.

Elishva got out of the deacon's car and waved goodbye. Walking down the street, she could hear her unhurried footsteps on the gravel. She was preparing an answer for when she opened the door and Nabu looked up as if to ask, 'So? What happened?'

More importantly, she was preparing to scold Saint George. The previous night he had promised that she would either receive some good news or her mind would be set at rest and her ordeal would come to an end.

2

Umm Salim was one of Elishva's neighbours who was convinced that Elishva had special powers and that God's hand was on her shoulder wherever she was. She could cite numerous incidents as evidence. Although sometimes she might criticize or think ill of the old woman, she quickly went back to respecting and honouring her. When Elishva came to visit and they sat with some of their neighbours in the shade in Umm Salim's old courtyard, Umm Salim spread out a woven mat for her, placed cushions to her right and left, and poured her tea.

Sometimes she might exaggerate and say openly in Elishva's presence that if it weren't for those inhabitants who had *baraka* – spiritual power – the neighbourhood would be doomed and swallowed up by the earth on God's orders. But this belief of Umm Salim's was really like the smoke she blew from her shisha pipe during those afternoon chats: it came out in billows, then coiled into sinuous white clouds that vanished into the air, never to travel outside the courtyard.

Many thought of Elishva as just a demented old woman with amnesia, the proof being that she couldn't remember the names of men – even those she had known for half a century. Sometimes she looked at them in a daze, as though they had sprung up in the neighbourhood out of nowhere.

Umm Salim and some of the other kind-hearted neighbours were distraught when Elishva started to tell bizarre stories about things that had happened to her – stories that no reasonable person would believe. Others scoffed, saying that Umm Salim and the other women were just sad that one of their number had crossed over to the dark and desolate shore beyond, meaning the group as a whole was headed in the same direction.

3

Two people were sure Elishva didn't have special powers and was just a crazy old woman. The first was Faraj the estate agent, owner of the Rasoul estate agency on the main commercial street in Bataween. The second was Hadi the junk dealer, who lived in a makeshift dwelling attached to Elishva's house.

Over the past few years Faraj had tried repeatedly to persuade Elishva to sell her old house, but Elishva just flatly refused, without explanation. Faraj couldn't understand why an old woman like her would want to live alone in a seven-room house with only a cat. Why, he wondered, didn't she sell it and move to a smaller house with more air and light, and use the extra money to live the rest of her life in comfort?

Faraj never got a good answer. As for Hadi, her neighbour, he was a scruffy, unfriendly man in his fifties who always smelled of alcohol. He had once asked Elishva to sell him the antiques that filled her house: two large wall clocks, teak tables of various sizes, carpets and furnishings, and plaster and ivory statues of the Virgin Mary and the Infant Jesus. There were more than twenty of these statues, spread around the house, as well as many other objects that Hadi hadn't had time to inspect.

Of these antiques, some of which dated back to the 1940s, Hadi had asked Elishva, 'Why don't you sell them, save yourself the trouble of dusting?', his eyes popping out of his head at the sight of them all. But the old woman just walked him to the front door and sent him out into the street, closing the door behind him. That was the only time Hadi had seen the inside of her house, and the impression it left him with was of a strange museum.

The two men didn't abandon their efforts, but because the junk dealer wasn't usually presentable, Elishva's neighbours were not sympathetic to him. Faraj the estate agent tried several times to encourage Elishva's neighbours to win her over to his proposal; some even accused Veronica Munib, the Armenian neighbour, of taking a bribe from Faraj to persuade Elishva to move in with Umm Salim and her husband. Faraj never lost hope. Hadi, on the other hand, had pestered Elishva repeatedly until he eventually lost interest and just threw hostile glances her way whenever she passed him on the street.

Elishva not only rejected the offers from these two men, she also reserved a special hatred for them, consigning them to everlasting hell. In their faces she saw two greedy people with tainted souls, like cheap carpets with permanent ink stains.

Abu Zaidoun the barber could be added to the list of people Elishva hated and cursed. Elishva had lost Daniel because of him: he was the Baathist who had taken her son by the collar and dragged him off into the unknown. But Abu Zaidoun had not been seen for many years. Elishva no longer ran into him, and no one talked about him in front of her. Since leaving the Baath Party, he had been preoccupied with his many ailments and had no time for anything that happened in the neighbourhood.

4

Faraj was at home when the massive explosion went off in Tayaran Square. Three hours later, at about ten o'clock in the morning, he opened his office and noticed cracks in the large front window. He cursed his bad luck, though he had noticed the shattered windows of many other shops in the area. In fact, he could see Abu Anmar, owner of the Orouba Hotel across the street, standing bewildered on the pavement, in his dishdasha, shards of glass from his old hotel's upper windows around his feet.

Faraj could see that Abu Anmar was shocked, but he didn't care: he had no great affection for him. They were polar opposites, even undeclared rivals. Abu Anmar, like many of the hotel owners in Bataween, made his living off workers and students and people who came to Baghdad from the provinces to visit hospitals or clinics or to go shopping. Over the past decade, with the departure of many of the Egyptian and Sudanese migrant workers, hotels had become dependent on a few customers who lived in them on a virtually permanently basis – drivers on long-distance bus routes, students who didn't like the university accommodation, and people who worked in the restaurants in Bab al-Sharqi and Saadoun Street, in the factories that made shoes and other things, and in the Harj flea market.

However, most of these people disappeared after April 2003, and now many of the hotels were nearly empty. To make matters worse, Faraj had appeared on the scene, trying to win over customers who might otherwise have gone to Abu Anmar's hotel or one of the others in the area. Taking advantage of the chaos and lawlessness in the city, Faraj had got his hands on several houses of unknown ownership. He turned them into cheap boarding houses, renting the rooms to workers from the provinces or to families displaced from nearby areas for sectarian reasons or because old vendettas had flared up again with the fall of the regime.

Abu Anmar could only grumble and complain. He had moved to Baghdad from the south in the 1970s and had no relatives or friends in the capital to help him. In the past he had relied on the power of the regime. Faraj, on the other hand, had many relatives and acquaintances, and when the regime fell, they were the means by which he imposed authority, winning everyone's respect and legalizing his appropriation of the abandoned houses, even though everyone knew he didn't have the papers to prove he owned them or had ever rented them from the government.

Faraj could use his growing power against Elishva. He had seen her house from the inside only twice but had fallen in love with it immediately. It had probably been built by Iraqi Jews, since it was in the style they favoured: an inner courtyard surrounded by several rooms on two floors, with a basement under one of the rooms that opened onto the street. There were fluted wooden columns supporting a balcony on the upper floor, and with its metal railings, inlaid with wood, it created a unique aesthetic effect. The house also had double-leaf wooden doors with metal bolts and locks, and wooden windows reinforced with metal bars and glazed with stained glass. The courtyard was paved with fine brickwork and the rooms with small black and white tiles like a chessboard. The courtyard was open to the sky and had once been covered with a white cloth that was removed during the summer, but the cloth was no longer there. The house was not as it once had been, but it was sturdy and had suffered little water damage, unlike similar houses on the street. The basement had been filled in at some point, but that didn't matter. The main drawback for Faraj was that one of the rooms on the upper floor had completely collapsed, and many of the bricks had fallen beyond the wall shared with the house next door, the total ruin inhabited by Hadi the junk dealer. The bathroom on the upper floor was also in ruins. Faraj would need to spend some money on repairs and renovations, but it would be worth it.

Faraj thought it would take only half an hour to evict a defenceless old Christian woman, but a voice in his head warned him that he risked breaking the law and offending people, so it might be better to first gauge people's feelings about her. The best thing would be to wait till she died, and then no one but he would dare to take over the house, since everyone knew how attached he was to it and acknowledged him as its future owner, however long Elishva lived.

'Look on the bright side,' Faraj shouted to Abu Anmar, who was wringing his hands in dismay at the damage to his property. Abu Anmar raised his arms to the heavens in solidarity with Faraj's optimism, or maybe he was saying 'May God take you' to the greedy estate agent whom fate had taunted him with day in day out.

5

Elishva shoved her cat off the sofa and brushed away the loose cat hairs. She couldn't actually see any hairs, but she knew from stroking the cat that its hair was falling out all over the place. She could overlook the hair unless it was in her special spot on the sofa facing the large picture of Saint George the Martyr that hung between smaller grey pictures of her son and her husband, framed in carved wood. There were two other pictures of the same size, one of the Last Supper and the other of Christ being taken down from the cross, and three miniatures copied from medieval icons, drawn in thick ink and faded s, depicting various saints, some of whose names she didn't know because it was her husband who had put them up many years ago. They were still as they were originally hung, some in the parlour, some in her bedroom, some in Daniel's room, which was closed, and some in the other abandoned rooms.

Almost every evening she sat there to resume her sterile conversation with the saint with the angelic face. The saint wasn't in ecclesiastical dress: he was wearing thick, shiny plates of armor that covered his body and a plumed helmet, with his wavy blond hair peeking out. He was holding a long pointed lance and sitting on a muscular white horse that had reared up to avoid the jaws of a hideous dragon encroaching from the corner of the picture, intent on swallowing the horse, the saint, and all his military accoutrements.

Elishva ignored the extravagant details. She put on the thick glasses that hung from a cord around her neck and looked at the calm, angelic face that betrayed no emotion. He wasn't angry or desperate or dreamy or happy. He was just doing his job out of devotion to God.

Elishva found no comfort in abstract speculation. She treated her patron saint as one of her relatives, a member of a family that had been torn apart and dispersed. He was the only person she had left, apart from Nabu the cat, and the spectre of her son, Daniel, who was bound to return one day. To others she lived alone, but she believed she lived with three beings, or three ghosts, with so much power and presence that she didn't feel lonely.

She was angry because her patron saint hadn't fulfilled any of the three promises she had extracted from him after countless nights of pleading, begging and weeping. She didn't have much time left on this earth, and she wanted a sign from the Lord about Daniel – whether he was alive and would return or where his real grave or his remains were. She wanted to challenge her patron saint on the promises he had given her, but she waited for night to fall because during the day the picture was just a picture, inanimate and completely still, but at night a portal opened between her world and the other world, and the Lord came down, embodied in the image of the saint, to talk through him to Elishva, the poor sheep who had been abandoned by the rest of the flock and had almost fallen into the abyss of faithless perdition.

That night, by the light of the oil lamp, Elishva could see

the ripples in the old picture behind the murky glass, but she could also see the saint's eyes and his soft, handsome face. Nabu meowed irritably as he left the room. The saint's long arm was still holding the lance, but now his eyes were on Elishva. 'You're too impatient, Elishva,' he said. 'I told you the Lord will put an end to your torment and bring you peace of mind, or you will hear news that will bring you joy. But no one can make the Lord act at a certain time.'

Elishva argued with the saint for half an hour until his beautiful face reverted to its normal state, his dreamy gaze stiff and immobile, a sign that he had grown tired of this futile discussion. Before going to bed, she said her usual prayers in front of the large wooden cross in her bedroom and checked that Nabu was asleep in the corner on a small tiger-skin rug.

The next day, after she had had breakfast and washed the dishes, she was surprised to hear the annoying roar of American Apache helicopters flying overhead. She looked up and saw her son, Daniel, or imagined she did. There was Danny, as she had always called him when he was young – at last her patron saint's prophecy had come true. She called him, and he came over to her. 'Come, my son. Come, Danny.'

CHAPTER TWO

The Liar

1

To make the stories he told more interesting, Hadi was careful to add realistic touches. He remembered all the details of the things that happened to him and included them every time he recounted his experiences. One day he was in Aziz the Egyptian's coffee shop, sitting on the bench in the corner by the front window and stroking his moustache and his forked beard. He ground the small spoon nervously around the bottom of the tea glass and took two sips of tea before starting to tell his story again, this time for the benefit of some patrons whom Aziz had encouraged to listen to Hadi. The guests were a slim blonde German journalist with thin lips and thick glasses perched on her small nose, her young Iraqi translator, a Palestinian photographer, and a swarthy young journalist named Mahmoud al-Sawadi, who came from the town of Amara in southern Iraq and was living in Abu Anmar's Orouba Hotel.

The German journalist was making a documentary about Baghdad journalists and was accompanying Mahmoud al-Sawadi on a normal working day. She hadn't planned to listen to a long, complicated story told by a junk dealer with bulging eyes, who reeked of alcohol and whose tattered clothes were dotted with cigarette burns. She was taking a risk by being out on the streets of Baghdad in such a conspicuous way, so she hadn't turned on her camera and was just listening as she drank her tea. Every now and then she turned to her Iraqi translator, who gave her a lengthy explanation of what Hadi was saying.

Hadi was rambling. It was a warm spring day, and the German journalist would have preferred to spend the rest of it outside. And at some point, she had to get back to the press centre at the Sheraton Hotel to transcribe the tapes she had recorded with Mahmoud al-Sawadi.

'That guy's recounting the plot of a movie,' she said to Mahmoud as he walked her out of the coffee shop. 'He's stolen his story from a Robert De Niro film.'

'Yes, it looks like he watches lots of movies. He's well known in the area.'

'Then he should have gone to Hollywood,' she said with a laugh as she got into the translator's car.

2

Hadi wasn't bothered. Some people walk out in the middle of movies. It's quite normal.

'Where did we leave off?' asked Hadi as Mahmoud returned and sat on the bench opposite him. Aziz stood, holding the empty tea glasses and smiling broadly, waiting for Hadi to resume his story.

'We'd got to the explosion,' said Aziz.

'The first one or the second?' asked Hadi.

'The first one . . . in Tayaran Square,' said Mahmoud,

waiting for Hadi to contradict himself by changing some of the details. That was the only reason Mahmoud was willing to listen to this story for the second or third time – to see if Hadi would contradict himself.

The explosion was horrific – and here Hadi looked to Aziz for confirmation. Hadi had run out of the coffee shop. He had been eating some of the beans that Ali al-Sayed made in the shop next door, which Hadi ate for breakfast every morning. On his way out of the shop he collided with people running from the explosion. The smell suddenly hit his nostrils – the smoke, the burning of plastic and seat cushions, the roasting of human flesh. You wouldn't have smelled anything like it in your life and would never forget it.

The sky was cloudy and threatening a downpour. The workers were lined up in large numbers opposite the grand white Armenian church with the cross-topped towers in the shape of octagonal pyramids. Smoking, chatting, drinking tea, eating cake from the street vendors on the wide pavements or pickled turnips or beans from the nearby carts, they waited for vehicles looking for day labourers for building or demolition work. Along the same kerb there were buses calling for passengers going to Karrada or to the University of Technology, and on the opposite kerb it was much the same: cars interspersed with stalls selling cigarettes, sweets, underwear and many other things. A grey four-wheel drive stopped, and most of the workers sitting on the kerb stood up. When some of them approached, the vehicle exploded in a ball of fire. No one saw it coming; it all happened in a fraction of a second. The people who weren't injured – because they were too far away, or screened by other people's bodies, or by parked cars, or because they were coming down the side lanes and hadn't reached the main street when the explosion went off – all these people and others – like those in the offices next to the Armenian church and some long-distance taxi drivers – witnessed the explosion as it engulfed the vehicles and the bodies of the people around them. It cut electricity wires and killed birds. Windows were shattered and doors blown in. Cracks appeared in the walls of the nearby houses, and some old ceilings collapsed. There was unseen damage too, all inflicted in a single moment.

Hadi was watching the scene after the commotion had died down and the huge cloud of smoke had lifted. Trails of black smoke continued to rise from the cars, and flames licked small burning objects scattered on the pavement. The police came quickly and set up a cordon. Injured people were groaning and bodies were lying in heaps on the asphalt, covered in blood and singed black by the heat. Hadi said that when he reached the scene, he stood at the corner by the hardware shops and calmly watched.

As he recounted the story, he lit a cigarette and started to smoke, as if trying to get rid of the smell of the explosion. He liked the idea of appearing on the scene as a kind of disinterested villain, and he waited to see from the faces of those who were listening whether they were similarly impressed. Ambulances came to pick up the dead and injured, then fire engines to douse the cars and tow trucks to drag them off to an unknown destination. Water hoses washed away the blood and ashes. Hadi watched the scene with eagle eyes, looking for something in particular amid this binge of death and devastation. Once he was sure he had seen it, he threw his cigarette to the ground and rushed to grab it before a powerful jet of water could blast it down into the sewer. He wrapped it in his canvas sack, folded the sack under his arm, and left the scene.

3

Hadi got home before the downpour began. He crossed the loose paving stones of the courtyard, went to his room, and put the folded canvas sack down on his bed. He had been breathing so heavily he could hear a whistling in his nose and a wheezing in his chest. He reached for the folded canvas sack, then changed his mind and decided to wait. He preferred to listen to the sound of the raindrops, which had started tentatively and then pattered steadily. Within moments the rain was pelting down, flushing the courtyard, the streets, Tayaran Square, and what remained of all the day's horrors.

Calling Hadi's place a house would be an exaggeration. Many people knew it well, especially Aziz the Egyptian before he got married and gave up the dissolute lifestyle. He and Hadi used to sit around Hadi's table and drink till late, or Aziz might find Hadi with one or two of the prostitutes from Lane 5. It was always fun with Hadi because he didn't deny himself when it came to pleasure.

Hadi's house wasn't really his and wasn't really a house. Most of what was in it was falling apart. There was only one room, right at the back; it had holes in the roof, and Hadi and a colleague named Nahem Abdaki had made it their base three years earlier.

Hadi and Nahem had been known in the area for years. They drove a horse-drawn cart around, buying household junk – pots and pans, and appliances that didn't work. Mornings they'd stop by Aziz's coffee shop for breakfast and tea before setting out on a grand tour of Bataween and the Abu Nuwas neighbourhood on the other side of Saadoun Street. Then they would head off in Nahem's cart, to other parts of the city, as far south as Karrada, where they disappeared into the backstreets.

After the American invasion, everyone noticed amid the chaos that Hadi and Nahem were rebuilding what they called 'the Jewish ruin', although nothing Jewish was ever seen there – no candelabra, no Stars of David or Hebrew inscriptions. Hadi rebuilt the ruin's outer wall with whatever was lying around and installed the big wooden door that had been hidden under dirt and piles of bricks. He and Nahem cleared the rubble from the courtyard, restored the ruin's only good room, and left the tumbledown walls and the collapsing ceilings of the other rooms as they were. The room above Hadi's had one wall left standing, with a window. The wall was in danger of collapsing and burying alive anyone who happened to be in the courtyard below, but the wall never did fall down. The locals eventually realized that Hadi and his friend had become part of the neighbourhood. Even Faraj, who was notorious for appropriating houses that had been abandoned by their owners, showed no interest in what the junk dealer had claimed for himself. To Faraj the place remained the Jewish ruin, as it always had been.

Where had these two men come from? No one gave much thought to the question because the area had plenty of outsiders who had moved in on top of each other over many decades; no one could claim to be an original inhabitant. A year or two later Nahem got married, rented a house in Bataween, and moved out of Hadi's place, although he and Hadi still worked together with the horse and cart.

Nahem was younger than Hadi – in his mid- to late-thirties – and they seemed like father and son, although they didn't look like each other. Nahem had big ears on a small head, with hair that was full and long and straight but like coarse wire, and thick eyebrows that almost converged. Hadi used to joke that even if Nahem lived to be 120, he would never lose his hair. Hadi was over fifty, though it was hard to judge his age. He was always dishevelled, with an untrimmed forked beard, a body that was wiry but hard and energetic, and a bony face with sunken cheeks.

Hadi called his partner Old Misery. Unlike Hadi, Nahem didn't smoke or drink, was fastidious about religious matters, and didn't touch a woman till his wedding day. Because of his religious scruples, he was the one who 'baptized' the house when they moved in, putting up on the wall in the main room a large framed copy of the Throne Verse of the Quran. He glued it to the wall to make sure it would be hard to remove, at least until it fell apart. Hadi had no regard for religion, but he didn't want to seem antagonistic, so he put up with the fact that the verse was the first thing he saw every day.

Nahem didn't live long enough to find out whether his head of hair would last as Hadi always predicted. By the time Hadi sat in Aziz's coffee shop with Mahmoud al-Sawadi and some old men, telling more of his story, Nahem had already been dead for several months – from a car bomb that had exploded in front of the office of a religious party in Karrada, also killing some other passersby and Nahem's horse. It had been hard to separate Nahem's flesh from that of the horse.

The shock of Nahem's death changed Hadi. He became aggressive. He swore and cursed and threw stones after the American Hummers or the vehicles of the police and the National Guard. He got into arguments with anyone who mentioned Nahem and what had happened to him. He kept to himself for a while, and then went back to his old self, laughing and telling extraordinary stories, but now he seemed to have two faces, or two masks – as soon as he was alone he was gloomy and despondent in a way he hadn't been before. He also started drinking during the day and always had quarters of arak or whisky in his pocket and the smell of alcohol on his breath. He grew dirtier, let his beard grow longer, and rarely washed his clothes.

Nahem Abdaki was never mentioned again, lest Hadi throw a tantrum and start shouting obscenities. So Mahmoud al-Sawadi didn't hear about Nahem till later, in the version of the story told by Aziz the Egyptian.

4

'Where did we leave off?' asked Hadi after relieving himself in the toilets next to the coffee shop.

'At the part about the big nose in the canvas sack,' Mahmoud al-Sawadi replied wearily.

'Oh yes, the nose.'

Hadi was zipping up his fly as he came towards the bench by the front window of the coffee shop. He sat down to resume his story, and Mahmoud, who was hoping to catch him out, was disappointed to find he hadn't changed any of the details. Before going to the bathroom, he had paused at the point in the story when the rain stopped and he went out to the courtyard with the canvas sack. Looking up at the sky, he saw the clouds breaking up like wisps of cotton wool, as if all at once they had released their water and were now departing. Some of the second-hand furniture was sitting in rainwater, which would damage it, but Hadi wasn't thinking about that. He went to the shed, which he had assembled out of scraps of furniture, iron bars, and sections of kitchen units he had leaned up against the piece of wall that still remained, and squatted down at one end. The rest of the shed was dominated by a massive corpse – the body of a naked man, with viscous liquids, light in colour, oozing from parts of it. There was only a little blood – some small dried patches on the arms and legs, and some grazes and bruises around the shoulders and neck. It was hard to say what the skin was – it didn't have a uniform colour. Hadi moved farther into the narrow space around the body and sat down close to the head. The area where the nose should have been was badly disfigured, as if a wild animal had bitten a chunk out of it. Hadi opened the canvas sack and took out the thing. In recent days he had spent hours looking for one like it, yet he was still uneasy handling it. It was a fresh nose, still coated in congealed, dark red blood. His hand trembling, he positioned it in the black hole in the corpse's face. It was a perfect fit, as if the corpse had its own nose back.

Hadi withdrew his hand, wiped his fingers on his clothes, and looked at the face with some dissatisfaction, but his task was now finished. Actually, it wasn't quite finished: he had to sew the nose in place.

The nose was all the corpse needed to be complete, so now Hadi was finishing the job. It was a horrible job, one he had undertaken without anyone's help, and somehow it didn't seem to make any sense despite all the arguments he used when trying to explain himself to his listeners.

'I wanted to hand him over to the forensics department, because it was a complete corpse that had been left in the streets like rubbish. It's a human being, guys, a person,' he told them.

'But it wasn't a complete corpse. You made it complete,' someone objected.

'I made it complete so it wouldn't be treated as rubbish, so it would be respected like other dead people and given a proper burial,' Hadi explained.

'What happened next?'

'To me, or the Whatsitsname?'

'To both of you.'

Hadi's listeners were completely wrapped up in the story. New listeners risked missing the pleasures of the story if they insisted on challenging it right from the start. The

25

logical objections were usually left to the end, and no one interfered with the way the story was told or with the sub-plots Hadi went into.

Hadi had an appointment with a man in Karrada. For several days he hadn't bought or sold anything, and his money was starting to run out. He had been pursuing the man for a while because there could be some money in it for him. He was another old person living alone in his own house, very much like Elishva, but this old one had a girlfriend in Russia who had persuaded him to sell his house and furniture and to emigrate so they could spend their retirement together.

No problem with that; may they live happily ever after. But whenever Hadi thought he and the old man had come to an agreement, the man would panic about losing his furniture, especially his chandeliers, reading lamps, and old-fashioned valve radios. He would cling to them as if he would drown without them. Hadi didn't want to put pressure on him or frighten him off, so he went away and then came back later to find him all smiles and enthusiastic about sealing a deal.

Hadi washed his hands after handling the corpse. He changed into clean clothes and went out to meet the reluctant old man, worried that someone else might convince him to sell his valuable furniture or might lease the house furnished, allowing the old man to retain ownership and collect rent while the tenant harboured hopes of assuming ownership when he died.

The man's house wasn't far – Hadi could jump on a bus and be there in five minutes. When there was traffic, he would make the trip on foot, along the way collecting empty soft drink and beer cans in a large canvas sack. He could sell them later to the peddlers who specialized in such things or save them in sacks at home and then hire a pickup to take them to the aluminium recycling plant in Hafez al-Qadi near Rashid Street.

'And the corpse, for God's sake, what happened to that?'

'Hang on a minute.'

Hadi reached the man's house and knocked on the door, but no one came to open it. Perhaps the man was asleep or out. Perhaps he was now dead: his time had come before he could see his Russian girlfriend again and touch her thin, wrinkled hands. Hadi kept knocking till he attracted the attention of the neighbours, then he turned back to Saadoun Street and went to a restaurant near the Rahma Hospital. He ate a kebab sandwich and ordered two kebab skewers to take home with him.

The clouds had completely cleared, but the wind blew in unpredictable gusts from various directions. The cigarette vendor's umbrella had toppled over, the block of cement in the large tin can it was in preventing it from flying away.

Buffeted by the wind, the pedestrians were having a hard time walking. Some looked as though a hidden hand were slapping them or pushing them along from behind. People sitting outside coffee shops soon went inside, and drivers with their car windows partly open wound them firmly closed. The newspaper and magazine sellers dispersed, and the people who sold cigarettes and sweets at traffic lights put their goods into their shoulder bags so they wouldn't blow away. People wearing hats pressed them down hard to keep them from flying away.

At the Sadeer Novotel hotel, overlooking Andalus Square, the palm trees swayed and the guard in the forecourt fastened his military jacket tight. He didn't have to stand in the open air, but his wooden sentry box didn't protect him from either the cold or the heat. If he had been a soldier or a policeman in one of the units posted throughout the streets of Baghdad, he would have lit a fire in an open oil drum to keep himself warm, covering his clothes in soot, but the hotel management had banned such things.

'And now he's going on about the hotel guard!'

'Be patient, man. He's coming to your part of the story.'

Hadi finished off his kebab, drank a can of Pepsi, and then crushed it with his hand and threw it into the canvas sack beside him. He didn't want to go out in the high wind, so he passed the time by picking through the restaurant's rubbish and removing all the soft drink cans. When the storm had died down, he went outside to find that the sun had disappeared and the sky had turned grey and was growing darker by the minute. He couldn't think straight. Then he remembered the corpse he had left at home, and he felt dizzy.

Without thinking, he walked towards the Andalus Square intersection. It was an extraordinary day. On the restaurant's television he had heard there had been explosions during the day in Kadhimiya, Sadr City, the Mansour district and Bab al-Sharqi. There was footage of the injured in the Kindi Hospital and images of Tayaran Square as the fire brigade hosed it down. Hadi expected to see himself on TV, on the corner by the hardware shop, smoking calmly like a criminal observing the aftermath of his crime. A government spokesman appeared, answering journalists' questions with a smile. He assured them that the government had thwarted the terrorists because, according to intelligence, al-Qaeda and remnants of the old regime had planned one hundred car bombings, but the coalition forces and the Iraqi security services had foiled all but fifteen of them.

The fat restaurant owner blew a long rumbling raspberry as he listened to what the government spokesman said. There had, in fact, been sixteen explosions, but the last one wasn't mentioned by the spokesman because he'd gone home by the time it happened.

Hadi was walking along with the sack of cans slung over his shoulder. When he reached the Sadeer Novotel, he usually crossed to the other side of the road so the guards didn't shout at him, but this time he forgot, preoccupied as he was with the thought of the corpse in his shed at home. What was he going to do? He had accomplished the task he had set himself. Should he hire a car to take the body to the forensics department? Should he take it out one night and leave it in some square or on the street and let the police come and finish the job?

As he was passing in front of the large metal gate of the hotel garage, he realized he was in a quandary. The only good solution was to go home, take the corpse apart, and restore it to what it had been – just disconnected body parts. Then he should scatter the parts around the streets, where he had found them.

Meanwhile, shivering from the cold, the guard considered stretching his legs. He stepped out of the sentry box, towards the gate, then grabbed on to the cold bars of the gate and watched as the creature with his suspicious bag walked past. He didn't think it necessary to warn him to move off.

'And you saw all this yourself, didn't you?' Hadi turned to Mahmoud.

'Yes, I was standing with some friends on the other side of the street when I saw a rubbish truck heading towards the hotel gate.'

'You saw it? There you are, so I didn't make any of it up. This guy's a witness.'

When he was twenty yards past the gate, Hadi saw the rubbish truck race past him towards the gate, almost knocking him over. A few moments later it exploded. Hadi, together with his sack and his dinner, was lifted off the ground. With the dust and dirt and blast of the explosion, he sailed through the air, turned a somersault and landed hard on the asphalt. Maybe a minute passed before he realized what had happened. He saw some young people running in his direction. The journalist Mahmoud al-Sawadi was among them and helped Hadi get up. Dust and smoke were everywhere. Terrified, Hadi started walking away. The people who had helped him shouted after him, thinking maybe he was injured and couldn't feel it, but he started running. He was clearly in a state of shock.

Darkness had fallen. In the distance Hadi could hear police cars, ambulances and fire engines. The cloud of dust and smoke dispersed into a thin fog that lit up in the headlights of the vehicles. Mahmoud and the other witnesses, shocked and confused, made their way down the street, crunching underfoot the unseen shards of glass, small pieces of metal, and other debris from the explosion.

5

Hadi walked with great effort. He had excruciating pain in his arms and his pelvis, and cuts on his forehead and cheekbone from falling on the asphalt. He was hobbling along, dragging his feet with difficulty. Had he been thinking clearly, he might have taken a taxi to Bab al-Sharqi. In fact, he wasn't thinking about anything at all. It was as if someone had pressed a button and he'd started walking, nothing more, and maybe when he ran out of energy he would collapse.

Hadi kept saying he wouldn't die – he had survived several other explosions. What mattered most to him was that his body hadn't been hit by shrapnel. All his injuries were from hitting the ground, and they were minor.

Upon arriving home – without his canvas sack or the dinner he'd bought from the restaurant; he'd dropped these at the scene of the explosion – he pushed open the heavy wooden door but forgot to close it behind him. When he looked in the distance at the door to his room, he felt it was much farther than usual. He walked across the courtyard's broken paving stones, frightened he might fall and die or faint. He wanted to reach his bed. When he got to his room, he threw himself on the mattress and quickly fell into a deep sleep, or perhaps it was a coma that he had managed to postpone.

The next day Hadi woke to the sound of the radio news bulletin. It might have been coming from the neighbours' house behind his, or maybe Umm Salim was sitting on the porch opposite his front door, hugging the radio and watching the people coming and going, as she sometimes did.

When Hadi lifted his head, he saw that the pillow was covered with saliva and spots of dried blood. At first he thought he must have been very drunk, but then he remembered the explosion. And then the body in the shed. It would be more decomposed today. Maybe people walking past the house would be able to smell it.

Hadi got up and could tell from the light that it was close to midday. He washed his face; the pain was intense as he moved his limbs. When he turned round, he saw the effect the storm had had on the courtyard during his absence. Some of the old kitchen and office units had been overturned. Pieces of the wooden roofing had been blown away. The ceiling was gone. When he looked closer, he discovered that many other things had disappeared.

The corpse, too, was gone. He turned everything upside down, then went back to his room and looked in there. His heart was beating faster and faster, and he forgot about the pains that racked his bones. Where on earth had the corpse gone? He stopped in the middle of the courtyard, afraid and confused. He looked up at the clear blue sky, then at the high walls of the neighbours' houses, then at the low roof that was left over from the room in Elishva's house that had collapsed. A mangy old cat had its gaze fixed on him. It gave a deep meow. Then it turned slowly and disappeared behind the crumbling wall.

'And then?'

'That's it. That's the end.'

'What do you mean, that's it? So where did the corpse go, Hadi?'

'I don't know.'

'That's not a nice story, Hadi. Tell us another one.'

'If you don't believe it, that's your choice. Okay, I'm off now. The teas are on you.'

CHAPTER THREE

A Lost Soul

1

Hasib Mohamed Jaafar was twenty-one years old, dark, slim, and married to Dua Jabbar. He lived with Dua and their baby daughter, Zahraa, in Sector 44 in Sadr City, in a room in the house of his large family. Hasib, who had been working for seven months as a guard at the Sadeer Novotel hotel, was killed in an explosion caused by a Sudanese suicide bomber driving a dynamite-laden rubbish truck stolen from the Baghdad municipality. The bomber was planning to crash through the hotel's outer gate, drive the truck into the hotel lobby, and detonate the explosives, bringing down the whole building. He failed because the guard bravely fired several rounds at the driver, causing him to detonate the explosives early. The guard's belongings were handed back to his family: his civilian clothes, a new pair of socks, a bottle of cologne, and the first volume of al-Sayyab's collected poems. In the coffin they put his burned black shoes; his shredded, blood-stained clothes; and small charred parts of his body. There was little left of Hasib Mohamed Jaafar; the coffin that was taken to the cemetery in Najaf was more of a token. Hasib's young wife wrapped her arms around it, wept bitterly, and wailed at length. Hasib's mother, sisters and brothers and neighbours did the same, and his stunned little daughter was passed from arm to arm whenever the person holding her was overwhelmed by grief.

Exhausted, every member of the family went to sleep dreaming of Hasib walking home with a cloth bag over his shoulder. They all dreamed something about Hasib. Parts of one dream made up for parts missing in another. A little dream filled a gap in a big one, and the threads stitched together to recreate a dream body for Hasib, to go with his soul, which was still hovering over all their heads and seeking the rest it could not find. Where was the body to which it should return in order to take its place among those who live in a state of limbo?

2

When Hasib saw the rubbish truck, many possible explanations flooded his mind. It was just a rubbish truck. The driver had made a mistake – he had lost control and veered off towards the hotel gate. There had been a traffic accident, and the driver had sped off and was unintentionally heading for the gate. No, it was a suicide bomber. Stop! Stop! One shot, then another. He didn't mean to kill the driver. He wouldn't dare kill anyone, but this was his duty. He was well aware of the strict orders about protecting the hotel. There were security companies and important people and maybe Americans in it. He had a licence to kill, as they say. The thoughts raced through his head in fractions of a second as his finger squeezed the trigger, maybe even before he had decided on the best course of action. The truck blew up, and Hasib was aware of himself observing the explosion, but not from his position between the wooden sentry box and the big hotel's outer gate. He was looking at the flames, the smoke and the flying pieces of metal from high in the air. He felt a strange calm.

He saw a man with a white canvas sack hurtling through the air and landing quite a distance from the explosion. He saw pieces of glass from the hotel windows and the lobby facade flying towards the hotel forecourt. A few moments later the cloud of smoke settled, and half an hour passed before the ambulances and fire trucks arrived.

He watched darkness engulf the city. He saw the distant lights of buildings, houses and vehicles. He saw some of the nearby flyovers. He saw the floodlights of the sports stadium and some minarets in the distance covered with bright lights.

He could see the river too, deep and black in the darkness. He wanted to touch it. He had never touched the river. He had lived all his life far from it. He had driven over it, seen it from a distance, and seen pictures of it on television. But he had never felt the coldness of the water or tasted it. He saw a man in a white vest and white shorts floating face-up in it. What bliss! He must be looking at the stars, clear in the night sky. He was drifting slowly with the current. Hasib moved towards him and looked into his face. 'Why are you looking at me, my son?' the man said. 'Go and find out what happened to your body. Don't stay here.'

He saw another dead body, floating face down in the water. It didn't say anything. It just floated slowly, in silence.

3

Hasib went back to the hotel gate and looked at the large hole the suicide bomber had made with his truck bomb. He recognized his burned boots but couldn't find his body. He looked in all the streets and in Firdaus Square, then went to Tahrir Square and saw birds perched on the bronze figures that make up the Liberty Monument. Then it occurred to him to go to the cemetery.

There, in the Valley of Peace in Najaf, he examined all the graves. He didn't find anything that offered him any certainty, but in the end he saw a teenager in a red T-shirt, with silver bangles on his wrists and a necklace of black fabric. He was sitting cross-legged on a raised grave.

'Why are you here?' the boy asked. 'You should stay close to your body.'

'It's disappeared.'

'How did it disappear? You have to find it, or some other body, or else things will end badly for you.'

'What do you mean?'

'I don't know, but it always ends badly that way.'

'Why are you here?'

'This is my grave. My body's lying underneath. In a few days I won't be able to get out like this. My body's decomposing, and I'll be imprisoned in the grave till the end of time.'

Hasib sat next to him, perplexed. What should he do? No one had told him about these things. What disaster could he expect now?

'Maybe you haven't really died and you're dreaming. Or your soul has left your body to go for a stroll and will come back later,' the boy said.

'I hope to God you're right. I'm not used to this. I'm still young, and I have a daughter, and . . .'

'Young! You're not as young as me!'

Hasib continued talking to the boy with the silver bangles. Every now and then the boy reminded him that he had to get back to his body, because maybe God intended him to have a new life.

'Sometimes the soul leaves the body and you die, but then the Angel of Death changes his mind or corrects the mistake he has made, and the soul goes back inside its body. Then God commands the body to rise from the dead. In other words, the soul is like the fuel in a car. It takes a spark to ignite it.'

They were silent for a while, and then Hasib heard weeping in the distance and saw some dogs as black as ink fighting with one another. The boy with the bangles looked at him anxiously. 'You better find out where your body's gone,' he said, 'or else things are going to end badly.'

4

Hasib went back to the hotel and looked up and down all the surrounding streets. After many hours there, he went home and saw everyone sleeping: his wife, his baby daughter and the rest of the family. Then shortly before dawn he returned to the scene of his death. He felt he was caught in a vicious cycle. In a house in Bataween he saw a naked man asleep. He went up to him and checked to see if he was dead. It wasn't anyone in particular; the man looked strange and horrible. Seeing the sky changing colour, Hasib felt for certain that sunrise would spell disaster for him. He wouldn't have the energy to roam the streets or go back to the scene of the explosion. With his hand, which was made of primordial matter, he touched the pale, naked body and saw his spirit sink into it. His whole arm sank in, then his head and the rest of his body. Overwhelmed by a heaviness and torpor, he lodged inside the corpse, filling it from head to toe, because probably, he realized then, it didn't have a soul, while he was a soul without a body.

5

So things didn't happen for no reason? The two of them were made for each other. Now he only had to wait for the family of the naked man to take the body to the cemetery, bury it in a grave, and cover it with soil. He didn't care what name they had inscribed on the gravestone.

CHAPTER FOUR

The Journalist

1

Mahmoud al-Sawadi was awoken at 7:30 a.m. by the explosion in Tayaran Square, but he didn't get out of bed. He had a terrible headache and was still sleepy. He didn't wake up again until about 10:00 a.m., when his mobile phone rang. It was the editor of *al-Haqiqa*, the magazine where he worked.

'Why are you still asleep?'

'I . . . I,' Mahmoud stammered.

'Mahmoud, get up right away and go to the Kindi Hospital to take pictures of the injured and speak with the doctors, the police, and so on. Understand?'

'Yes, I'll head there now.'

'*Now*, now, not tomorrow, as Fairuz sings. Okay, Mahmoud?'

Leaving his room in the Orouba Hotel, Mahmoud found Abu Anmar, the owner, wringing his hands in the street, surrounded by broken glass. In the centre of Bataween, he crossed the main street and stopped in at Aziz's coffee shop for a glass of tea but didn't want to stay too long. He had all his equipment with him – camera, digital recorder, notebook, pens – in a black leather bag that hung from his shoulder and hit his bottom gently as he walked.

Reaching Tayaran Square, Mahmoud saw the blackened stalls and carts and a shallow crater six feet in diameter. The square was deserted, and he imagined how big the explosion had been and how much death and destruction it had wrought.

Mahmoud stopped on the central reservation, took a deep breath, then brought his digital recorder up to his mouth and, as he had often seen in American movies, he pressed Record. 'Damn you, Hazem Abboud,' he said. 'Damn you right now and always.'

Hazem was a freelance photographer who supposedly shared Mahmoud's room on the second floor of the Orouba Hotel, but he was rarely there – he used it as a rest station or a refuge in emergencies. Abu Anmar, the hotel's paunchy owner, was an old friend of Hazem's and didn't treat him as a customer. Maybe he was grateful to Hazem for bringing Mahmoud to live at the run-down hotel, making him the third or fourth guest in a place that in the good old days would have had more than seventy guests at a time.

The previous afternoon Hazem Abboud had insisted on celebrating, though there was no reason to do so, and he had dragged his poor friend by the collar to a house in Lane 5 in Bataween. Mahmoud was wary but went along. They knocked back beer for two hours, and although it was cold outside, two blonde girls were sitting right next to them in skimpy summer clothing. Mahmoud's heart skipped a beat whenever one of the girls brushed up against him, when picking up her glass or taking nuts from the bowl. Mahmoud had never been to this kind of party and had never been so close to a woman. Hazem kept goading him to drink more.

'If you're not comfortable here, we could leave,' Hazem said every now and then.

But Mahmoud had no desire to leave. Eventually, the girls got up and pulled Mahmoud by the hand, taking him to a bedroom on the second floor. One of them came out laughing half an hour later and sat down to finish her beer. The other one stayed another hour.

'Why didn't you go with them too?' Mahmoud asked Hazem as they went outside into the cold air.

'Me? I'll go back and see them another time. The important thing is that you're now relaxed.'

'Yes, you're a good friend,' said Mahmoud with a troubled smile. His head was spinning slightly from drinking so much, and his whole body felt numb. It was a strange combination of feelings. Reaching the Orouba Hotel, Hazem stopped to light a cigarette. He blew smoke through his nostrils; then he turned to his young friend, pointing at him with the fingers holding the cigarette.

'Anyway,' he said, 'never talk about that woman Nawal al-Wazir in front of me again, okay? God damn Nawal al-Wazir.'

'Sure, I promise. God damn her,' Mahmoud agreed.

2

Nawal al-Wazir was a film director, or so she claimed. She was about forty, light-skinned with jet-black hair, plump with a double chin that gave a touch of oriental beauty to her face, which was always covered with a thin layer of slightly tacky make-up. She liked dark red lipstick, a thick line of kohl around her eyes, and black eyebrow pencil to accentuate the arch, and wore a loose scarf on her head, matching tops and skirts, and an ever-changing array of colourful plastic accessories. If anyone had asked Mahmoud al-Sawadi about her, he could have rattled off a long list of details that would have been of interest only to those equally as obsessed with her as he was. There was also an annoying detail that Mahmoud tried to ignore: the fact that she was a close friend of Mahmoud's editor, Ali Baher al-Saidi, who was a well-known writer, an opponent of the old regime, and an associate of many of the politicians whose faces often appeared on television.

On some afternoons Nawal al-Wazir would come to the magazine's offices in Karrada, stay half an hour or more, and leave with the editor in his car. During that half hour Mahmoud couldn't help seeing her every time he went into the editor's office. When she was there, the editor might invite him to sit down, to talk about something or other, and Mahmoud would always agree to his ideas and requests without discussion because he felt uncomfortable and confused in Nawal's presence.

'She's the boss's fuck buddy,' Farid Shawwaf, his colleague at the magazine, once said. Mahmoud quarrelled with him because he had no evidence. Later he accepted Farid's assessment, because what else but sex could have brought this woman and Ali Baher al-Saidi together?

Occasionally, when Saidi was away or hadn't yet arrived at the office, Mahmoud had a chance to sit alone with Nawal in the editor's office. From their conversations, Mahmoud gathered she was working on a feature film about the crimes of the Saddam Hussein regime. She made it out to be one of the most important Iraqi movies in development and said Saidi was helping with some of the formalities, such as obtaining permits, through his connections with the political class, ministries and other institutions. This gave him reason to feel more comfortable and to dismiss the horrible theory that the malicious Farid Shawwaf had planted in his mind.

His mind at ease, he continued to steal glances at Nawal, examining her closely and noting the daily changes she made to her appearance. He also continued to talk about her in front of his close friend Hazem Abboud. To make matters worse, Mahmoud had become the editor's favourite journalist. When Saidi said, 'Go there', 'Do this interview', 'Attend this conference' or 'Look into this for me', Mahmoud would usually oblige. Mahmoud alone ended up doing as much work as all the other journalists combined.

3

Mahmoud had started his life as a journalist in April 2003 at the weekly paper *Sada al-Ahwar* in the city of Amara, where he lived. For reasons he was still secretive about, he had suddenly moved to Baghdad. He came to the capital at a time when other people were leaving. 'Stay where you are until things calm down in the capital, then come,' Hazem Abboud had said to him.

But things didn't calm down. They got much worse. And Mahmoud didn't take his friend's advice. He badly needed to move to Baghdad, or, to be more precise, he needed to escape Amara. His friend Hazem didn't discover the reason until later.

Mahmoud had been working at a small newspaper in Baghdad called *al-Hadaf* for some months when Ali Baher al-Saidi asked him to work with him at the magazine. He contacted Mahmoud through his friend Farid Shawwaf, who was already working at the magazine. From his first meetings with Saidi, Mahmoud found he was drawn to the man, who was at least twenty years older than he was, though it was hard to judge his age. Saidi was extremely stylish, the embodiment of elegance. Over months of observation, not once did Mahmoud spot a flaw in his appearance. He was also active and energetic, always on the move, with a permanent smile and a talent for smoothing over crises, however serious they might be, and treating them as minor obstacles that could be overcome with a quick leap. On top of that, he inspired those around him, too, to be active and energetic.

Maybe that was why Mahmoud hardly ever challenged the orders Saidi gave him. Mahmoud hadn't worked as hard in any of the other jobs he had held over the previous two years. He was always exhausted, but he believed in Saidi and knew deep down that he was pushing him in the right direction.

4

'God damn you, Hazem Abboud, now and forever.'

Mahmoud repeated these words into the digital recorder, this time in the tone of those who recite tragic stories about the death of Hussein in Shiite meeting halls. He still had a headache when he reached the gates of the Kindi Hospital, perhaps because he hadn't eaten anything, or perhaps because of all the alcohol he had drunk the night before to relieve the tension he felt after his experience at the brothel. Now he was at the hospital reception desk, and he was still turned on. He was looking at the bottoms of the female staff and the cleaning women; he wanted all the women in the world at once. He pictured every woman in some lewd position, with him on top. Tired, he rubbed his face and played with his soft beard. Saidi would be critical if he saw him in this state. He would say, 'You mustn't make people who look at you feel depressed. Always be positive. Be a positive force and you'll survive. Shave off your beard, change your shirt, and comb your hair. Take every opportunity to look at yourself in the mirror, any mirror, even in the windows of parked cars. Compete with women in this, and don't be too oriental.'

'And what does "too oriental" mean?'

'Being oriental can be summed up in a line of poetry by Antara ibn Shaddad: "Are you surprised, Abla, that I haven't washed or anointed myself with oil for two years?"'

Mahmoud had never heard this before. But it had a big impact on him. He memorized it and repeated it often to himself. And he realized that on that day, that morning, he was a true disciple of the poet Antara.

Mahmoud had trouble reaching the victims of the explosion that had taken place in Tayaran Square that morning. He saw other journalists and the cameramen and correspondents of satellite channels. He kept following them and going into the rooms they went into. They were trying to wrap up brief spot stories, while he needed to carry out more detailed interviews and get photos that would be exclusive to the magazine.

He finished his work there without great satisfaction, then left. He felt more and more exhausted. After buying a disposable razor, he went to a restaurant on Saadoun Street, had lunch, washed his hands and mouth at the basin, then took out his razor and had a quick shave amid inquisitive looks from the restaurant staff and customers. He combed back his coarse hair with his wet fingers, then went out into the street, where he took the digital recorder out of his bag and spoke into it: 'So, Riyadh al-Sawadi, Father, may you rest in peace. Because of you I'm here. Because of you I've reached this place. But I'm tired. My joints hurt, and I haven't had enough sleep. All this has to come to an end before I reach my twenty-third birthday.'

In fact, an ending was very close indeed, or at least a pivotal moment. When Mahmoud got to the magazine offices, he set about typing up his notes and recordings, and downloaded the photos he had taken onto his computer. He was chatting with Farid Shawwaf and his other colleagues when an old messenger came to tell him that the editor wanted to see him.

Mahmoud went into the editor's office to find Saidi alone, holding a remote control and flicking through the channels on the large television screen facing his grand desk, while in his other hand he held a cigar like a thick pen. Saidi asked Mahmoud about his day and what he had accomplished, then asked him about the status of stories it was agreed would be written over the next few days. There was a large folder on the desk. Saidi reached for it, turned it over, examined it, and said, 'These are the stories your colleagues have written in the past month. None of them is fit for publication.'

Saidi lit his cigar and took deep drags on it till it produced thick smoke. He blew smoke casually into the air, then went back to talking to Mahmoud, who seemed uneasy.

'I'm going to get rid of Zaid Murshid, Adnan al-Anwar, and that thin girl, Maysa, and tell your friend Farid Shawwaf to stop being so lazy. He's a good writer, but he doesn't believe in his work here,' Saidi said.

'What should I do with him? I thought you had a good relationship with him,' Mahmoud replied.

'I don't want to argue with him. He's a real pro at arguing. I wish he would channel that energy into writing, and then he would be in a better position. Drop him a hint. You're his friend. Make it clear to him indirectly.'

Mahmoud tried to come up with an indirect way to send the message but he couldn't think of anything. In silence he looked at Saidi for a moment, then turned towards the television.

'There's something else, my friend,' Saidi said. 'You're working too hard.' Mahmoud was taken aback. The remark came as a great relief.

The cigar went out, and Saidi placed it on the edge of a

large ceramic ashtray. He kept looking at his watch: it was time for Nawal al-Wazir to come, Mahmoud assumed. He hadn't noticed that Saidi hadn't finished his sentence yet – the man loved to punctuate his meticulously constructed sentences with dramatic pauses. Saidi looked at Mahmoud for a second and then continued: 'You're tenacious. That's why, starting tomorrow, you are editor-in-chief of *al-Haqiqa*.'

5

Three of his colleagues sat in front of Mahmoud at a wooden table with a red tablecloth covered by a thick sheet of plastic. Each had a can of Heineken, a glass mug and a bowl of boiled beans. Mahmoud had ordered a bottle of soda, and the others had failed to persuade him to drink even one can of beer. His stomach was unsettled after the previous day's adventures. Mahmoud looked at their faces as they laughed: Zaid Murshid, Adnan al-Anwar, and Farid Shawwaf. Saidi had made up his mind that the first two should be fired and the third was at risk of dismissal, while Mahmoud had been promoted to the second most important position at the magazine. How could he break this news without them overturning the table on him? Should he tell them now, before they got drunk? Or should he wait until their reflexes were dulled and they could take the shock more easily?

Might it help if he, too, had a drink? It felt like a major ordeal, and he decided to put it off until the next day.

They were laughing. Farid Shawwaf was talking enthusiastically about something he was working on – an anthology of the one hundred strangest Iraqi stories.

Why don't you first try to finish what you get paid to do, Mahmoud thought as he listened to his friend explaining how these weird but real stories had to be saved from oblivion.

'Why don't you write them as features for the magazine? We need stories like that,' Mahmoud said.

'For the magazine?' Farid replied scornfully. 'But that's just journalism. It gets published one day, and the next day it's gone. That's just a way to make a living. I'm talking about a book.'

'Okay. Publish them here first, and then put them together as a book,' said Mahmoud.

'No. You have to think of them as a book from the start.'

'Write them as a book from the start, and then serialize them in the magazine.'

Zaid Murshid and Adnan al-Anwar laughed. Farid Shawwaf looked at them and shouted, 'This guy's killing himself for the magazine. God damn the magazine!'

Mahmoud lost interest in pursuing the argument. The place was dark and full of smoke, crowded with young men and middle-aged men with paunches, moustaches and shiny bald patches. Some of them, Mahmoud later discovered, came from outside Baghdad, possibly from remote towns and provinces. A short distance from Andalus Square, it felt like a secret, unlicensed tavern; it could be reached only through a small restaurant. Despite being seedy, it was Farid Shawwaf and his friends' favourite place.

The four of them left without getting completely drunk. They resented the fact that Mahmoud had only drunk a soda.

They walked lazily towards the square because from there Farid Shawwaf could get a bus to his apartment in Karrada, while Zaid Murshid and Adnan al-Anwar could catch one to Bab al-Sharqi.

The sky was grey and rapidly growing darker. They stood in Andalus Square, opposite the Sadeer Novotel hotel. Farid Shawwaf was still chatting about his hypothetical book. If he had crossed to the other side of the street at that moment, he would have met a certain death: an orange rubbish truck loaded with dozens of pounds of dynamite turned off the main street and slammed into the metal gate of the hotel, setting off an explosion the likes of which these four journalists had never seen.

Everyone fell back from the blast. They were battered by a gust of dust and pebbles. It took them a minute to realize they hadn't been hit. Without thinking, they ran to the other side of the street. On the asphalt beyond the central reservation they saw a body. They went up to it, and Mahmoud touched it with his hand. The body suddenly moved. They lifted the man to his feet, and Mahmoud recognized him at once. It was Hadi the junk dealer, or Hadi the liar, as the customers in Aziz's coffee shop called him. Hadi looked at their faces in horror, brushed their hands off his body, and hurried away, ignoring their calls to stop because he might have a serious injury.

They didn't see anything else. There didn't seem to be any victims from this explosion. The bomber who was driving the rubbish truck had probably been vaporized. That's what they told themselves when they saw the hotel staff coming out to the forecourt and heard the sirens of the police cars. They preferred to walk away to Bab al-Sharqi.

When they reached Nasr Square, Zaid Murshid and Adnan al-Anwar took a bus towards Bab al-Sharqi. Farid said he preferred to take a taxi. He was troubled and confused, and the stupor he was in when he left the secret bar had completely lifted.

'You could be dead now. You were eager to keep chatting. Your wonderful stories saved you, my friend,' said Mahmoud, with a stutter and dramatic pauses between the sentences, rather like the way Saidi spoke. Farid widened his eyes in a daze, maybe because what Mahmoud had said was true.

Farid left, and Mahmoud felt he had enough energy to walk

all the way to the Orouba Hotel. He took out a cigarette and put it to his lips but didn't light it. He felt strangely relaxed despite the disaster that had taken place before his eyes, but didn't bother to examine this apparent contradiction. He remembered a single phrase and repeated it to himself. The phrase caught his imagination. He took out his digital recorder:

'Be positive. Be a positive force and you'll survive. Be positive. Be a positive force and you'll survive.'

He repeated the words several times like someone obsessed, until he noticed that the batteries in the recorder were dead.

CHAPTER FIVE

The Body

1

'Get up, Daniel,' Elishva shouted. 'Get up, Danny. Come along, my boy.'

He stood up immediately. So this was the command that the dead boy with the silver bangles in the cemetery in Najaf had talked about the night before. With her words the old woman had animated this extraordinary composite – made up of disparate body parts and the soul of the hotel guard who had lost his life. The old woman brought him out of anonymity with the name she gave him: Daniel.

Daniel saw the old woman standing in the upstairs room that had collapsed. Wisps of grey hair stuck out from under the black headband she had tied loosely around her small head. She was wrapped tightly in a dark woollen jacket with torn sleeves, and at her feet the moulting grey cat looked at Daniel with wide, frightened eyes, mewing softly as if talking to itself. It was almost six o'clock in the morning, and the air was very cold. The sounds coming from outside were still faint; the daytime bustle hadn't begun yet. Hadi the junk dealer, asleep in his room and in pain, wouldn't wake up till noon.

Daniel clambered over piles of bricks to what had been the floor of the room before it collapsed. He followed the old woman and her cat downstairs.

Elishva put the heater close to Daniel in the sitting room, then went away for a few minutes and came back with a creased white shirt, an old green sweater and a pair of jeans, all smelling strongly of mothballs. She had taken the clothes from Daniel's chest of drawers, where they had been kept for many years. She threw the clothes at him and told him to put them on. Before leaving him to himself, she gave him a final glance. She didn't ask him anything – she had promised her patron saint that she wouldn't ask too many questions. All this time she had left her thick glasses dangling from her neck, but she still knew this man didn't look much like Daniel. No matter. Not many people came back looking the same as when they left. She had heard enough stories to explain the differences and the changes – stories told by a succession of women ravaged by the effects of time and by the realization that they would never again see the missing faces they remembered so well. What was happening was a miracle, she believed, and it was hard to predict where it might lead. She had been preparing to remove the big picture of the saint from the wall and stash it away in some corner of the house. Maybe she would put it in one of the dusty rooms on the upper floor. With his beautiful eyes and his white horse, Saint George could watch the specks of dust come in through the cracks in the windowpanes overlooking the street. He would regret ignoring her all those years and failing to recognize that, given the depths of her despair, it was time the Lord and His holy images listened to the bleating of His lost sheep.

Elishva left the strange, naked man staring at the walls and furniture. Daniel stood up and looked at the pictures – one of a man in his fifties with a thin black moustache and wearing a Western-style suit, another of a clean-shaven young man with thick hair and big sideburns. His sleepy, cloudy eyes were looking away from the camera. Daniel moved closer to this picture. It must have been taken twenty years earlier. He noticed the reflection of his own face in the glass. It rather surprised him – this was the first time he had seen himself. He ran his finger over the stitches on his face and neck. He looked very ugly. How come the old woman didn't seem startled by his dreadful appearance? He moved on to another picture. It was a warrior-saint on a white horse, thrusting his lance into the throat of a mythical dragon. He studied it. The saint's face was soft and gentle and beautiful, like the holy men in all icons. The old woman was inside, making something for breakfast. He could hear the clatter of pots as she went about her business. Slowly, he put on the three garments. They fitted him perfectly. He went back to look at his reflection in the picture of Daniel Tadros Moshe and noticed, even though it was a black-andwhite photograph, that Daniel was wearing the same clothes: a white shirt with a wide, slightly raised collar under a V-neck sweater. Apart from the crude stitches on his face and neck, he looked almost like him. The old woman had had that in mind. Given that her sight was definitely weak, when she came back into the sitting room she would see only what she wanted to see.

Daniel turned his attention to the picture of the martyred saint, studying it in the daylight streaming in through the window. He noticed the skill with which the artist had rendered the folds in the bright-red cloak that fluttered behind the strapping warrior-saint. It was a wonderful picture of a handsome saint with delicate lips, and now those lips began to move.

'You have to be careful,' it said.

The saint's lips really were moving.

'She's a hapless old woman. If you harm her or make her sad, I swear I'll plunge this lance in your throat.'

2

The new version of Daniel slept on the sofa in the sitting room. Elishva covered him with a thick duvet and left him to resume her daily chores, which usually meant cleaning things she had already cleaned, dusting the furniture, the icons, and the pictures, and sweeping the courtyard – that took up half her day.

The cat escaped once more to the roof and looked out over the courtyard of Hadi's dilapidated house. Hadi scratched his head in puzzlement and looked all over the place for the body he had made. He imagined finding it hanging from a wall or hovering in that morning's pure blue sky.

Despite the pains in his joints and his head, Hadi went outside and looked up and down the lane for a sign that something strange had happened, but he wasn't willing to stop any of his neighbours to ask, 'Excuse me, have you seen a naked corpse walking down the street?'

Hadi was a liar, and everyone knew it. He would need witnesses to corroborate a claim of having had fried eggs for breakfast, let alone a story about a naked corpse made up of the body parts of people killed in explosions.

Hadi looked up at the roof of Elishva's house and those of the neighbouring houses, thinking someone might have dragged the body up there, but he couldn't see anything. He opened all the wardrobes and cupboards in the courtyard of his house. Then he walked up and down the nearby lanes. He stopped when he got to Abu Zaidoun, the old barber, who was slumped on a white garden chair outside his shop, but Hadi doubted he would have seen anything even if the body had walked right in front of him. The owner of the Akhawain laundry shop told him the police had been raiding houses all morning in search of armed gangs that were trafficking women out of Iraq. A worker at the bakery said there were 'terrorists' coming from the provinces to stay at a local hotel and that the police and the Americans were searching the hotels one by one. Hadi also heard that two young prostitutes he had slept with had travelled that day to Syria to work in the nightclubs – apparently Baghdad was no longer lucrative. He heard lots of other news. In fact he spent half the day listening, but he didn't hear anything about his mysterious disappearing corpse.

3

Umm Salim took it as a good omen when she saw Elishva at the butcher's. Elishva bought half a pound of beef and two pounds of well-cleaned sheep's tripe, then went to the greengrocer's shop next door. Having removed her widow's mourning headband, she was wearing a red headscarf with white flowers, like a young woman. Umm Salim wondered what had happened to her.

The two women did their shopping together and walked slowly back to the lane. Umm Salim was talking about what had happened the previous morning and how the dreadful explosion had made cracks in the walls of some of the houses. She gathered from Elishva that she'd been at church at the time. Elishva said she had heard the explosion but hadn't seen anything when she got back. This was further evidence for Umm Salim that Elishva had special powers.

When Umm Salim asked about her striking red headscarf, Elishva looked down at the street and said quietly, 'The time to be sad is over. The Lord has finally heard my prayer.'

'I'm delighted to hear it. What good news.'

Elishva couldn't help but drop her bombshell, telling Umm Salim straight out that her son had come home. Umm Salim just walked on in stunned silence. What was this old woman talking about, she wondered?

When Elishva reached the door of her house, Umm Salim, whose house was a few yards farther down the lane, stopped. 'Is he at home now?' she asked.

'Yes, he's asleep. He's very tired.'

Umm Salim curled her lips like someone deep in thought, but she didn't go into the house to check, a major mistake that she would later regret. She was busy thinking about the lunch she had to prepare for her husband, who sat on the balcony all day in silence, reading old newspapers. She didn't take seriously what Elishva had said – the news was too big to take in after such a cursory announcement. Umm Salim told herself she'd drop in on Elishva later, perhaps in the afternoon, to find out more.

But it turned out she wouldn't find out anything more. In the afternoon she was too busy after her middle son suddenly announced the name of the girl he was planning to marry, leaving her no time to see the old woman's son, who had come back from a war that had ended twenty or more years ago. Eventually, Umm Salim would defect to the group that believed the old woman was senile, and Elishva would lose the last of her loyal allies.

4

Hadi went back home. He felt around on the floor of the courtyard for blood or bits of the body parts he knew he had held in his hands when he was cutting them up or stitching them together to get the body into a reasonably finished state. He couldn't find anything: the heavy rain that had fallen the day before had washed everything away. He spent the late morning stretched out in bed, looking up at the water-damaged ceiling. Then he looked at the far wall where his late friend Nahem Abdaki had hung the Throne Verse of the Quran. One of the cardboard edges had come loose and was curling downward from the moisture. If someone pulled it, they could peel the whole verse off the wall. At the end of the day, he thought what had happened might prove convenient: he had wanted to get rid of the body, and it had disappeared, sparing him another demeaning task – cutting it up and unstitching all the thread, then throwing the parts away in various bins around the neighbourhood.

In the afternoon Hadi went to Aziz's coffee shop, but it was too crowded and his Egyptian friend wasn't free to chat with him, so he headed to the home of the old man from Amirli in another attempt to persuade him to sell his old furniture. As usual, he was back at square one in his negotiations. For the tenth time he heard the history of how the old gramophone player was made and where he had bought it and the stories of whatever piece of furniture or object stood before them.

What if this well-dressed, clean-shaven old man had known he was standing next to a criminal who tampered with human body parts? He would have taken him down the concrete path to the outer gate, said goodbye to him then and there, and shut the door on him once and for all.

Hadi would later narrate these details several times, because he loved details that gave his story credibility and made it more vivid. He would just be telling people about his hard day's work, but they would listen as though it were the best fable Hadi the liar had ever told.

Sitting in the coffee shop, he would tell the story from the beginning, never tiring of repeating himself. He immersed himself in the story and went with the flow, maybe in order to give pleasure to others or maybe to convince himself that it was just a story from his fertile imagination and that it had never really happened.

5

Elishva was busy making *kashka*. She boiled the bulgur wheat and added the chickpeas, spices, and cubes of meat. She was good at making traditional dishes but rarely had much occasion to do so – she wouldn't make them just for her cat. But that day was different. She was honouring a special guest and fulfilling an old vow. As the old woman stirred the *kashka*, she repeated to herself, 'A blessing and peace from God our Father and the Lord Jesus Christ, who loved us before we loved Him.'

Having adopted many of the customs of the neighbourhood, Elishva saw it as a vow she was now fulfilling, although Father Josiah always corrected her.

'We don't set conditions for the Lord, as Muslims do,' he would say. 'We don't say, "If You do this, then I'll do that."'

Elishva knew what he meant, of course, but she saw no harm in setting conditions for God, as Umm Salim and her other Muslim neighbours did. She didn't see the Lord in quite the same way as Father Josiah did. The Lord wasn't 'in the highest'; she didn't see him as domineering or tyrannical. He was just an old friend, and it would be hard to abandon that friendship.

Elishva's special guest didn't eat any of the food she put in front of him. She had a little of it herself, and Nabu finished off the remaining pieces of meat and licked the bowls. She wasn't bothered that her son, or his ghost, hadn't eaten a bite. Perhaps he was like Abraham's guests in the Quranic version of their visit, or perhaps he didn't have an appetite. She wouldn't pepper him with questions, lest he run away.

Elishva spent the rest of the day until late at night muttering intermittently to her taciturn guest. Nothing important happened in the meantime. The man who sold cooking gas came, and Elishva swapped an empty bottle for a full one; the man carried it to the end of the corridor to help the old lady out. Some American helicopters flew noisily over the house, causing it to shake and the birds that belonged to Abdel Razzaq, the boy in the house at the back, to flap their wings in a panic, sending feathers up into the air. Umm Salim didn't come by, nor any of the other neighbours – not even Diana, the pretty Armenian girl from the next lane, whose mother, Veronica Munib, sometimes encouraged her to visit Elishva to find out if she was short of anything or needed anything done.

As she chatted with her guest, Elishva opened up the boxes inside her that had long remained closed and took out everything that was in them. She dozed off on the sofa opposite the one where the strange, silent man was sitting. When she woke up, she saw him staring at the faint light coming through the window overlooking the lane.

Elishva opened up to Daniel about her conflict with her husband, Tadros, who buried an empty coffin for Danny against her wishes. Tadros, a junior clerk in the public transport department, went with some relatives, friends and acquaintances to the cemetery of the Assyrian Church of the East in eastern Baghdad and buried a coffin containing only some of Daniel's clothes and pieces of his broken guitar. They prayed for him, then laid a gravestone reading in Syriac and Arabic, 'Here lies Daniel.'

Elishva hadn't agreed to go with them because her heart told her that her son was not dead. She didn't look at the grave until Tadros himself died and was buried next to the grave of his son. It broke her heart to read the name of her son on the limestone marker, and even then she wouldn't acknowledge that he was dead, despite the passing of the years.

During that time Ninous Malko's family moved into one of the rooms on the upper floor of the old woman's house. They had left their rented house in Bataween. Eventually, Matilda, Elishva's second daughter, married Ninous's younger son, and a strong friendship developed between Elishva and Ninous Malko and his wife. They almost made up for the succession of losses that Elishva had suffered, because apart from Daniel and his father, Elishva's two daughters were also planning to leave. It wasn't hard for her new relatives to believe that Daniel might come back one day. There were many missing people, and some of them were bound to come back. That kept happening. One of Ninous's brothers had come back after years in prison in Iran, and at the time many people had talked about the shock of learning that he had abandoned his original religion and become a Shiite Muslim of the Twelver branch. He remained a Shiite for several years but gradually converted back to Christianity, or at least that's what he had his family believe in order to put an end to the strife that his conversion had caused.

Many prisoners came home after the war over Kuwait and in the middle of the 1990s. Because of the severity of the economic sanctions imposed on Iraq, the husbands of Hilda and Matilda decided to emigrate. The two sisters wouldn't move away unless their mother came too. But like a stubborn mountain goat, Elishva refused. The disagreement continued for a full year, but the old woman wouldn't relent. Finally she convinced her daughters that she would join them when they had settled down and she had completely given up hope that Daniel might come back. But she never did give up hope, and the presence of Ninous Malko's family was some consolation for the loss of her daughters. But on the eve of the declaration of the last war, Ninous's wife accused Elishva of practising some kind of black magic on her two little boys and said she had prevented one of them from speaking even at the age of six. She was frightened of the old woman, especially after she found her talking to pictures or to the many cats that roamed the house. Once she told her husband that one of the cats spoke back to the old woman and had a conversation with her. She even said she suspected the cats were in fact human and that Elishva had transformed them into cats with satanic magic.

Ninous didn't believe such superstitious nonsense, but he couldn't take his wife's complaining about the house, and after US forces invaded Baghdad he took his little family to Ankawa in Erbil. He didn't tell Hilda or Matilda, and Elishva didn't object – she seemed supportive, or indifferent. Her daughters were shocked when they found out that their mother was alone in a big house in a troubled city where the demons had broken out of their dungeons and come to the surface all at once – at least that was how they imagined it.

At the time, they were calling Elishva every Sunday on the Thuraya phone at the Church of Saint Odisho, and if Elishva didn't turn up for some reason, then Father Josiah himself would call to reassure them. The phone call wouldn't last more than a minute – the priests wanted to be fair to all the people who needed to use the phone, and there were many. Sometimes Elishva and one of her daughters would start arguing halfway into the call, and the minute would run out just as the argument was getting heated, forcing Father Josiah to pull the phone out of Elishva's hand. The daughters said they wanted to come back to Baghdad and carry their mother off by force, but they didn't go beyond threatening this. If the argument was interrupted, Elishva would argue with herself instead or grab hold of one of the women in the church to listen to her fiery sermon about how she refused to leave her home and move to a place she knew nothing about. Father Josiah encouraged her to stay, because he saw it as a religious obligation. It wasn't good that everyone should leave the country. Things had been just as bad for the Assyrians in previous centuries, but they had stayed in Iraq and had survived. None of us should think only of ourselves. That's what he said in his sermon sometimes.

At the beginning of that year, Father Josiah asked Elishva if she could put up the Sankhiro family, who had fled sectarian cleansing in the southern Baghdad district of Dora. The family took the room that Ninous Malko's family had been living in, but only a few weeks later they left for Syria, with plans to emigrate to Europe. Soon afterwards, three of Elishva's cats disappeared, and then Elishva found a fourth cat dead on the roof, its body all inflated. She suspected that a piece of shrapnel had hit it or it had eaten poisoned meat.

Elishva chatted for half an hour about her cats and how Nabu was the only one left. Then she suddenly remembered Abu Zaidoun, the Baathist responsible for sending her son off to war. Abu Zaidoun used to track down people avoiding military service, and Daniel had been late in responding to the draft. He had refused to sign up and go to the training camps, wanting instead to finish studying music. He loved to play the guitar and kept one in his wardrobe, although he didn't play it well.

Abu Zaidoun took Danny away by the collar. From the training camp, Daniel went straight to the front and never came back. From then on, Abu Zaidoun was Elishva's sworn enemy. When the Baathists brought an empty coffin for Daniel, along with some clothes and personal belongings, old Tadros smashed his son's guitar in grief.

Some pieces of the guitar were put in the grand red-teak coffin that Tadros had bought and were lowered into the grave with it. So there was a smashed guitar in an empty coffin, a house that had lost the ghost of its only son, and an enemy who made merry in the neighbourhood, imposing his authority on everyone with few people standing up to him. But Elishva stood up to him. She cursed him in her prayers and whenever she saw him on the street. Abu Zaidoun no longer went down Lane 7 in case Elishva suddenly came out of her house to curse him. Some of the women had vowed that if the evil man died, they would slaughter a sheep to God Almighty. Elishva also made a vow, but she never told Father Josiah about it. Now she was revealing it, to her silent guest, for the first time ever.

As night fell Elishva was winding up one part of her rambling monologue. She told him several times that she knew he would come back. Antoinette, one of her relatives, hadn't believed her, or Martha, or the wife of her brother Youaresh. Now they had all died or emigrated. She took out an old photo album to show him. In the lamplight she showed him pictures of himself as a child, standing with the church choir in his choirboy vestments. There were pictures of him with his friends at school. At a bar or a restaurant. Wearing team uniforms, his foot on a ball in the same way as the famous footballer Ali Kadhim. All the boys who wanted a picture like that would put their right foot on the ball, put their right hand on their hip, and smile. The picture wouldn't be any good unless they did exactly that. There was another picture of him with his football team, their arms all wrapped around each other. The picture was faded and had water stains. When Daniel had finished flipping through the pictures, he got to his feet and, suddenly curious, went to roam through the other rooms. Elishva stayed seated, looking at the picture of her patron saint by the light of the lantern. It didn't look like it was going to move or speak that night.

From the kitchen came the clatter of pots and pans falling. He must have tripped on something in the dark. Elishva heard him go to the roof. He was away for a few minutes, then came back, carrying something in his hand. He quickly hid it in his trouser pocket. Then he opened his mouth to speak for the first time. At last Elishva heard his voice. It was croaky, as though he hadn't said anything since he was born. Pronouncing the words with difficulty, he told her that he had to go out. She wanted to say, 'Why are you going? You've just come back. Why would you leave me? Whenever anyone goes out that door, they never come back. It's like a door that opens into a hole.' Feeling like screaming, she gently held on to the sleeve of his green sweater. She could feel how firm his arm was, like the branch of a tree. She looked up at his face, but it was too dark to see anything. He looked away. The cat walked between them, rubbing itself against his trousers and purring softly.

'I'll be back. Don't worry,' he said hoarsely.

He slipped out of her grasp and walked towards the door. She heard his footsteps as he tramped across the courtyard and then along the path that led to the door. She heard him open the door and then close it gently. Silence reigned again in the large, lonely house. She felt very thirsty and more tired than ever before. Sitting despondent on the sofa before the picture of Saint George the Martyr, she wanted to ask her patron saint some questions or chat with him but couldn't summon the energy. She noticed that the saint's metal shield had a new shine, as though someone inside the picture had given it a polish. Then the shine faded, and she had nothing to say. She had said everything she had to say. She wouldn't speak again for the next few days. Blinking, she looked at the patches of yellow lamplight on the rippled surface of the old picture, while the old cat curled up between her legs in search of warmth.

CHAPTER SIX

Strange Events

1

Two police tanker trucks arrived, blocking off access to Lane 1. Five armed Iraqi policemen and a US military police-man got out. They pushed onlookers behind the two tankers. The lane had been empty since morning, and many of the residents had managed only a silent, wary peek through the wooden latticed windows of the rickety old *mashrabiya* that overlooked the lane. All was calm while a policeman took photographs.

A few minutes later Faraj the estate agent arrived out of breath, his thick beard swaying with every step he took. Under his arm was a small leather briefcase in which he kept documents and official papers for his visits to government offices.

The American immediately accosted Faraj and asked him about one of the houses – who lived there and whether he knew anything about an incident that had taken place outside. An Iraqi in police uniform was translating the American's questions into Arabic and looking accusingly at Faraj, who appeared stunned. Although he had clout in the neighbourhood, he was still frightened by the Americans. He knew they operated with considerable independence and no one could hold them to account for what they did. As suddenly as the wind could shift, they could throw you down a dark hole. Faraj opened his dry lips and explained that he owned the house, or rather he had been renting it from the government for fifteen years, and he paid the rent regularly to the lawyer in the department of frozen assets. As he spoke he took some papers out of his bag and, with a trembling hand, showed them to the policemen.

The American left him to talk. Nearby sat the bodies of four beggars who had been found sitting upright in the lane. He turned back to Faraj to ask again if he knew them. Faraj nodded. He felt the blood in his veins run cold. What a terrible start to the day. Who had killed these poor beggars? Had an act of God struck them dead in an instant while they were sitting like that?

Each of the beggars had his hands around the neck of the man in front of him. It looked like some weird tableau or theatrical scene. Their clothes were dirty and tattered, and their heads hung forward. If Hazem Abboud had seen this and taken a picture, he would have won an international prize for it.

More and more onlookers gathered at the ends of the lane, and timid heads started to look out cautiously from behind the *mashrabiya* screens. The American didn't like that there were so many onlookers. With a wave of his hand he urged the Iraqi policemen to speed things up. They took Faraj's phone number and asked him to drop in at the Saadoun police station if he came across any information about the crime or found any witnesses. Faraj breathed a sigh of relief and started to stroke his thick beard. He took out his prayer beads, plucked up his courage to move closer to the beggars' corpses, and looked at them with disdain.

Some of the policemen put on white rubber gloves and started to unlock the hands gripping the necks. They carried the bodies quickly to one of the vehicles, and then they all left.

People suddenly poured into the lane and gathered around Faraj to ask him about the incident. He dismissed them with a wave, hit some of the boys with his long string of black prayer beads, and walked away.

Up above, from a wooden window of the derelict old house opposite the one where the beggars had been squatting, another old beggar was furtively watching what was happening. He had been in the same place the previous night when the crime took place, drinking by himself, and had drunk half a bottle of Asriya arak when he heard the fighting in the dark lane. He dismissed it at first as just one of the usual drunken brawls between beggars returning to their wretched rooms at the end of the night. They had insulted one another and suddenly remembered what a terrible state they were in, and they got it into their heads that the problem lay with the creature that happened to be standing in front of them, who was usually one of their fellow beggars.

The brawling continued and the curses grew louder, mixed with gasps, groans and screams of pain. The drunken beggar poked his head out the window, but he couldn't see anything. Then, in the headlights of a car that was turning at the far end of the lane, he was able to see five figures holding hands and moving in a circle.

On the evening of the same day that the bodies of the beggars were found, the drunken beggar was brought to Faraj's office. He started to blabber, and word soon reached Faraj, who saw him as a possible opportunity to enhance his authority. The man still hadn't recovered from his drinking binge. In fact, he was always drunk and it didn't make sense to rely on what he said, but there was no harm in taking advantage of it.

Faraj shouted a string of invective at the beggar, insulting him and all the drunks in the world. He prayed that God would rid the country of them and their disgusting behaviour. He blamed the government, saying it was frightened of the Americans and wouldn't apply sharia law to save people from this scourge. As Faraj issued this frightening tirade, the drunken beggar looked on like a terrified, helpless mouse.

Faraj asked the beggar what he had seen, and the beggar repeated what he had started spreading in the neighbourhood an hour after the police patrol left: that one of the five men was a horrible guy with a big mouth.

'But there were four of them!'

'No, five. Each of the four wanted to grab the throat of the fifth man, but they grabbed each other's throats instead.'

'What kind of nonsense is that, for God's sake?'

Faraj slowly took a sip of tea and looked with contempt at the old beggar. At the same moment someone else was drinking his tea – Brigadier Sorour Mohamed Majid, the director general of the Tracking and Pursuit Department. One of the brigadier's assistants came into his office and put the 'four beggars' file on his desk. The brigadier put his glass of tea back on the saucer, picked up the file, and turned it over to check that the case was the responsibility of his department. It was a summary of a police report indicating that the four beggars had died by strangling one another.

2

Mahmoud and Ali Baher al-Saidi left the office in Saidi's black Mercedes. Saidi invited Mahmoud out sometimes, and Mahmoud didn't have much choice about whether to go. Saidi would call Mahmoud, who would find Saidi standing at his door, holding his black leather briefcase and about to depart.

'We have to go on a small errand, and I want you with me,' Saidi usually said, and Mahmoud would be curious to find out what he meant by this mysterious expression. Saidi was addicted to expressions like this, ones with hooks to pull the other person along behind him. He would never tell you the whole story in one sentence: he would tease it out in dribs and drabs. When he was with Saidi, Mahmoud might end up going into the Green Zone and being thoroughly searched. Or they would take an elevator with familiar-looking senior officials. He once met the minister of planning in an elevator and saw how the minister shared a laugh with Saidi. Wow, they were friends! Many women shook Saidi's hand – translators, civil servants, journalists, and others who worked in parliament. Mahmoud looked at himself in the mirrors that were everywhere, but what he saw meant nothing. All he saw was Saidi and his network of relationships.

'Where are we going?' Mahmoud asked as they got into Saidi's car. Daylight was fading, the sky gradually turning black. Mahmoud had had to cancel an appointment with his friend Hazem Abboud. In the morning Hazem had invited him to an exhibition of photographs by some of his friends who worked for the news agencies. Maybe he would go the next day, he said to himself.

'We're going to meet an old friend. You might get some useful information out of him.'

'Information about what?'

'I've been working on him for a while. There are things happening on the ground that we know nothing about. What's behind all the insecurity? We need to exploit any piece of information we can get to embarrass the Americans and the government,' said Saidi.

Mahmoud clearly didn't understand anything. He had

imagined Saidi was friends with the Americans and the government; why did he want to embarrass them? He didn't have the courage to ask. He would find out when they met this old friend, as Saidi described him. They drove into Karrada and ran into a traffic jam created by a patrol of American Hummers. The troops on top of the vehicles were pointing their weapons at the cars behind, which kept at least twenty yards back.

Saidi turned on the stereo, and a Whitney Houston song came on. Saidi didn't seem bothered by the scene in front of him. In fact, he rarely seemed bothered by anything. He believed in the future, as Farid Shawwaf put it. But Farid said that with a touch of sarcasm, meaning Saidi knew he himself would be better off in the future. It had nothing to do with the country or what was happening in it. Mahmoud was confused about what Farid said. He didn't want to think too much about his own attitude towards Saidi or Saidi's attitude towards the general situation. These things required a level of effort, concentration and mental distance that Mahmoud just didn't have right now, or else he was just trying to trick himself into thinking he didn't. He knew that Farid Shawwaf was spiteful and hard to please and always trying to discredit people. He wasn't even grateful for the trouble Mahmoud had taken to keep him on at the magazine and save him from being fired along with Zaid Murshid, Adnan al-Anwar, and Maysa, the thin girl, who had wept bitterly when she was told she was being dismissed.

Saidi's car approached an imposing gate flanked by enormous concrete walls of a kind Mahmoud had never seen before in the streets of Baghdad. Night had fallen, and Saidi had taken a series of turns in Jadriya to avoid the traffic jam, so Mahmoud no longer knew where they were. The gate opened, and they drove down a long, deserted street lined with eucalyptus trees. The farther they went, the quieter it became. The sound of the traffic and police sirens faded into the distance.

At the end of the street they turned into a side lane, and Mahmoud saw police cars parked alongside an American Hummer and some civilian cars. A man in uniform waved them into a parking space.

Mahmoud and Saidi got out of the car and were escorted into a two-storey building by a man in civilian clothes. Saidi turned to Mahmoud. 'So, you don't have any appointments or anything?' he said with his usual smile. 'Today we're going to have lunch together.'

They went into a grand office, and as soon as they entered, Mahmoud could smell an apple-scented air freshener. A short white man with a shiny bald patch, dressed in civilian clothes and chewing something, stood up behind his desk. He and Saidi laughed and embraced; then he shook hands with Mahmoud, and they all sat down on plush sofas in front of the man's desk. Mahmoud learned that the man was Brigadier Sorour Mohamed Majid, the director general of the Tracking and Pursuit Department. But tracking and pursuit of what, Mahmoud wondered? He assumed he would find out in the course of the meeting.

Saidi had said the visit would be short, but it lasted over two hours. The conversation ranged widely, and sometimes they laughed so much they cried. Mahmoud laughed too; he had no problem with that. He had nothing else on his schedule; he was his own man. All he had to look forward to was going back to his miserable hotel room in Bataween. But he did want to have a smoke, and the smart man whose office smelled of apple didn't look like he would welcome smokers. Saidi himself hadn't lit a cigarette. Mahmoud gathered from the meeting that Brigadier Majid was an old friend of Saidi's. They had gone to middle school together, but the years had kept them apart. Now they were meeting up again, perhaps as part of the same assignment: serving the new Iraq.

Brigadier Majid had been a colonel in the intelligence service of the old Iraqi army, and for his new position, he had obtained an exemption from the de-Baathification regulations, as well as a promotion to a sensitive post that was rarely mentioned in public. He was in charge of a special information unit set up by the Americans and so far kept largely under their supervision. Its mission was to monitor unusual crimes, urban legends, and superstitious rumours that arose around specific incidents, and then to find out what really happened and, more important, to make predictions about crimes that would take place in the future: car bombings and assassinations of officials and other important people. The department had provided a good service in that field over the past two years. They were doing it all undercover, and the information they obtained was being used indirectly. The Tracking and Pursuit Department was never mentioned in public, to preserve its secret status and protect the people working there.

Mahmoud couldn't understand why Saidi had arranged for him to be briefed on all this. Why did Saidi trust him so much that he would take him along on these mysterious missions? It wasn't the first time, and it didn't look like it would be the last. He had spent the last two months driving around with Saidi in his black Mercedes, going from one place to another. He knew, and he thought Saidi also knew, that the recent assassinations targeted not just prominent people but anyone like Saidi who wore a smart suit and drove a fancy car. Someone was bound to assassinate him one day. Whoever was with him at the time might well die too. The story of Mahmoud al-Sawadi and his dreams of professional advancement could come to an abrupt end.

Saidi might be a fool or a hero, someone oblivious to what was happening around him or a courageous adventurer.

Mahmoud preferred to see himself as stupid, at least in his dealings with himself if not with others, because the turning points in his life had come about because of stupid things, not because of planning or intelligence. His coming to Baghdad, for example, was due to a big mistake he had made back in Amara.

A muscular young man put a tray with some bulbous tea glasses on the table next to them. Mahmoud came out of his reverie. Brigadier Majid kept declining to give Saidi any information that could be published.

'We have analysts in parapsychology, astrologers, people who specialize in communication with spirits and with the djinn, and soothsayers,' said the brigadier.

'Do you really believe in such things?'

'It's work. You don't know how many weird stories we have to deal with. The aim is to get more control, to provide information about the sources of violence and incitement to hatred, and to prevent a civil war.'

'A civil war?'

'We're now in the middle of an information war. An information civil war. And some of my soothsayers are talking about a real war within the next six or seven months.'

Mahmoud's heart raced when he heard what Majid was saying. His head was spinning like a jet engine. He tried to digest this deluge of strange ideas but couldn't. He was frozen silent, holding the handle of his tea glass but not drinking. He felt as if he had become nothing more than a pair of ears.

'Should I buy that printing press I told you about? Should I or shouldn't I expand my operations?' asked Saidi.

Brigadier Majid stood up to turn off his mobile phones, which had all started ringing. He looked over his glasses at Saidi in the distance. 'I don't think so,' he said. 'I'd leave that aside for now.'

Saidi didn't press the subject. He went back to trying to obtain information to report in the magazine. Brigadier Majid picked up a folder from his desk and waved it around. 'This is the file on four beggars who were strangled to death a few days ago in Bataween. They strangled one another. It was meant to send a message. There are people who are trying to convey something. We don't have much information yet, but you can follow the case by keeping in touch with the Saadoun police station.'

Saidi looked at Mahmoud as if to say he should take on that task. Then he looked back at the brigadier, who was still standing by his desk. From the sofa, Saidi asked him about similar stories, but the brigadier said he couldn't say any more. After a pause, the brigadier came back to stand in the middle of the room.

'There are reports about criminals who don't die when they're shot,' he said. 'Several reports from various parts of Baghdad. The bullet goes into the criminal's head or body, but he just keeps walking and doesn't bleed. We're trying to collate these reports because I don't think they're just exaggerations or fabrications.'

He went up to the edge of the desk and pressed a buzzer. Before the muscular young man had time to respond, Brigadier Majid looked at his old friend and smiled. 'You came about the printing press, didn't you?' he said. And then, as if he realized his confidences might lead to trouble, he added: 'If you were to write a story for the magazine, who would believe you?'

The older men laughed, and Mahmoud noticed that he was laughing with them.

3

In the evening, lying on the bed in his room at the Orouba Hotel, Mahmoud turned on his digital recorder and spoke into it:

'Very strange . . . Saidi was making fun of his friend's bizarre responsibilities. He was making fun of the djinn and the fortune telling, but then he asked his advice on whether to buy the printing press. He must have obtained some information based on predictions. He didn't dispute it. He just took what the man said as given. He must be receiving similar information at regular intervals, so he feels safe moving around Baghdad. He isn't frightened of going out openly, not because he's courageous but because he knows he's not going to die.

'He spoke about civil war as if it were a film they were waiting to see in the cinema. They were laughing. So things definitely won't get too bad. If I stay close to Saidi, I can be sure that things won't go badly, at least for me.

'Saidi's an Islamist, and his friend's a Baathist. But Saidi's a lapsed Islamist. His ideas changed while he was living abroad. And his brigadier friend is a lapsed Baathist. He has strong feelings towards Saidi and is an old friend, and they seem close. But why was Saidi making fun of Majid on the way back? He made fun of the apple scent that the air freshener on the wall squirted out in small doses every minute or so, saying that Baathists loved the smell of apples. "The chemical weapons they dropped on Halabja smelled of apple," he said with a laugh.

'That was pretty sick. My God. But why did he allow me to witness all this? I asked Abu Anmar about the four beggars, and he confirmed it. Everyone in the area had heard the story, and the local people were afraid and on the lookout because the killer had killed the beggars, who had become famous in death if not in life. He had strangled them, and then, by some bizarre and complicated operation, he'd put their hands around each other's throats.'

Mahmoud turned off his recorder. He recalled Saidi's explanation: 'There are certain points on the shoulders, the back, and the spinal column, and if you put acupuncture needles in them, all the muscles in the body tense up and go rigid. Maybe that's what happened to the four madmen.'

'The beggars,' Mahmoud had corrected him. He had then asked Saidi whether he should pursue that story.

'There are other stories that are more worthwhile. Forget about that one,' he had replied.

Mahmoud went over in his head the interesting conversations he had heard, especially over lunch. It was a fine lunch that Brigadier Majid had prepared in honour of the visiting journalists. The table was covered with food and drink, everything except alcohol. Mahmoud gathered that the brigadier wanted to keep his image intact in the eyes of the parties in the ruling coalition. He was in a sensitive position. Just as he was spying on ordinary people, there were people spying on him and reporting on him to the government parties, which did not look kindly on him because of his past and his work serving the old regime. But they had to accept him because of his acknowledged competence and because the Americans supported him and protected him from the whims and reckless excesses of their Iraqi counterparts.

Saidi and the brigadier had gone over all the country's problems, and unlike those in power, they seemed to know the solutions. There was stupidity and shortsightedness among the new rulers. Solutions were readily available. All these problems could be solved in half an hour, at least in theory, if people genuinely had the will to solve them.

But there were two fronts now, Mahmoud said to himself – the Americans and the government on one side, the terrorists and the various anti-government militias on the other. In fact 'terrorist' was the term used for everyone who was against the government and the Americans.

Mahmoud turned his digital recorder back on and brought it close to his lips. 'Aren't they both, in one way or another, working with the Americans?' he said. 'Why did they want to give me the impression they were such patriots? What is this chaos? Oof! I'll have to say no to Saidi next time he invites me on one of his trips, which always make me dizzy. My work at the magazine ends at three or four in the afternoon. That's when my relationship with Saidi ends too. I have a job on his magazine, not in his life.'

In the morning Mahmoud put on his last two clean pieces of clothing and put his dirty clothes in a large bag to give them to the Akhawain laundry next to the hotel when he went out. He went down to the lobby and was surprised to find Hazem Abboud sitting with Abu Anmar and Luqman, the only Algerian in the whole of Iraq and a long-standing resident of the Orouba Hotel. It would have been hard to detect that Luqman was Algerian because he spoke the Iraqi dialect so well. Everyone was gathered around the table, chatting over thick cream, pastries and cups of strong tea. Veronica, the plump chambermaid, and her teenage son were flitting from room to room with a mop and a bucket, making their weekly cleaning rounds.

Had Hazem slept the night at the hotel? Mahmoud greeted him and Luqman and Abu Anmar, and they asked him to have breakfast with them. He sat down with a hot glass of tea, then thought back over some of the mysterious exchanges of the previous evening. He took a large gulp of the tea, as if he wanted to erase those uncomfortable memories.

Mahmoud turned to Hazem to ask where he had spent the night, when he had come to the hotel, and how the exhibition of photographs was. But Abu Anmar interrupted him.

'Mr Sawadi,' he said, 'I'd be careful going out – the police are all over the place. A man was killed this morning.'

4

The man was none other than Abu Zaidoun, the old barber, who was all skin and bones. They found him slumped on his white plastic chair in front of the barber shop that had once been his – he had handed it over to his youngest son years ago when he could no longer stand on his own two feet. He looked to be asleep, at least to anyone seeing him from afar, but the handle of a pair of stainless steel scissors protruded from the top of his breastbone, at the base of his neck. Someone had slipped into the shop while the son was out having a cup of tea at the cart on the corner, where the lane met the main street, and had grabbed the scissors and jabbed them into the old man, who was far off in the fantasy world of those with advanced dementia.

There were those who had long expected him to meet such an end. Abu Zaidoun wasn't going to die quietly in bed: divine justice wouldn't allow it. The medical report said he had died of a heart attack. Maybe the criminal had killed a man who was already dead. The old man's sons were satisfied with this explanation, not having the energy to pursue a vendetta.

When Faraj the estate agent heard that Abu Zaidoun had been killed, he said, 'Poor man! It only took a little push for him to meet the Supreme Comrade.' He spoke with a touch of sarcasm, stretching out the word 'comrade' with a wry smile.

Others recalled the man's long career and how he had been responsible for sending so many young men off to war. He had been active in Baath Party organizations, doggedly pursuing all those who deserted from the army or tried to avoid military training. He may have taken part in raids on some houses, and he wasn't short of enemies, but no one knew who had killed him. It clearly wasn't random. At the condolences ceremony people did their best to cite Abu Zaidoun's virtues – how he had helped others and done favours for those in need and how, in the end, his record as a zealous, merciless party member applied only to the first years of the Iran–Iraq War. That's how everyone wanted to remember him; death gives the dead an aura of dignity, so they say, and makes the living feel guilty in a way that compels them to forgive those who are gone.

There was at least one person who wasn't prepared to make excuses for Abu Zaidoun. Justice at some later stage wouldn't do. It had to happen now. Later there would be time for revenge, for constant torment by a just god, infinite torment, because that's how revenge should be. But justice had to be done here on earth, with witnesses present. Elishva had a vague sense of this when her friend Umm Salim told her in amazement how the wicked old man had been murdered. Umm Salim herself had once vowed to slaughter a sheep at her front door if God took revenge on Abu Zaidoun, but now she had forgotten all that. It had been more than twenty years since Salim, her eldest son, had been killed in battle. But Elishva hadn't forgotten. Umm Salim had three other children and a house bustling with life, whereas old Elishva had only a mangy cat, some photographs and old furniture. When she heard about the murder of Abu Zaidoun, she thanked God and remembered one of her solemn vows – she would light twenty pink candles on the altar of the Virgin Mary in the Armenian church, and she wouldn't leave the altar till all the candles had burned down and the twenty wicks had sunk into the molten wax. Then the heartache at the loss of her son would also come to an end: she would see the justice of the Lord, and He would deserve her thanks.

If she asked Father Josiah, he would tell her to ask for forgiveness for Abu Zaidoun – she never would. If she asked God or Saint George the Martyr or the ghost of her son, they would tell her she didn't need to ask forgiveness for Abu Zaidoun. She was fully entitled to seek revenge because it would strengthen her faith and give her ailing spirit the energy it needed to keep on living.

5

Two young men were sitting opposite Hadi at his usual bench in Aziz the Egyptian's coffee shop. They were plump with downy moustaches and were both wearing pink shirts and black linen trousers, like fellow members of a sports team or club. They had short hair and sideburns trimmed level with their ears, and they laughed often and told jokes. Since arriving that morning and sitting down in front of Hadi, they had drunk four cups of tea. One of them placed a small digital recorder in the middle of the wooden table. They both looked at Hadi. 'Tell us the story of the corpse,' they said in unison.

'The story of the Whatsitsname, you mean.' Hadi insisted on correcting them, using the name he had given his creation. It wasn't really a corpse, because 'corpse' suggested a particular person or creature, and that didn't apply in the case of the Whatsitsname. Hadi could tell his story at length, and he usually did, but the sight of the digital recorder made him nervous, and the mood in the neighbourhood at the time was unsettled and confused. Aziz brought over a fresh glass of tea and put it in front of Hadi. He gave him a double wink, a gesture that Hadi immediately understood. Aziz was uneasy with the two young men. They were from the Mukhabarat, or military intelligence, or some other security agency, and the meeting would no doubt end in Hadi being arrested.

'The Whatsitsname has died, I'm sorry to say,' said Hadi.

'Died how?' one of them said. 'No, tell us from the start – how did you make the corpse?'

'The Whatsitsname,' Hadi corrected them again.

'Yes, the Whatsitsname. Tell us the story, and the drinks are on us.'

'I tell you. He's dead.'

At that point Hadi stood up and called out to Aziz to take away the fresh tea and put it back in the pot. He walked out of the coffee shop, leaving the two young men puzzled. They tried to persuade Aziz to talk, but his lips were sealed. They stayed another half hour, talking to each other in whispers. Their broad smiles were gone. They gave Aziz five thousand dinars, much more than the price of all the teas, and left.

At midday Hadi went back to the coffee shop. He sat in his usual place, and a tray of rice and beans arrived from Ali al-Sayed's restaurant next door. Hadi sat there eating, and when Aziz had finished cleaning some glasses and plates behind the counter, he came over and sat opposite Hadi, a serious expression on his face.

'What's the matter with you, man?' he said. 'You should forget that bullshit story of yours.'

'Why? What's happened?'

'What's happened! They're looking for the guy who killed the four beggars and Abu Zaidoun and the officer they found strangled in the whores' room in Umm Raghad's house.'

'And what's that to do with me?'

'Those stories of yours are going to get you into trouble. When the Americans grab you, you've no idea where they'll take you. God alone knows what charge they'll pin on you.'

Hadi's heart started pounding, but he finished his lunch. Without informing Aziz, he made a private decision not to mention the story of the corpse ever again. Aziz told him the story the drunken beggar had told – about the criminal who killed the four other beggars and how horrible he looked, with a mouth like a gash across his face. He told him what Umm Raghad and her girls had said too – about the person who burst in on them in the dark and strangled the officer who was sleeping in the room of one of the girls. Its body was sticky, as if it was smeared with blood or tomato juice. When it jumped onto the roof, some of the young men fired at it with their rifles. Everyone has weapons these days. They fired many shots, but the bullets just went through its body. It didn't stop running, skipping from roof to roof until it disappeared. No one knows what will happen in the coming days. The story may or may not end with what Umm Salim said. She claimed that as she was sitting on her front stoop in the lane she saw a strange-looking person in a faded army jacket and with a headscarf wrapped so tight that nothing of his face would be visible to someone in the distance. He was looking at the ground, coming from the direction of Abu Zaidoun's barber shop. He walked past her, and she glimpsed part of his face – it was the most horrible thing she had ever seen. It's hard to believe God would create such a face; just looking at it was enough to make your hair stand on end. She spoke about this strange person to anyone who happened to be around and claimed that he had killed old Abu Zaidoun. But one evening Abu Zaidoun's sons came to her house and had words with her, making threats if she went on telling her story. Their father had died of a heart attack, they said.

'Your stories have started frightening people. You'd better keep a low profile,' Aziz finally said to Hadi. He then got up to take orders from some elderly customers who had just come into the shop. Hadi sat in his place, looking through the front window at the cars and the passersby in the busy street. He took a cigarette out of his pocket, lit it, and smoked for half an hour – the longest time he had ever spent in sustained silence. For a while he forgot about the errands he usually ran in the afternoon. A seed of fear had started to grow deep inside him, and he couldn't get it out of his mind. Because lies can come true. He remembered a dream from the distant past. He went over the dream in his mind's eye and thought again about what Aziz had said. He was sure Aziz had received some information. Except for what was said about the blood or tomato juice, the other details were familiar: the big mouth like a gash right across the jaw, the horrible face, the stitches across the forehead and down the cheeks, the big nose.

Hadi left the coffee shop, saying goodbye to Aziz, his most trusted friend. All the others saw him as insignificant: no one would miss him if he disappeared, and this was a time when many people were disappearing for no logical reason, and he didn't want to disappear. He wanted to stay alive, buying stuff that people wanted to get rid of, restoring it, and selling it again, without thoughts of amassing a fortune or expanding his operations, because that would be too much trouble, like having a disease. He was interested in having cash in his pocket, nothing more, enough to sleep with women whenever he wanted and to buy a drink. To eat and drink what he wanted, to go to sleep and wake up without anyone watching over him and without responsibilities.

He went to the junk market at Bab al-Sharqi. He had left some radios and Japanese tape recorders with one of the stallholders. The man had declined to buy all the stuff outright but agreed to take it on consignment – he would give Hadi the money for the things he sold and give back the stuff he hadn't sold whenever Hadi wanted.

Shortly before sunset Hadi went back to his neighbourhood and was shocked to see American soldiers, in uniform
with helmets and other gear, walking down the lanes, carrying their rifles across their chests and looking at everyone
suspiciously. He saw Faraj in his grey dishdasha and with
his black prayer beads, talking with one of the interpreters.
He knew they were doing one of their routine sweeps for
weapons – there had been reports of some heavy shooting
the night before. He walked slowly along the wall, trying not
to look any of the soldiers in the eye. Entering his house, he
pushed the heavy wooden door firmly closed, then waited in
dread, listening for movement in the lane and for the moment
when they'd knock on the door to carry out their search, or
force it open with their heavy boots, as in the scenes broadcast on television. He passed the time repairing some small
wooden tables. He knocked in some nails here and there,
then varnished them and put them in the courtyard to dry in
the open air. At sunset he left home and went to see Edward
Boulos, the man who sold alcohol. Edward had closed his
little shop overlooking the Umma Garden because someone
had thrown a hand grenade at it early one morning, setting
fire to it. After that he moved his business, the only one he
knew, into his house. Hadi bought half a bottle of arak from
him and then went shopping for some white cheese, olives,
and other things in the shops nearby, before heading home.

He spent the night hours drinking slowly and quietly, sitting
on his bed, with the bottle of arak, his glass and the plate of
mezes on a high metal table. In a gloom lit only by a feeble,
sooty lantern, he listened to the soft warbling from the radio.
Raising his last glass high, as always, as if he was in a noisy
bar, he toasted his companions – the ghosts of people he
knew who were gone and of others he had never met. And
he toasted the darkness and the contents of his cluttered, rat-
infested room. Downing his last glass, he heard a movement

and looked in the direction of the door. The door swung wide open and beyond the doorway loomed the dark figure of a tall man. His blood froze in his veins as he saw the figure approach.

The yellow light of the lantern struck the strange man's face – a face with lines of stitches, a large nose and a mouth like a gaping wound.

CHAPTER SEVEN

Ouzo and a Bloody Mary

1

In the early morning hours, one of Faraj's assistants came and told him that some people were walking round the area marking the walls of the houses he owned with blue spray paint. They were in fact from a charity that specialized in preserving Baghdad's old houses and were accompanied by some civil servants from the city council and the provincial council. Faraj was uneasy: he picked up his small leather briefcase and went out to find them, accompanied by some of the young people who lived in the area and helped him in his work.

He found the strangers in front of Elishva's house. They were knocking on the door but no one was answering. Eventually, Umm Salim came out of her house and told them that Elishva had gone to church. One of the young men shook up the can of paint and sprayed a blue X on the wall. They went on to Hadi's house and sprayed an X on the wall, but this time in black. This meant the house was unsuitable for renovation and could be demolished. Faraj didn't understand what the people were saying. They obviously wanted to take over his houses, or the houses he had rented from the state under contracts that were legal and in good order. They told him it was just a routine procedure for statistical purposes and to identify the historic houses, especially the ones that had wooden *mashrabiya* windows. But Faraj, who had got his hands on four or five of these old houses, took it as a plan to wrest the properties from him, so he had rushed to the scene to argue with the young men. One of them raised his finger in Faraj's face and warned him that he was obstructing the work of a government employee in the course of his official duties. Some of the neighbours intervened and dragged Faraj away. Feeling uneasy, the people from the charity and the government officials who were with them left.

Faraj would later find out that some of these people had been coming to the area individually and had visited Elishva to try to persuade her to sell her house to the state, with the concession that she could remain there, for as long as she lived, without paying any rent. The state would automatically acquire unrestricted ownership of the house when she died or vacated it.

What if she accepted this offer? It would be a disaster for Faraj. But the old woman had apparently turned it down. She had told them she couldn't make any decisions about the house in the absence of her son. The more they heard what she had to say, the more confused and mystified they became. Because they were dealing with several similar houses in various parts of central Baghdad, they didn't stay with her too long. In their notebooks they wrote a few things about the house and who owned it, and perhaps they set a date for checking what Elishva said more carefully. Unlike the people from the charity, Faraj understood what Elishva meant when she talked about her son, but he hadn't yet seen him for himself. Elishva had been standing outside the bakery and the cheese shop and talking about the meals she was making for her son. The same thing happened in the courtyard of Umm Salim's house when they were breaking walnuts open with a hammer and eating them with hot tea. The old women were sad at first, because poor, crazy Elishva with that strange red scarf on her head had finally lost her mind. But late at night some people did see a young man coming out through her front door, wrapped in the darkness.

When the news spread, some of the young men lay in ambush at a corner of the lane in the hope that the strange visitor might come out again, but he didn't appear. Within a week they had forgotten, but then by chance they did see a man come out of the house. When they ran after him, the man ran off faster than they did and disappeared.

Umm Salim told her neighbours that her husband knew the true story. He spent most of his time sitting by the balcony window on the upper floor, reading old newspapers and looking up from time to time to monitor people coming and going down the lane and in and out of the houses. That was his only pleasure. The taciturn old man confidently asserted that this visitor was a thief or some other kind of criminal who had tricked Elishva into believing that he was her son and was using her house as a hiding place. A young woman who came to Umm Salim's gatherings heard this version from Umm Salim and shouted that Faraj the estate agent must be behind it. Umm Salim gasped in surprise. The young woman said spitefully that Faraj was behind everything bad that happened in the area. And why not? He had evicted her one dark night, she said, without pity for her or her children. During other sessions in Umm Salim's courtyard, the story became more coherent.

As if she had forgotten what she had said earlier, the spiteful neighbour said the young man had climbed the low wall of Hadi's house and jumped up to the open area where the two rooms had collapsed on the upper floor of Elishva's house. He had intended to go downstairs and strangle her in her bed. No one would bother to ask why such an old woman had died. They would say that God had snatched her soul as she slept, and then forget all about it. The young criminal came down the stairs and saw her sitting with her oil lamp in the big room next to the street, praying and talking to Saint George. What she said struck a chord in his heart, even though he didn't understand the language. She was speaking Syriac to the large picture hanging on the wall, and the young man felt that someone was answering her. He moved closer to the door and listened more carefully. It definitely sounded like a conversation between two people. He looked into the room. In the dim light, all he could see was the old woman clasping the metal cross on her rosary and lifting it to her lips. She turned towards him and saw him standing in front of her. An emaciated cat rubbed against his legs, then walked on and sat at Elishva's feet. The young criminal was motionless, as if the old woman had pinned him to the spot with her tender, maternal glances. 'Come on, my boy,' she said. He stepped forward obediently and submissively, walking like a child, then threw himself into her arms, weeping.

Of course Umm Salim and the other old women didn't believe this story, but in quick succession they all said, 'Bless the Prophet and the Prophet's family.' The story sent shivers down their spines. That spiteful woman had won people over with her story. It didn't matter that it was made up; it was moving, and the reason they spent part of the day in the courtyard of Umm Salim's house was to escape Bataween and its daily routines and float in another world. This damned woman with a grudge against Faraj was doing her duty as well as she could, and they were grateful to her.

'God curse you this evening, Faraj. God take you,' cried Umm Salim. The other women repeated the curse and brought down on his head various other curses and insults. The woman with a grudge felt a great sense of relief because of their reaction, and suddenly she didn't hate Faraj so much.

2

The weather was warm, so Elishva took off the dark sweater she had been wearing. Instead, she put on a dark-blue summer dress. She didn't take off the red headscarf with the white flowers, which had become a symbol of her transformation. She hadn't gone to her church for the past week. Instead, she preferred to go to the Saint Qardagh Church in Akad al-Nasara in Sheikh Omar, to fulfil some of her overdue 'Islamic' vows. She put a handful of henna paste on the metal knocker of the large wooden door of the Anglican Church of Saint George in Bab al-Sharqi. She sprinkled water on the small rose garden in the Syriac Orthodox church. These complicated tasks took her the whole week. She put another handful of henna on the wall of the abandoned Jewish synagogue and a third handful on the door of the Orfali Mosque near the start of Saadoun Street, the only mosque in Bataween.

In the Church of Saint Odisho, she lit sticks of Indian incense at the altar of the Virgin Mary before Father Josiah arrived. Now all her vows had been fulfilled. In the past week Father Josiah had received two calls for Elishva from her younger daughter, and he had been planning to send the old deacon, Nader Shamouni, to Elishva's house if she didn't turn up the following Sunday either.

Before starting the church service, Father Josiah went up to Elishva with a smile and told her that her daughters had been asking after her and that Matilda would call her at midday. Elishva beamed contentedly and thanked Father Josiah. Then she followed the Mass, mouthing her favourite prayer silently: 'Glory to God in the highest, and on earth peace, goodwill towards men.' But her mind was on the phone call that was three weeks late.

After Mass, Elishva helped give out the food that the women in the congregation had brought from home and laid out on big tables in the church hall. She ate with them, and when the food was finished, everyone said goodbye to Father Josiah, the young sacristans, the caretaker, and the policemen who were parked in their government vehicle at the gate to protect the church. Most people went out, but Elishva stayed behind, sitting and waiting for her daughters to call. When she felt the place falling quiet, she began to despair. Father Josiah's phone rang two or three times with calls from his house and from other priests and friends. Eventually, the call Elishva had been waiting for came through. Father Josiah heard the voice on the other end, smiled, and handed Elishva the phone.

'Hilda's been ill. We didn't want to tell you. Mentally unwell. She's in the hospital, but she's better now,' said Matilda.

'Daniel's come back, Matilda,' said Elishva. 'My son's come back.'

'Hilda's upset, to tell the truth. She says she'll never speak to you again. She's not here with me now. She's not listening to what I'm telling you, and she'd be upset if she found out I'd spoken to you.'

'He's with me now,' Elishva continued. 'He refuses to go out when people can see him. He goes out at night. From the roof. He disappears for days, but then he comes back.'

'Are you in good health? I call one hundred times a day but can't get through. I was going crazy. Sometimes I get strange people answering. I don't know what the problem is,' said Matilda.

'I'm well. How are Hilda and her children? How are your children? Have they grown? Let me speak to them.'

'Hilda's in the hospital. She's better now. Her elder son looks just like Daniel. He wants to start studying medicine this year.'

'Daniel's the apple of my eye. My lovely boy. My dear.'

'We've sent you five hundred dollars. I sent it myself to the office of Ayad al-Hadidi, the money changer in Karrada. In Father Josiah's name. He can withdraw it and give it to you. Do you need anything?'

'I need you to come back and bring some life to the house.'

'We won't come back. You need to come here. You'll be more comfortable here,' said Matilda. 'Here in Melbourne there's an Assyrian church called Saint George's. Does that mean anything to you? I've told the priest, Father Antoon Mikhail, and he would welcome you coming.'

'I'm not going. I'm here with Daniel.'

'Tell this Daniel that your daughters need you. He'll understand.'

'You understand, Matilda.'

'The country's in flames around you. My God! Okay, from now on I'm going to train myself not to be sad and not to cry. You're going to kill us here. You love to torment us.'

'Don't torment yourself and don't be sad,' replied Elishva. 'And don't call until you've calmed down.'

'What do you mean, *don't call*?' shouted Matilda. Elishva gave the phone back to Father Josiah. Her feet felt stiff from standing for so long, because she always stood during these phone calls. She felt a little swirl of anger stirring in her chest. She sat down, still listening to what Father Josiah was saying as Matilda told him about the money transfer and Elishva's material needs. She had questions about the pension Elishva received every three months and about the assistance to the needy according to the register that was in the church.

Matilda kept complaining that they weren't well off but were planning to visit to take Elishva out before things got worse.

'We'll have to take her by force if necessary. She can't keep torturing us like this,' Matilda told the priest.

Father Josiah tried to calm her down. He wouldn't support Matilda's plan. His religious vocation didn't allow him to encourage members of the congregation to emigrate. But he wouldn't stop anyone from emigrating, and he would normally certify religious documents related to marriages, births and so on that people who were emigrating might need in order to simplify the process of joining an Assyrian church wherever they went.

The phone call ended, and Elishva looked dissatisfied. The priest escorted her to the church gate and offered to have one of the sacristans drive her home, but she said she would take the bus. Before she left, she turned to Father Josiah, took off her large glasses, and, with eyes flashing, announced firmly that she didn't want any more phone calls. She wouldn't answer calls from her daughters, and she wouldn't ask to call them. Father Josiah laughed and tried to pat her on her skinny shoulder, but she replied that if he didn't comply with her request, then next week she would go to the Saint Qardagh Church and would never go back to his.

3

The weather had turned surprisingly warm, and Mahmoud tossed and turned on his bed in his room at the Orouba Hotel. It was dark, and the electricity had been off for many hours. He guessed that the approaching summer would be very hot, but it wasn't clear what plans Abu Anmar had for installing air conditioning in the rooms.

He knew that some of the hotels in Bataween, Saadoun Street and Karrada had started to make preparations for the intense summer heat, especially the ones that had regular guests. They had set about buying diesel generators that could be commissioned from private workshops. The generators combined a Kia bus engine with a generator head and were much cheaper than similar, imported generators. But Abu Anmar wasn't like the owners of those hotels. He didn't have enough money to buy a generator of that kind and pay for the fuel it would need. There were now only four guests left in the hotel, each of them paying the equivalent of only ten dollars a day.

Mahmoud had experience from previous summers of scorching nights that made sleep impossible and left you feeling exhausted and hopelessly lethargic all day long. He didn't need complications like that right now, especially when he was trying hard to improve his position at the magazine and to keep winning the confidence of the editor.

Saidi dragged Mahmoud off on various outings, besides the journalistic assignments and trips to check the page layout. When Saidi was out, Mahmoud would sit in Saidi's office and answer phone calls from the printers or advertisers. Saidi always left one of his mobile phones charging in the office, and when it rang no one but Mahmoud dared to take the call. Once he took a call from an official in a large parliamentary bloc, who was accusing the magazine of publishing what he said was a fabricated story about an armed group loyal to this official assassinating some of his rivals. Frightened, Mahmoud apologized and explained that the editor wasn't in the office and that the magazine had taken the story from Agence France-Presse, the French news agency.

'Aren't you on our side?' the man said. 'Why do you do things to upset us?'

Mahmoud was profusely apologetic, but he silently cursed

the turn of events that had put him in this embarrassing situation. He made up his mind to call Saidi and tell him about it, but Saidi took it coolly and told Mahmoud not to pay too much attention.

Once Mahmoud answered a call from a private number. On the screen it showed up as 666, and he knew from an American film that this was the number of the 'beast from the sea' in the book of Revelation.

What did the beast want? Had the magazine published something hostile to beasts, or what? 'Hello . . .'

It was Nawal al-Wazir, but she didn't seem to have noticed that it wasn't Saidi who had picked up. Her words came out in a tirade and struck Mahmoud like a thunderbolt, but he didn't want to say anything, or else he would have to reveal his identity.

'Why don't you answer?' she said.

She grew increasingly angry, and in his embarrassment Mahmoud decided to hang up on her. What would happen if Saidi heard about the call? Why had he left his phone there? Why didn't he get a phone just for the magazine? Nawal would think it was Saidi who had cut her off. Apparently they weren't on good terms, and apparently she really was his 'fuck buddy', as Farid Shawwaf had said that day.

Mahmoud finished his work at noon. Farid Shawwaf and the other editors left the building. The caretaker brought him lunch from the restaurant next door. Mahmoud felt numbed and exhausted. The cold air from the air conditioner hit his face and made him feel sleepy. He didn't want to meet his friends in a coffee shop or go back to the Orouba Hotel, so he lay down on the red leather sofa in Saidi's office, closed his eyes, and tried to sleep. In an attempt to relax, he imagined Nawal al-Wazir coming into the office, throwing off her clothes, stretching out alongside him on the sofa, and wrapping her soft, plump arms around his waist.

4

Saidi woke Mahmoud up at sunset. He had called on his mobile phone several times. He was in an ecstatic mood, so he didn't question Mahmoud about why he hadn't picked up his calls. Mahmoud followed Saidi as he moved around the office. Saidi opened some of the drawers in his vast desk, took some papers out, and put them in his briefcase. He told Mahmoud he had made an excellent deal that day.

'What Brigadier Majid said was true,' he said, without explaining what part of what the brigadier had said he was referring to. Saidi then went into the toilet for a few minutes, and Mahmoud took the opportunity to pull himself together. He washed his face at the basin outside and rearranged his hair and clothes. When Saidi came out of the toilet, he told Mahmoud to come along with him on an errand and then they would go and celebrate.

Mahmoud left with Saidi in his fancy car. First they went to a real estate office in Karrada, and Saidi negotiated with the real estate agent over a piece of land overlooking the Tigris. They were held up in the office and drank four cups of tea. Mahmoud watched television while Saidi was busy negotiating. By the time they left, Mahmoud was hungry and he didn't know what plans Saidi had for the night or what kind of celebration he intended.

They set off into the darkness in the black Mercedes, heading to somewhere in the Arasat area. Every now and then the river was visible through gaps in the walls, sparkling with dancing spots of light that were the reflections of lights on the other bank. Mahmoud expected they were going out to some exclusive place. They went into a tall building with guards at the gate and then more guards at the end of a long corridor. They were searched for weapons, and then they heard Iraqi pop songs in the distance and smelled a mixture of alcoholic drinks, shisha pipe tobacco and cigarette smoke. Saidi had booked a table close to the dance floor in the main hall. He usually did that by phone, spending money liberally. Money was the key to everything; it was the magic lamp in this life, Mahmoud thought, as he sat in the noisy hall. The sound level was unbelievable, and yet Saidi had no problem leaning towards the young journalist to talk to him. Mahmoud couldn't hear anything but nodded as if he could. Saidi looked at the band with a smile. There wasn't anything to stop him from smiling, and Mahmoud didn't hide from himself his feelings of envy towards this man.

He wanted to tell Saidi about the phone call from Nawal al-Wazir. He also wanted to ask him about some other things to do with the magazine. But Saidi certainly wouldn't hear him amid all the noise, and Mahmoud was worried about spoiling Saidi's good mood by bringing up work. A waiter brought them glasses of some mysterious blood-coloured drink. Saidi picked his up, took a sip, then leaned over towards Mahmoud. 'Bloody Mary,' he shouted.

Yes, Bloody Mary, delicious, great, wonderful – what bliss! What other little delights did this man dabble in? No doubt he was a happy man. So now Nawal al-Wazir was the devil incarnate. Saidi must have exchanged her for some other woman. Someone like Saidi couldn't not have a woman. Definitely, wonderful, beautiful.

The waiter came back with a large bottle of dark whisky, fresh glasses, and a metal bucket full of ice. Another waiter sprang out from behind him with some plates of mezes and gave a little bow as he listened to Saidi. The waiter smiled gratefully and withdrew.

They drank. Then the band stopped playing, and Mahmoud could hear other noises – the clinking of glasses and the murmur of people talking at the nearby tables. So they had been able to talk despite all that noise? Is this place really in Baghdad?

Farid Shawwaf had warned Mahmoud about being too deferential towards Saidi. 'Don't be his lapdog' was the phrase that stuck in his mind, but Farid never actually said that. Mahmoud just worried that he might say it. It was an offensive expression, and Mahmoud always caught a whiff of it in what his old friend said. Besides, Mahmoud wasn't Saidi's lapdog, or anyone else's. He didn't follow Saidi around. It was Saidi who dragged Mahmoud around with him, Saidi who needed him. But what did he need him for, Mahmoud wondered?

So far Saidi had introduced Mahmoud to half the people in the government, many senior officers, and foreign diplomats. He had introduced him to mysterious characters he had never heard of before, such as Brigadier Majid. He had let him in on some terrible secrets. What was Saidi's purpose in all this? What did Saidi gain from it at the end of the day? Mahmoud needed to be a little more daring and ask his boss some questions. He needed answers, though he believed the answers would come one way or another.

Mahmoud plucked up his courage and made a start. 'What did Brigadier Majid say that was true?' he asked.

Saidi seemed to be rummaging around in his memory for anything relevant to Mahmoud's question. Then he broke into a serene, toothy smile. 'About the printing press,' he said. 'It would have been a disaster. Many of those working in the printing business are waiting for the security situation to improve and hoping the worst doesn't happen. Don't forget that this year there'll be unprecedented elections. There'll be lots of work on election posters and leaflets.'

'Are you going to buy another printing press, or have you decided against it?'

'No, I've bought a house close to Andalus Square. That's the deal I made today. A furnished house from an old man from an Amirli family,' Saidi replied.

Mahmoud had established that Saidi would answer his questions, so he saw no problem in asking more, or maybe it was just the combined effect of his good mood, the whisky and the Bloody Mary. He tried to be more daring and ask him about personal matters – about Nawal al-Wazir, for example. But then the band started up again: a song by Hussein Neama but at a higher tempo. Mahmoud brought his glass to his mouth and took a large sip. He ate from the plates of meze and turned to Saidi every now and then. He felt he really liked this man and wanted to be like him.

'You have to understand, Farid Shawwaf. I want to be like him, not be his underling.' That's what Mahmoud would say when he next saw his old friend. He didn't need any of Farid's confusing advice.

Mahmoud kept drinking steadily. Then he noticed Saidi giving him a strange look. He was smiling as he drank and looked as if he wanted to say something.

'How I wish I was in your place,' he finally said. 'If some power could arrange for us to change places. But it's too late for that.'

Mahmoud gaped in amazement. The words alone were like the wave of a magician's wand, fulfilling his impossible dream. He wished he had the courage to answer Saidi by saying that he too wanted to become him, that he wanted to change places with him, that his life would mean nothing unless he became like Saidi, if he didn't, at some later stage, turn into Ali Baher al-Saidi.

5

Hadi the junk dealer was resentful and disappointed when the old man from Amirli told him he had sold his house and his furniture and was moving to Moscow in two weeks to marry the girlfriend he had met decades ago when he was studying chemistry in Russia.

This shouldn't have happened. He had spent a long time trying to persuade the man to sell some of his battered old furniture, but the man had been very sentimental about the memories contained in these old pieces of wood. Yet now he was announcing that he'd got rid of everything – his memories, his furniture, his life in Baghdad – all to have a belated honeymoon in what was left of his life.

Hadi needed whatever money he could raise to meet his basic needs. He had spent the last few days in a state of permanent drunkenness, ever since that dark night when the frightening guest had visited him and he had tricked himself for a moment into believing it was a figment of his imagination and not his own creation.

Hadi crossed Andalus Square and walked slowly past the Sadeer Novotel. He recalled the night when he was thrown through the air by the force of the explosion. He wished he had died right then.

For a while he sat on the pavement, smoking. He assumed a car bomb or some other explosive might go off at any moment and that this was a good place to get killed by one. He sat there till darkness fell, deep in thought about the possibility that dozens of bombs had either exploded or been defused during that day. No day passed without at least one car bomb. Why did he see other people dying on the news and yet he was still alive? He had to get on the news one day, he said to himself. He was well aware that this was his destiny.

When Hadi was back in Bataween, he heard from Aziz in the coffee shop that Abu Anmar was looking for him. Hadi went to see him and found him sitting in the lobby of his hotel, in his dishdasha, with his big paunch and his white headdress, reading a thick book. Abu Anmar took off his glasses, closed the book, and stood up to shake hands with Hadi.

Over the past few years, Hadi had run into Abu Anmar in the neighbourhood only a few times and had talked to him once or twice. He knew some of the rumours about him, the most important of which, as far as Hadi was concerned, was about his long-term relationship with Veronica, the Armenian woman who cleaned the hotel so thoroughly every week. Some people said that her teenage son, Andrew, who often accompanied her, was Abu Anmar's son.

Abu Anmar told Hadi that he was thinking of selling the furniture in some of the rooms because he was preparing to renovate the hotel. In fact, he wanted to replace everything and was hoping to find a buyer for the beds, the wardrobes, and other pieces of furniture. Hadi perked up when he heard this and quickly tried to remember the things that might be relevant in a transaction such as this. He told Abu Anmar he was willing to buy, and Abu Anmar thought a tour of some of the rooms might give Hadi a more accurate idea of what was involved.

The tour was disappointing for Hadi. The rooms occupied by Mahmoud al-Sawadi, Luqman the old Algerian and two other guests were the best rooms in the hotel. The furniture in them was still usable, but the rest of the furniture was just old junk, some of it eaten by termites and some water-damaged. But he didn't change his position and assured Abu Anmar that he would find a buyer for it all.

Hadi sat with Abu Anmar in the lobby. For the first time he noticed a small wooden table behind the big reception desk. In the middle of it was a full bottle of arak, a glass and a plate of cucumbers. Hadi wasn't in a position to drink just then – his body was saturated with alcohol, and he reeked of it. He had dragged himself out of bed in the early afternoon to go and see the old Amirli man. He had walked down the street with difficulty, and it took a while for the effects of the alcohol to wear off. But what could he do? He had at that moment an intense thirst for that wonderful bottle.

Abu Anmar went on talking about his plans to replace the hotel's furniture and didn't think of inviting Hadi to sit down and have a drink with him. Although he wore glasses to read, Abu Anmar wasn't blind and could see that the junk dealer was mentally unbalanced. If he were ever to hear that Hadi was a thief and a murderer, it wouldn't greatly surprise him. He had called Hadi for a purely commercial transaction.

Abu Anmar had said what he had to say, but Hadi had no strong desire to leave. If Mahmoud al-Sawadi hadn't come in, an awkward situation might have arisen.

Mahmoud was drunk but was trying hard not to show it. He noticed the blast of air from the ceiling fan in the lobby and thought of the depressing atmosphere he had been trying to escape all day. He had drunk more than he could handle in his evening out with Saidi and was planning to go straight to bed. He was so out of it that he wouldn't notice the humidity, the bad ventilation and the unpleasant smells in his room.

Mahmoud raised his hand in greeting and gave a big smile. He was surprised to see the celebrated storyteller in the hotel. He sat down in the sitting area, slapped Hadi on the thigh, and asked how things were.

Mahmoud didn't notice how serious Abu Anmar looked. He wasn't happy that Hadi was staying so long. He wanted to go back to drinking at his leisure and reading books about astrology and fortune telling, his favourite genre. Without the other two people in the room noticing, he poured himself some arak, put in a lump of ice and some water, and slowly started to drink. On previous occasions he had invited Mahmoud and Hazem to drink with him. He enjoyed spending the evening with them, but tonight things were different.

Mahmoud had a heavy feeling in his stomach. As he was walking down the dark lane towards the hotel, he had thought of trying to vomit in the bathroom. Maybe it would help if he sat down and chatted, to distract himself from his stomach until he felt better. He started to ask Hadi about his extraordinary story, about the body he had stitched together, and so on. Abu Anmar looked up from his book and peered over his glasses at Mahmoud with a mixture of curiosity and amazement.

Until that night Hadi had kept the promise he had made to himself during his conversation with Aziz in the coffee shop – he would forget about his story and never mention it to anyone again. But then he'd discovered the story was true, and he no longer found it amusing to tell it in front of other people.

No one knew, not even Aziz, that the Whatsitsname, as Hadi called it, had come back to Hadi alive and standing on its own two feet. There were serious things happening, and Hadi was merely a conduit, like a simple father or mother who produces a son who is a prophet, a saviour or an evil leader. They didn't exactly create the storm that followed. They were just the channel for something that was more powerful and significant than themselves.

Now, what would he tell this young journalist, whose head was lolling drunkenly and who was trying to cover up his drunkenness by resting his forehead on his clenched fist or by changing his posture when he felt a little off balance?

Mahmoud was expecting casual nonsense of the kind that Hadi's listeners were used to hearing from him. An amusing story for free, and then Mahmoud would go off to his room to sleep like a log till the morning. But Hadi was going to go way beyond what Mahmoud had in mind.

'I'll tell you a sequel to the story,' Hadi said. 'Just for you. But on two conditions.'

Hadi's eyes were flashing. Mahmoud had thought Hadi was crazy from the beginning, so he felt more tempted, more curious to let him continue, in case he knew something significant. Abu Anmar looked up from his book and started to listen to this strange conversation.

'And what are your conditions?' asked Mahmoud.

Hadi stroked his moustache and his thick beard. 'You have to tell me a secret in exchange for my secret,' he said, deliberately earnest and lucid. 'And the other thing is, you buy me dinner and a bottle of ouzo.'

CHAPTER EIGHT

Secrets

1

The preliminary reports that had been prepared the evening before by the team of astrologers in Brigadier Majid's office spoke of ghostly figures gathering on the Imams Bridge, which crosses the river Tigris between the districts of Kadhimiya and Adamiya. The brigadier had some suspicions that the fortune-tellers and astrologers had confused these ghostly figures with the people who for the past two days had been setting off from various parts of Baghdad and heading for Kadhimiya for the ceremonies celebrating the anniversary of the death of the imam Musa al-Kadhim.

The final report from the senior astrologer came at noon, in a pink envelope, and it gave an approximate number for these ghostly figures: about one thousand. As the brigadier read the report, the big television screen in his grand office flashed breaking news that dozens of people had been killed on the Imams Bridge. A rumour that there was a suicide bomber among the pilgrims had caused panic, and some of the pilgrims were trampled to death while others threw themselves into the river and drowned.

The brigadier was frustrated that he hadn't been able to do anything to prevent the disaster. Then he remembered something that made him even more upset: he was always providing valuable information, but the authorities didn't make good use of it. He had sent reports on many criminals, after painstakingly identifying their locations, but not a single one had ever been arrested, or if they were arrested, then some officer in the National Guard or in the Ministry of the Interior would appear on television or in front of his subordinates and take all the credit for the success of the security operation, with no mention of the curious Tracking and Pursuit Department or of the diligent work by a team led by a dedicated and meticulous man called Brigadier Sorour Majid.

He spent most nights in the office. He had a small room as an annexe to his large office, with just a bed and a closet for clothes. Everything he needed was there – except for a woman's body, and he didn't usually think about that. He thought about success and about continuing to be 'irreplaceable' and 'indispensable'. He was waiting to pull off a major coup with his own personal stamp on it so that maybe he would be promoted to a higher position. A coup in the sense of arresting a criminal who was a threat to everyone. That's what he'd been working on for two months now. The team of astrologers and analysts that he headed had managed to collate all the information available about strange murders in Baghdad, and all signs pointed to one perpetrator. In every crime there was one victim, and the victim had usually been strangled. Accounts by witnesses were almost unanimous on the criminal's appearance.

The brigadier had concluded that one person was behind all these crimes. There were usually one or two such crimes every day, and as the days and months passed, the numbers had mounted. A day before the story of the ghostly figures on the Imams Bridge, the senior astrologer had come to the brigadier with some good news: he had discovered the name of the criminal. He had enslaved the djinn and familiar spirits and made use of Babylonian astrological secrets and the sciences of the Sabaeans and the Mandaeans to find the aura of the name surrounding the body of the criminal.

'It's . . . it's the One Who Has No Name,' the senior astrologer said, raising his arms in the air – a gesture that suited his flamboyant appearance: he had a long white pointed beard, a tall conical hat and flowing robes.

'What does that mean, the One Who Has No Name? So, what's his name?'

'The One Who Has No Name,' said the senior astrologer, who then took a few steps back and turned to leave the brigadier's office. The brigadier didn't stop him or ask him to provide more information, because he was used to strange behaviour in his department, and he had to treat these astrologers with kid gloves, since they were his main sources. Tomorrow the One Who Has No Name, he mused, might become He Who Has No Identity, and then He Who Has No Body, and then He Who Can't Be Caught and Thrown in Jail.

But today he could ignore this criminal who didn't have a name, because the disaster on the bridge had turned out to be a big one, and he would have to prepare a report on his department's monitoring of the Imams Bridge, in case the Americans or the Iraqi government asked for one, so he called together the officers on his team. One of the junior officers mentioned an important piece of information that had been picked up two hours before the meeting: these figures hovering over the bridge were ghosts that lived in people's bodies. They slept and rested in those bodies without the people being aware of them, or they could wake up and break free for a little and wander around outside the people's bodies but only when the people were frightened. According to the astrologers, these ghosts were called *tawabie al-khouf*, the 'familiars of fear'.

The team of assistants finished preparing the report, then placed it in a pink envelope on Brigadier Majid's desk. The brigadier wasn't sure the government or the Americans would ask for it, but he was doing his job and always had to be ready for anything. The astrologers went back to their living quarters in the department, and some of the officers left at the end of the workday. The brigadier turned off his television, went into the side room where he slept, turned on the air conditioning, and lay on his bed. Closing his eyes, he could hear only the whirring of the air conditioning. Out of nowhere, he had a strange feeling that his thoughts had left his head and were swirling around near the ceiling, and they included a ghostly figure that was his own personal 'familiar of fear'. A familiar that didn't have a name. Its name, in fact, was the One Who Has No Name. It went round and round: he was seriously worried he would wake up one morning to see an order dismissing him from his position, signed by the prime minister; worried that the Americans would wash their hands of his department and leave it to the mercy of the political parties in power. There was also a deeper and more personal fear: if he had recruited the djinn, the ghosts, the spirits, the astrologers, and the fortune-tellers against multiple enemies, he couldn't be sure his enemies wouldn't mobilize them against him in the same way. Perhaps his enemies were now making a major effort to create and nourish these fears deep inside him.

Without thinking, he stretched out his arm to grab the 'familiar of his fear' by the neck, but when he opened his eyes, he couldn't see anything between himself and the ceiling.

2

Mahmoud said he was in love with his boss's woman and wanted to sleep with her. But Hadi said that was nothing to be embarrassed about.

'I told you my terrible secret. I told you about the Whatsitsname and what he has done. If the police get wind of it, it might be the end of me. I want you to tell me a real secret in return.'

Mahmoud didn't say anything for a long while. He peered around at the wreckage of the house where Hadi lived. He thought back to some old memories. Then he made up his mind.

'I'll tell you something. I don't think my family were originally Arabs. We weren't Arabs or Muslims,' he said.

'Then what were you?'

'I think my great-grandfather or my great-great-grandfather was a Sabaean who converted to Islam for the woman he loved. My father wrote all this down in his diaries, but my brothers and my mother burned them after he died.'

'So, what's the problem?'

'It's a big problem. We're not real Arabs.'

'I was saying in the coffee shop that my great-grandfather was an Ottoman officer, but now I don't know whether that was just a lie.'

'And the story you told me just now, isn't that a lie too?'

'No. I'd be upset if you thought that.'

'Give me some evidence that your story's true. I'll believe you if you give me some evidence.'

'What exactly do you want?'

'Let me meet this Whatsitsname.'

'No, impossible. He might kill you.'

'Put me somewhere in the middle of all this, so I can have a look at him.'

'I don't know when he'll show up. He might never come again.'

'What then? You're avoiding the subject.'

'Not at all. Tell me what you want, and I'll do it.'

'Take a picture of him. I'll give you a camera.'

'Impossible. He'd kill me.'

Mahmoud stood up from the wooden chair in the court-yard of Hadi's dilapidated house. Mahmoud hadn't expected the conversation to go this far. The evening before, in the lobby of the Orouba Hotel, he had been in a different mood. When Hadi left the hotel, Mahmoud had given him ten thousand dinars for dinner and a bottle of arak, and had made an appointment for the next day to exchange confessions of dangerous secrets. Mahmoud had made the arrangement very light-heartedly, and had then stayed on for a quarter of an hour, talking to Abu Anmar in the lobby.

The next day, after dozens of people died on the Imams Bridge, Mahmoud forgot about everything. Saidi had left him in charge of the next issue of the magazine and gone off to Erbil that morning with a delegation of politicians and economists for something to do with oil. Saidi had said he was depending on him and that he had great confidence in him, that everything would be fine and he had complete authority.

The streets were mostly blocked because of tight security for the religious ceremonies in Kadhimiya, so Mahmoud walked to the magazine offices. No one had arrived yet, except for the old caretaker. He found Saidi's second mobile phone connected to the charger. He turned on the phone and found fourteen missed calls, half of them from the number 666.

What would happen if Mahmoud called that number now? He could tell her that he had taken her previous call and found out what kind of relationship she and Saidi had, and that he was now offering her some advice: 'Forget Saidi, because he has no memory. He's just a man of pleasure. You can try your luck with other men if you like. Try your luck with me, you devil woman.'

He struggled with himself over whether to call her, just to hear her voice, especially as he hadn't seen her for about ten days. He finally persuaded himself to wait till she called again – she had already called seven times that day. He would answer her call and reveal his identity to her.

He didn't find much that he could do. The caretaker wanted to make him some tea or coffee, but he made it clear he didn't want any. He asked the caretaker to lock the doors so they could both leave. He took his stuff from Saidi's table and looked at Saidi's phone. He had an overwhelming desire to do something stupid. Something stupid but minor. He would listen to Nawal al-Wazir's voice, nothing more. He wouldn't tell anyone. No one would ever know.

He picked up the phone, found the list of recent calls, and selected 666. He heard ringing on the other end, and the blood started coursing through his veins and his heart beat faster and stronger. The ringing continued for several seconds, and then she picked up: 'Hello, hello?'

It was her voice, with those sensuous cadences that so agonized him. But he couldn't answer. He couldn't control his throat or his lips or even blink. He was transfixed, frozen.

'Hello?' said Nawal. 'Baher,' she added. 'Who is it that comes and uses your phone in your office?'

'I don't know,' came Saidi's voice in the background. 'Please give the phone to me. Hello, hello? Is that you, Abu Jouni?'

Mahmoud hung up, turned off the phone, and tossed it on the editor's table as though it had given him an electric shock.

So she was with him now. A political and economic conference, huh! But she was a film director? Maybe she'd gone to film some footage for her next film, which they chatted about so much. Maybe it was a film about the links between money and politics and oil, and about getting out of Baghdad to escape the religious rituals that brought life to a standstill. Maybe she was adding some realistic bed shots to include in her great film.

Mahmoud turned and saw the old caretaker, Abu Jouni, watching him, or waiting for him to finish his business so they could go out and lock up the building from the outside.

He didn't speak for a whole hour and walked back. He ate at a restaurant on the way. He thought of calling his friend Farid Shawwaf and bringing up Nawal al-Wazir in passing, but then he thought that if he did that, he would make a laughing stock of himself. So he'd call his friend Hazem Abboud, the photographer. But Hazem would ridicule him for talking endlessly about Nawal, as he had done that time they went to the brothel together.

'It's all to do with your cock,' Hazem would say, trying to shock him and to deny the emotional aspect of his attachment to Nawal. 'Find a permanent flesh hole for it.'

Mahmoud reached Aziz's coffee shop and found Hadi, who reminded him of the agreement they had made the previous evening. Mahmoud ordered a tea and, out of a desire to forget everything, surrendered himself to Hadi's crazy story. Hadi was speaking quietly, stopping and looking around every now and then. He wasn't behaving his usual way when playing the role of the old storyteller. Now he was speaking as if he were revealing a secret. Then, when he came to a critical point in his story, he asked Mahmoud to come home with him so that they could speak more openly.

When he had finished narrating the new details in his story of the Whatsitsname, it had quite an effect on Mahmoud. For half a minute Mahmoud went over in his head everything that Hadi had said. It was a truly appalling story, and this crazy old man couldn't have made it up all by himself. It

112

included things that were too complicated for the simple mind of this junk dealer. Hadi woke Mahmoud from his reverie. 'Now you,' he said. 'Tell me your dangerous secret.'

3

Mahmoud did tell him a real secret. He had never told anyone, not even his close friend Hazem Abboud, of his suspicion about his family's origins. He had never had occasion to mention it, or else he simply wasn't brave enough to. Anyway, it was a real secret that was buried inside him, and he couldn't remember the last time anyone in his family in Amara had spoken about it. So he was honest with Hadi, even if Hadi didn't seem to appreciate the significance of his confession. For the rest of the day Mahmoud kept thinking about what Hadi had said. He promised himself he would play back the recording on his digital recorder, in his hotel room, so he wouldn't forget the details. He believed that emotions changed memories, that when you lost the emotion associated with a particular event, you lost an important part of the event. So he had to write down things that he thought were important or record them on his little recorder when the emotions that went with them were still strong.

He recorded almost everything on his new Panasonic recorder, which he had bought from a shop in Bab al-Sharqi about six months earlier. The recorder struck him as being an evolutionary advance over the school notebooks in which his father, Riyadh al-Sawadi, used to write his diaries. In the end, on the eve of his death, his father had filled twenty-seven notebooks of one hundred pages each. On a few rare occasions, Mahmoud had looked at some of the pages. But then his mother had done the unthinkable: she put them all deep in the oven, poured paraffin over them, and set them on fire. She then made twenty-seven loaves of flat bread, baking them gently on the ashes of his confessions. His father had written down everything. He had written the naked truth in black ink, in elegant handwriting of the kind you would find in a calligraphy book. There were passages about the times his father had masturbated when he was married, about the women he dreamed of sleeping with, some of them old women from the neighbourhood. What he said in his diaries couldn't be squared with the way people saw him in the Jidayda district of Amara. He was highly respected and revered, but maybe that wasn't an image Mahmoud's father liked very much. It was an image that had been imposed on him and that he had finally managed to live with, but only by expressing his real self in his secret confessions.

When Mahmoud's brothers looked at the notebooks, they were shocked and embarrassed. Mahmoud heard them say things about origins and changing religion and so on. He wasn't sure what he heard, and the subject was completely closed once the ashes of the twenty-seven notebooks had cooled down in their mother's oven. But Mahmoud sometimes remembered some of what his father had written and tried to piece it together with scraps of information that had been suppressed forever, in an attempt to understand things, even if there was no longer any way to verify the information. One of those things was the family name Sawadi, which Mahmoud's father, an Arabic teacher, had invented, completely ignoring the usual name that indicated tribal affiliation. Many people started referring to the family house as the house of the Sawadi clan. But Mahmoud's father's death meant death for the invented family name as well, because Mahmoud's brothers reverted to their tribal name, which they were proud of. But Mahmoud, outraged by the ruthless way they had tried to expunge their father's life story, retained the Sawadi name and established it as the name by which he was known in newspapers and magazines.

4

Mahmoud got up from the wooden chair Hadi had placed for him in the courtyard of his run-down house and looked up at the sky, which was growing darker as sunset approached. He took a long breath and told Hadi he wouldn't believe his story until he provided some material evidence that the Whatsitsname he'd been talking about really existed.

Mahmoud put his hand in his pocket, pulled out the Panasonic recorder, and gave it to Hadi, saying he should do an interview with this creature. He should turn on the recorder and ask him what he was doing, where he was going, and where he was living.

Mahmoud invited Hadi to examine the recorder. He explained how to turn it on and off. Hadi spent five minutes recording and then playing his voice back, checking that he had understood the instructions.

'Mind the batteries. They run out very quickly,' Mahmoud said before leaving, unsure what exactly he had just done – this junk dealer would probably sell the recorder the next day. Perhaps it was the effect of the exhausting day, or the effect of Hadi's strange story and the promise of hearing more details. What if Hadi produces real evidence that a mythical creature of this kind existed? Would he really believe it?

Mahmoud walked towards the Orouba Hotel, thinking about Saidi and his female devil Nawal and his friends and his father who had been dead for ten years.

When he reached the hotel, he found that someone had put a small generator on the pavement. Abu Anmar had brought it; it was enough to power the fans and lights in the four hotel rooms that were occupied, as well as the reception area and the private room that Abu Anmar lived in.

Mahmoud went up to his room and lay flat on his bed for a full hour. His feet hurt from all the walking. He closed his eyes to the swirl of air from the ceiling fan. Out of his memory streamed a clear image of his father, wearing a dishdasha and sitting in the parlour at home. He had on his glasses, and there was a large wooden board on his crossed legs. On the board he had an open notebook, and he devoted hours to writing in it silently.

When Mahmoud opened his eyes in the pitch dark, he didn't know how much time had passed. He went downstairs and then to a nearby restaurant for dinner. When he came back he saw Luqman, the Algerian who lived in the hotel, sitting in the lobby with another old guest, as well as Abu Anmar and Andrew, the teenager who helped his old mother Veronica with the weekly cleaning. They were all watching television; the little generator was purring outside. Mahmoud said hello to them and sat down to watch too. What a surprise it was when he saw his friend Farid Shawwaf on the screen, in a grey suit, black shirt and red tie. He looked smarter than Mahmoud had ever seen him before.

Abu Anmar raised his fat hand and ordered the boy to go and get four cups of tea from the tea stand in the street.

Everyone in the lobby was watching the talk show on television anxiously and in silence. It was a big disaster, the biggest disaster that had struck Iraq so far, as Abu Anmar put it. About a thousand people had been killed, either from drowning or being trampled to death, and no one knew who the culprit was. The government spokesman came out smiling as usual to announce that an attempted suicide bombing on the Imams Bridge had been prevented and that the criminal had escaped.

'If the criminal had blown himself up, there would have been thousands of victims today,' the spokesman said. A loud, rumbling fart echoed through the lobby and even outside. Soon everyone realized it was just the horn of a truck driving down Bataween's main street, warning off a child who had run out in front of it.

The host of the talk show returned to his guests after showing a clip of the government spokesman, and Farid Shawwaf, smartly dressed, jumped in to express his view. 'As I said earlier, responsibility for this incident lies with the government, which installed concrete barriers on the bridge itself. It should have carried out the searches at the entrance and exit of the bridge so it wouldn't get crowded there.'

The host put up his hand to interrupt Farid, turned to his other guest – a bald old man with a small white beard – and asked him the same question: who was responsible?

'It's definitely some al-Qaeda cells and remnants of the old regime,' the man said. 'Even if they didn't personally carry out this crime, they are responsible for it because there have been criminal incidents in their name in the past, so the mere mention of their name is a factor in creating insecurity and confusing people.'

The host cut in: 'Some people say the person responsible is the one who started the rumour that there was a suicide bomber on the bridge.'

'No, I don't think he is to blame,' replied the older man. 'No one knows who started the rumour, but the idea was very much in the air. Perhaps the person thought there was a suicide bomber and warned the others with good intentions.'

The host turned to Farid to give him a chance to elaborate. 'Honestly, I think everyone was responsible in one way or another. I'd go further and say that all the security incidents and the tragedies we're seeing stem from one thing – fear. The people on the bridge died because they were frightened

117

of dying. Every day we're dying from the same fear of dying. The groups that have given shelter and support to al-Qaeda have done so because they are frightened of another group, and this other group has created and mobilized militias to protect itself from al-Qaeda. It has created a death machine working in the other direction because it's afraid of the Other. And we're going to see more and more death because of fear. The government and the occupation forces have to eliminate fear. They must put a stop to it if they really want this cycle of killing to end.'

5

Brigadier Majid was watching the talk show on television and was impressed by the way Farid Shawwaf was dressed – the grey suit with black shirt and red tie. Maybe he should send one of his staff to go and buy him a similar outfit, but he doubted there would be an occasion to wear clothes like that, because for most of the week he lay low in his office like a prisoner.

He flicked through all the Iraqi television channels and saw they were still preoccupied with the incident on the Imams Bridge. Something told him they were all wrong and that the real culprit was still at large. He might even be arrested that very night.

He took a sip of tea. There were a few light taps on the door, and two fat young men with short hair came in, both wearing pink shirts and black linen trousers. They saluted him and stood at attention.

The brigadier took another sip of tea, then turned to them and spoke with great insistence, because his big coup might take place that night. He had summoned the men only to give himself the satisfaction of feeling he was in control of the operation, and the conversation between them was devoid of content.

'Are you going to go?' he asked.

'Yes, sir,' they replied in unison.

'Don't do anything weird. Act normal. Arrest him and come back as quickly as possible. I want you to be tough. Off you go, and God be with you.'

'Yes, sir.'

The two fat young men gave him another firm, sharp salute then hurried off.

The brigadier went back to his tea and found it had gone cold. He reached for a file on the table and looked through it again. It contained a prediction by the team of astrologers and fortune-tellers in the Tracking and Pursuit Department. It had landed on his desk a quarter of an hour ago, which meant he urgently needed to prepare a team to arrest the criminal – the One Who Has No Name, as the laconic senior astrologer had dubbed him.

He would spend the night in the office, waiting for the hit squad to come back, in the hope that this would be the end of the story, the end of the headache, the anxiety, the tension. Then he would be in an excellent position with respect to the Americans and the parties in power, both of which looked at him with suspicion. He might be promoted or be able to come out into the limelight, from the dark, mysterious shadows where he had been lurking for the past two years.

What would the criminal look like, the brigadier wondered? Deep in thought, he paced around his large office. This man who could take bullets without dying or bleeding, how horribly ugly would he be? How would he be arrested if he wasn't afraid of death or of gunfire? Did he really have extraordinary powers? Would he breathe fire at his men and burn them to ashes? Or did he have hidden wings to take off and fly away from his pursuers? Would he suddenly disappear before their eyes as if he had never existed?

He knew he would have the answers to these questions in two or three hours.

CHAPTER NINE

The Recordings

1

Mahmoud slid open the window overlooking the balcony of his second-floor room in the Dilshad Hotel. The warm air hit his face, and he saw the heat rising from the asphalt on Saadoun Street. The harsh glare of the sun, reflecting off the passing cars, hurt his eyes. Just seeing from above the effect of the heat on what was happening below was enough to discourage him from leaving the hotel.

Mahmoud had finally managed to move from the Orouba Hotel to the Dilshad, with encouragement from Saidi, who wanted his assistant to live in better conditions, apparently in preparation for bigger assignments.

Mahmoud closed the sliding window, shutting out some of the street noise and the rumble of the traffic. He picked up the remote for the air conditioning and set the thermostat to seventy-five degrees. Settling into a wooden chair, he rested his elbows on the round coffee-coloured table, brought his old digital recorder to his mouth and pressed Record. He wanted to go over the details of what had happened over the previous two days, especially his strange conversation with Hadi the junk dealer.

Hadi had seemed willing to answer any of Mahmoud's questions. He was eager to convince Mahmoud that his story was true. His manner was different from his usual one, when he had an audience. Typically he'd seem relaxed and cheerful while knowing deep down that others didn't believe what he was saying, the fact that they didn't believe him seemingly part of the ritual he enjoyed while telling the story. When he was telling Mahmoud the story of the Whatsitsname, he wasn't enjoying it. It was more like he was fulfilling an obligation or conveying a message.

The Whatsitsname had visited Hadi on the very night that several murders took place in the Bataween area, after Aziz had warned him to stop telling his story about the body he had sewn together. The story was no longer funny: it now aroused suspicions, Aziz thought. Hadi was drinking his last glass of arak when the Whatsitsname appeared at the door to his room. When Hadi saw him standing a few feet away, he thought it was just a bad dream. If the dream came true before his eyes, the creature's intentions would not be good. It would have come to kill him.

The first sentence the Whatsitsname spoke confirmed Hadi's fears: he really was visiting him that night in order to kill him.

'You're responsible for the death of the guard at the hotel, Hasib Mohamed Jaafar,' the Whatsitsname said. 'If you hadn't been walking past the hotel – the guard wouldn't have come out to the gate. He might have stayed close to the sentry box, which was relatively far from the outer gate, and opened fire from a distance on the suicide bomber driving the rubbish truck. The explosion might have caused him some injuries, or the blast might have thrown him, but he definitely wouldn't have died, and the next morning he could have gone home to his wife and his little daughter. While having breakfast with them, he might have considered giving up his dangerous job and selling sunflower seeds on the pavement in Sector 44.'

The Whatsitsname seemed intent on carrying out the mission for which he had come. Hadi argued with him, plucking up all his courage to defend himself. In a sense Hadi was his father; he had brought him into the world, hadn't he?

'You were just a conduit, Hadi,' the Whatsitsname replied. 'Think how many stupid mothers and fathers have produced geniuses and great men in history. The credit isn't due to them but to circumstances and other things beyond their control. You're just an instrument, or a surgical glove that Fate put on its hand to move pawns on the chessboard of life.'

Such eloquent talk! Everything Hadi had done – things that no one in his right mind would have undertaken – made him just a conduit, just a paved road that Fate's car could speed along on.

The argument went on for some minutes, and that in itself showed the Whatsitsname wasn't quite sure of what he was doing. If he had decided to kill Hadi, he wouldn't have spoken to him in the first place. He would have come in and, as with the four beggars, have squeezed his throat with his strong, steady hands until Hadi gave up the ghost. Then he would have thrown Hadi's lifeless body onto his dirty bed. He would have left him there and gone, and people would have found Hadi's body maybe a month later because so few people had visited Hadi since the death of Nahem Abdaki, and no one liked him much or would miss him.

The Whatsitsname looked at the Throne Verse on the far wall of the room. He needed to do something to distract himself and give his brain a chance to decide a course of action. He kept looking at the Throne Verse and at the cardboard edge that was hanging down. He took a few steps towards it and pulled at the cardboard edge. The other corners that were pasted to the wall came off too. The whole frame broke into pieces and came off the wall easily, as if it had been waiting for ages for someone to come along and pull it down. Hadi couldn't remember why or when Nahem had put up the verse, but it had been there since they built the room. The Whatsitsname threw the inscription aside, and a dark hole appeared in the wall behind where it had been, about a foot and a half high and a foot across. The next morning Hadi would find out what was in the hole.

Time was passing slowly for Hadi in the awkward company of the Whatsitsname, but the course of events suggested to Hadi that his creation wasn't sure what his mission was that night. The Whatsitsname turned to him and admitted he was confused, because the soul of Hasib Mohamed Jaafar was demanding revenge, and he had to kill the person who had caused Hasib's death.

'It was the Sudanese suicide bomber who caused his death,' Hadi said confidently, trying to exploit the situation to his own advantage.

'Yes, but he's dead. How can I kill someone who's already dead?'

'The hotel management, then. The company that ran the hotel.'

'Yes, maybe. But I have to find the real killer of Hasib Mohamed Jaafar so his soul can find rest,' said the Whatsitsname, pulling up a wooden crate and sitting on it.

2

Mahmoud picked up the latest issue of *al-Haqiqa* magazine and read a paragraph of Ali Baher al-Saidi's weekly column:

There are laws that human beings are unaware
of. These laws don't operate around the clock
like the physical laws by which the wind blows,
the rain falls, and rocks fall down mountains, or
like other laws that human beings can observe,
verify, and define because they apply to things
that recur. There are laws that operate only
under special conditions, and when something
happens under these laws, people are surprised
and say it's impossible, that it's a fairy tale or
in the best case a miracle. They don't say
they're unaware of the law behind it. People
are deluded and never admit their ignorance.

Mahmoud imagined that this passage might summarize
the Whatsitsname's ideas about the reasons he existed. But
Hadi adhered to a more imaginative formula – that the
Whatsitsname was made up of the body parts of people
who had been killed, plus the soul of another victim, and
had been given the name of yet another victim. He was a
composite of victims seeking to avenge their deaths so they
could rest in peace. He was created to obtain revenge on
their behalf.

The Whatsitsname talked about the night he met the
drunk beggars. He said he tried to avoid them, but they were
aggressive and charged towards him to kill him. His horrible
face was an incentive for them to attack him. They didn't
know anything about him, but they were driven by that latent
hatred that can suddenly come to the surface when people
meet someone who doesn't fit in. They fought for half an
hour, trying to hit him with their fists or get hold of his
neck to strangle him. In the darkness, one of them grabbed
one of his friends by the neck and, given new strength by
his delirium, finished him off. Then he noticed that another

beggar had done the same thing. The two dead beggars were victims of acts of stupidity, and the two surviving beggars were criminals, so the Whatsitsname strangled them to avenge the beggars they had killed. Because they had been secretly planning to do the same thing to him, and because the four of them would have failed in any attempt to kill him anyway (and this is the underlying significance of what happened on that strange night), they were intent on suicide but hadn't found a good way to commit it until the Whatsitsname appeared, strolling down the dark lane in Daniel's old clothes.

Daniel, or the Whatsitsname, was just a means by which they went to their deaths, which was a fate that appealed to them at every serious drinking session they had, including the one they had had that night.

They had died because they wanted to die, and that explained the strange posture they were in when the locals found them the next morning, in a square, with each one strangling one of the others.

Mahmoud recorded all this on his digital recorder, aware that he was paraphrasing the words that Hadi had attributed to the Whatsitsname and that he was adding his own personal gloss as well.

'It's hard to convince anyone of this nonsense, but organized nonsense of this kind stands behind all the crimes committed,' said Mahmoud. He then resumed a re-narration of the strange details. The Whatsitsname had been planning something completely different, instead of getting involved in fights with people who weren't his enemies in the first place. He had no doubts about his ability to survive, however hard the others tried to kill him, but he wasn't looking for stardom or a chance to show off or display his strength. Nor did he intend to frighten people. He was on a noble mission and had to carry it out with as few complications as possible, so after the incident with the four beggars and another incident in which a police vehicle accidentally hit him in the street near the Liberty Monument, he decided not to move around in the open and to avoid people as much as possible.

There he was, sitting on an upturned wooden crate in Hadi's room, seeing and hearing how stories about him had spread through the neighbourhood and other parts of Baghdad. The stories portrayed him as a dangerous criminal, but really he was nothing like that.

He had killed Abu Zaidoun to avenge Daniel Tadros, and he had killed the officer in the brothel because he was responsible for the death of someone whose fingers Hadi had taken for the Whatsitsname's body. He would keep on doing his work till the end.

'What is the end?' asked Mahmoud. 'When can it stop?'

After a moment's silence, Hadi replied, 'He's killing them all, all the criminals who committed crimes against him.'

'And what will he do after that?'

'He'll collapse and go back to how he was before. He'll decompose and die.'

Hadi himself was on the Whatsitsname's list. But the Whatsitsname's time wasn't unlimited, and he had to complete his mission quickly. He should really have stood up right then, strangled Hadi on his bed, and made him vomit onto his pillow all the arak he'd drunk, but the Whatsitsname didn't have the resolve for that. With his foxlike intuition, Hadi sensed this and took advantage of it.

'Leave me till the end,' he said. 'I don't want to live anyway. What's living to someone like me? I'm nothing, whether I live or die. I'm nothing. Kill me, but at the end. Make me the last one.'

The Whatsitsname just looked at Hadi from his dark eye sockets. His silence was enough to reassure Hadi that he wouldn't die that night.

3

The day after the Whatsitsname's visit, Hadi had met up with Mahmoud and told him he had given the digital recorder to the Whatsitsname. Mahmoud immediately had visions of the junk dealer selling the recorder in the Harj market in Bab al-Sharqi. But ten days later Hadi belied Mahmoud's doubts by giving the recorder back to him. So he wasn't a thief or a liar. Now, in his comfortable new room at the Dilshad Hotel, Mahmoud turned on the recorder and found that the memory was completely full.

After Mahmoud had given the recorder to him, Hadi had been sitting as usual in the courtyard outside his room. He had brought his bed out into the open air and thrown himself down on it to look at the few stars visible in the night sky. Meanwhile, close to midnight, while Mahmoud was trying to sleep under the roar of the ceiling fan in his wretched room in the Orouba Hotel, gunfire broke out.

There was nothing exceptional or strange about that, but the shooting sounded as if it was nearby. Hadi was worried that a bullet falling from the sky could kill him.

It was a terrible mistake by the team from the Tracking and Pursuit Department, which was led by two young officers in pink shirts. Brigadier Majid had made it clear to them that they should keep a low profile, but, accompanied by one of the astrologers from the department, they had been able to identify the location of the criminal and had gradually tightened the noose around him until they spotted him in a dark alley. Forgetting that he couldn't be killed by bullets, they fired at him and ran after him as he climbed walls and jumped from roof to roof. One of the officers managed to intercept the criminal and grab hold of his clothes. They wrestled for a few minutes, with the officer hoping that the rest of the team would soon arrive to handcuff the criminal, but the Whatsitsname won the upper hand. He grabbed the throat of the officer, whose eyes almost popped out of their sockets. When the Whatsitsname saw that the rest of the team was closing in on him, he smashed the officer's head against the wall. The officer collapsed, and the Whatsitsname ran off, disappearing from sight.

Half an hour later there was no sound of gunfire or any other sounds, for that matter. Hadi came out of his room, which was hot and full of damp smells, to lie down again in the courtyard, but he saw someone sitting on his bed. It was his friend the Whatsitsname.

For a moment Hadi thought the Whatsitsname had finished his task and had only Hadi left to take revenge on. But before he could speak, the Whatsitsname told him the area was surrounded by police and men from the special intelligence unit. He would stay at Hadi's place for a while until he was sure they were gone.

The Whatsitsname was discovering new things every day, he told Hadi. He had found out, for example, that each piece of dead flesh that made up his body fell off if he didn't avenge the person it came from within a certain amount of time. But if he did avenge someone, then that person's piece would fall off anyway, as if it was no longer needed.

Hadi felt so at ease that he sat next to the Whatsitsname on the bed, where he could smell his putrid body. He told the Whatsitsname he was prepared to help in any way he wanted. The Whatsitsname said he needed to replace the parts that were falling off, so he needed new flesh from new victims. Hadi said he would try to help, starting the next day, but in fact he had other ideas. It would be good, he thought, if the Whatsitsname's body fell to pieces quickly so that he could be done with him and with the terror he inspired.

The Whatsitsname turned to Hadi. 'That's not everything,' he said. 'What's worse is that people have been giving me a bad reputation. They're accusing me of committing crimes, but what they don't understand is that I'm the only justice there is in this country.'

Hadi suddenly remembered Mahmoud's digital recorder. He stood up and offered the Whatsitsname a drink, which he declined. He went into his room, lit the paraffin lamp, brought out his drinking stuff, and poured himself a glass of arak. He looked at the Whatsitsname and said, 'You should do an interview with the press to explain your cause.'

'An interview? I'm telling you I don't want to draw attention to myself, and you suggest an interview with the press!'

'You've already drawn attention to yourself,' Hadi said. 'You should defend yourself, to win some friends to help you in your mission. Right now, you're everyone's enemy.'

'But who could I do the interview with? You mean I should just walk into the television station? What kind of nonsense is that?'

'I can do the interview,' said Hadi, taking out the recorder. He tried to turn it on but couldn't remember how to. The Whatsitsname, sitting on Hadi's bed, took the recorder and fiddled with it as Hadi tried to enjoy a glass of warm arak without ice or mezes. Then more gunshots broke out, and the Whatsitsname stood up.

'I'll interview myself,' the Whatsitsname said, turning to Hadi. 'Would that work?'

'That would be fine,' said Hadi, watching his strange companion skip across the stones towards Elishva's house. He disappeared into the house as the sporadic shooting came closer, along with the sound of footsteps and indistinct shouting from men running in the street.

4

The next morning the area was surrounded by the Iraqi National Guard and the US military police. An African American soldier yelled at Mahmoud and pointed his gun at him when he tried to approach and explain that he was from the press. Frightened, Mahmoud went back to the hotel. He found Abu Anmar in the lobby, talking with some people about what had happened the night before. Several houses had been raided, their doors kicked in and locks smashed. Entering with flashlights, the soldiers came and arrested some men they thought were suspect, but not the criminal. The area was quickly sealed off, so the criminal was still within the confines of Bataween.

Mahmoud called Saidi, his editor, filled him in, and said he couldn't come to the magazine that day. Saidi urged him to go out to see what was happening, to interview people, and try to find out from the Iraqi soldiers the purpose of the operation.

Mahmoud was resentful of Saidi's insistence, but he left the hotel anyway. The information he managed to gather was worthless: that an intelligence officer had been taken to the hospital after sustaining a serious head injury during the hunt for a major terrorist who had been spotted in the area at night.

At midday they called off the search and relaxed the security cordon. Mahmoud saw some young and middle-aged men being herded into army trucks, their hands tied behind their backs. What they all had in common, Mahmoud soon noticed, was that they were ugly. Some had genetic defects, others had been disfigured by burns, and others seemed to be insane: their faces were relaxed, with no signs of fear or anxiety.

Mahmoud returned to his room in the Orouba Hotel. In the afternoon the ceiling fan stopped because of a problem with

131

the generator Abu Anmar had bought for his four guests. Mahmoud felt he was starting to drown in his own sweat. He headed for Aziz's coffee shop, which since the beginning of summer had a large air-conditioning unit secured with metal brackets above the big front window. There Mahmoud ran into Hadi smoking a shisha in his usual seat next to the front window.

Mahmoud sat down with Hadi and ordered a shisha and a glass of tea. Hadi seemed to have recovered his customary cheerfulness. He told Mahmoud that the police had targeted the Whatsitsname but hadn't arrested him. He said it with considerable confidence, and then told Mahmoud that he had persuaded the Whatsitsname to do the interview.

'He's going to interview himself,' he said.

Mahmoud now knew for sure that Hadi had lost his recorder, which was worth one hundred dollars. Laughing and cheerful, Hadi seemed like the liar and con artist everyone described him as.

But ten days later, Hadi did in fact return the recorder. Mahmoud spent hours just listening, and then listened again. The recording was sensational and shocking. The Whatsitsname came across as a physical presence – a real person made of flesh and blood, like Mahmoud or Hadi or Abu Anmar. He wasn't as Hadi had described him with his fanciful talk.

Mahmoud listened again and again, immersing himself in the Whatsitsname's dramatic story while drowning too in the humid heat at the Orouba Hotel. On the second day Saidi noticed the dark rings around Mahmoud's eyes.

'I have lots of work and other assignments for you. Leave that cave of a hotel,' Saidi said, insisting that Mahmoud move to the Dilshad Hotel in Atibbaa Street. When Abu Anmar saw Mahmoud standing in front of him with his suitcase, his books and his other possessions, determined to leave, he didn't say anything. Mahmoud thought it must be quite a shock for Abu Anmar, but Abu Anmar behaved professionally, closing Mahmoud's account after Mahmoud paid his balance.

Saidi was fascinated by the details of Mahmoud's dealings with Hadi and invited Mahmoud for tea in the office's inner garden so he could hear the story directly.

'You should appreciate the plants and the greenery,' Saidi said. 'It's good for you, important for your psychological and physical health.' Then he added, 'At least it's a change from the grey of the concrete barriers throughout the city.'

Mahmoud didn't know what to do with this digression – whether he should continue with his story or wait for Saidi to give him a sign.

Neither of them spoke for thirty seconds, but then Saidi turned to Mahmoud and said, 'Write me a story about all this. Do a feature or an interview with this person. Do something for the next issue.'

Two days later Mahmoud gave Saidi an article headlined 'Urban Legends from the Streets of Iraq'. Saidi liked it immediately. When Mahmoud did the layout for the magazine, he illustrated the article with a large photo of Robert De Niro from the film of *Mary Shelley's Frankenstein*. Mahmoud wasn't happy when he got a copy of the issue, especially when he saw that his headline had been changed.

'Frankenstein in Baghdad,' Saidi shouted, a big smile on his face. Mahmoud had been trying to be truthful and objective, but Saidi was all about hype. He had even written his own article on the same subject for the same issue.

With the latest issue in his hands, Mahmoud was lying on his bed on the second floor of the Dilshad Hotel. The cold air gave him the shivers, so he turned down the air-conditioning. It was his day off, and he tried to sleep. But he kept staring at the cover of the magazine, with Robert

De Niro's grim face looking out at a world that turned on him, and he wondered what the Whatsitsname, if he really existed, would make of the article. Would he see it as another misunderstanding of his prophetic mission?

And what would Hadi say about it? Would he insult Mahmoud or praise him?

5

As Mahmoud was lounging on his bed, Brigadier Sorour Majid was in his grand office in the Tracking and Pursuit Department, standing in front of the air-conditioner. He knew it wasn't good for his health, but he was unbearably hot. Maybe he had high blood pressure. His staff had waited till he'd finished his siesta before confronting him with the latest issue of *al-Haqiqa*, which was edited by his childhood friend Ali Baher al-Saidi.

He had read Mahmoud's article twice and thought it contained information that shouldn't have been disclosed without approval from the Tracking and Pursuit Department, but what could he do about the freedom of the press that had suddenly descended on the country? Saidi had made a mistake with this article and should have discussed it with him before publishing it.

His plump cheeks were icy from the air-conditioner, but Brigadier Majid still felt on fire. He threw the magazine onto his vast desk, picked up one of his mobile phones, and called Saidi.

As usual, Saidi was laughing.

'What's the problem, man?' Saidi asked.

'Did your journalist actually meet this criminal?'

'I don't think so. He spoke to some local guy with a wild

imagination. It's a simple story, my friend. The guy's a liar,' said Saidi.

'Yes, but maybe this is the criminal we're looking for. What colour was his skin? Did he have scars from bullet wounds or injuries that had been stitched up?'

'I have no idea. It's all based on the fantasies of some low-life, my friend.'

'This is not fantasy. Where can I find your journalist?'

'It's Friday today, my friend. Aren't you at home?'

'Where does this kid live?'

Brigadier Majid wrote down the address on a scrap of paper and hung up. He pressed the service bell, and a young muscular man came in, gave a military salute, and stood at attention.

'Call Ihsan for me,' the brigadier said.

About a minute later, a plump, close-shaven young man came in. He had short hair and was wearing a pink shirt and black linen trousers.

'Go right away to this address and bring me this journalist, Mahmoud Riyadh Mohamed al-Sawadi,' said the brigadier.

CHAPTER TEN

The Whatsitsname

1

'Hello, hello, test, test, test.'

'I've started recording.'

'I know. Hello, hello, test, test.'

'Mind the battery.'

'Please be quiet. Hello, hello, yes.'

'I don't have much time. I might come to an end and my body might turn into liquid as I'm walking down the street one night, even before I accomplish the mission I've been assigned. I'm like the recorder that journalist gave to my father, the poor junk dealer. And as far as I'm concerned, time is like the charge in this battery – not much and not enough.

'Is that junk dealer really my father? Surely he's just a conduit for the will of our Father in heaven, as my poor mother, Elishva, puts it. She's a really poor old woman. They're all poor, and I'm the answer to the call of the poor. I'm a saviour, the one they were waiting for and hoped for in some sense. These unseen sinews, rusty from rare use, have finally stirred. The sinews of a law that isn't always on the alert. The prayers of the victims and their families came together for once and gave those sinews a powerful impetus. The innards of the darkness moved and gave birth to me. I am the answer to their call for an end to injustice and for revenge on the guilty.

'With the help of God and of heaven, I will take revenge on all the criminals. I will finally bring about justice on earth, and there will no longer be a need to wait in agony for justice to come, in heaven or after death.

'Will I fulfil my mission? I don't know, but I will at least try to set an example of vengeance – the vengeance of the innocent who have no protection other than the tremors of their souls as they pray to ward off death.

'When I'm alone, deep inside I'm not very interested in having humans listen to me or meet me, because I'm not here to be famous or to meet others. But in order to make sure that my mission isn't misrepresented and doesn't become more difficult, I find myself compelled to make this statement. They have turned me into a criminal and a monster, and in this way they have equated me with those I seek to exact revenge on. This is a grave injustice. In fact there is a moral and humanitarian obligation to back me, to bring about justice in this world, which has been totally ravaged by greed, ambition, megalomania, and insatiable bloodlust.

'I'm not asking anyone to take up arms with me or to take revenge on the criminals on my behalf. And please don't panic when you see me. I'm saying this to good, peace-loving people. I ask you to pray and to pin the hopes in your hearts on my winning and accomplishing my mission before it is too late and everything is out of my hands and—'

'Look, the battery's died.'

'Why are you interrupting me? What's wrong with you?'

'The battery's dead, my lord and master.'

'Yes, no problem. Leave the building and don't come back till you have a big bag full of batteries.'

2

'I'm living in an unfinished building close to the Assyrian quarter in Dora, south of Baghdad. It's an area that's become a battleground between three forces: the Iraqi National Guard and the American army on one side, and the Sunni militias and the Shiite militias as the second and third sides. I could describe the building I live in No Man's Land because it and the buildings around, in an area about a half-mile square, have never been under the full control of any of the three forces, and because it's a war zone without any inhabitants. So it's the right place for me.

'I have safe corridors in the form of big gaps in the walls of the houses that have been damaged and deserted. I use them to go out on my nightly missions, alert for the moment when I come face-to-face with a group of armed men from one of the three groups I mentioned. All of us use a complicated network of routes that is like a labyrinth in daytime and even more complicated at night. We try to avoid meeting one another, although we are moving around in search of one another.

'I have a number of assistants who live with me. They have banded together around me over the past three months. The most important one is an old man called the Magician.

'The Magician used to live in an apartment in Abu Nuwas, just west of Bataween, and he says he was part of the team of magicians that worked for the president of the old regime and that he cast spells to keep the Americans away from Baghdad and to prevent the city from falling into their hands. But the Americans, besides their arsenal of advanced military hardware, possessed a formidable army of djinn, which was able to destroy the djinn that this magician and his assistants had mobilized.

'When I met him, he was in deep grief and pain, not because the former regime had fallen but because he had failed the biggest test he had ever faced. As far as he was concerned, his magic is now useless.

'But one of the djinn that had survived the massacre that took place during the battle for Baghdad airport continued to hover around him to console him in his loneliness. The djinn told him that he had one important mission left. He told him about me and gave him a description of my appearance.

'The Magician told me that he had been thrown out of his apartment because of accusations related to crimes committed under the old regime, and that there was someone following him wherever he went. Even the djinn that served him couldn't help, and now he hardly ever left our base in the damaged building. His role is now to make sure it's safe for me to move around inside Dora and out into other parts of Baghdad. He does this with dedication and selflessness because he says that I represent vengeance against anyone who has wronged him.

'The second most important of my assistants is the Sophist, as he calls himself. He's good at explaining ideas, promoting the good ones, polishing them, and making them more powerful. He's good at doing the same for bad ideas too, so he's a man who's as dangerous as dynamite. I've often sought his help to understand the mission I'm now carrying out, and I consult him when I have doubts about some course of action. He makes everyone feel reassured and strengthens their faith – because he doesn't fully believe in anything himself. I ran into him one evening when he was sitting drunk on the pavement in Saadoun Street, and he told me that although he had no respect for belief, he was prepared to believe in me – for one reason: that others had no faith in me and didn't even believe I existed.

'The third most important person is the one I call the Enemy – because he's an officer in the counterterrorism unit. He provides me with a living example of what the enemy looks like and how the enemy thinks and behaves. Because he's so well placed, he also leaks important information to me that helps me on my difficult excursions. He has taken refuge with me because of his strict morality: after working in the government's security agency for two years, he became convinced that the justice he was looking for wasn't being achieved on the ground at all.

'Now he's with me, offering his valuable services because it's the only way, he thinks, to bring about the justice that he longs for.

'There are three other people who are less important: the young madman, the old madman and the eldest madman. It was the young madman who kept interrupting me when I started recording this. I made him go buy some batteries from a shop a few miles from our base. To get there you have to go through several dangerous intersections.

'The young madman thinks I'm the model citizen that the Iraqi state has failed to produce, at least since the days of King Faisal I.

'Because I'm made up of body parts of people from diverse backgrounds – ethnicities, tribes, races and social classes – I represent the impossible mix that never was achieved in the past. I'm the first true Iraqi citizen, he thinks.

'The old madman thinks I'm an instrument of mass destruction that presages the coming of the saviour that all the world's religions have predicted. I'm the one who will annihilate people who have lost their way and gone astray. By helping me in my mission, he is accelerating the arrival of the long-awaited saviour.

'The eldest madman thinks I am the saviour and that in the coming days he will acquire some aspects of my immortality and his name will be engraved next to mine in any chronicle of this difficult and decisive phase in the history of this country and the world.

'When I consulted the Sophist, he told me that this eldest madman, because he is completely mad, is a blank page that can assimilate wisdom that transcends the bounds of reason and that, without knowing it, he speaks with the tongue of pure truth.'

3

'I go out at night, an hour or two after sunset. I keep my head down because of the constant crossfire. I'm the only person walking down long streets where even stray cats and dogs dare not venture. In the short interludes of silence between the bursts of gunfire, which grow more and more intense as midnight approaches, there is nothing but the sound of my footsteps. I'm equipped with everything I might need – identity cards and documents provided to me by the Enemy, so well made that they are impossible to distinguish from the real thing, and a detailed map of the best route through the residential areas, the streets and the lanes, provided by the Magician. The route enables me to avoid running into people I don't need to see and who don't need to see me.

'My preparations include dressing in clothes appropriate to the place I'm heading to, always provided to me by the three madmen, and applying make-up to hide the scars and bruises and stitches on my face. The Sophist usually does the make-up, and he gives me a mirror so I can see the results before I go out.

'I'm getting close to accomplishing my mission. There's a man from al-Qaeda living in a house in Abu Ghraib, on the edges of the capital, and a Venezuelan officer who's a mercenary with a security company operating in Baghdad. Once I've taken revenge on them, everything will be over. Except that things haven't been moving to a close in the way I had assumed they would.

'One night I went home with my whole body riddled with bullets. It had been a fierce battle and a perilous chase, and I only just managed to get my hands around the neck of my target, a criminal who was supplying many of the armed gangs with dynamite and other explosives regardless of their ideological or political background. He was a merchant of death par excellence and was living with some other members of his gang in a house close to the Shorja market in central Baghdad.

'The three madmen extracted many of the bullets from my body. The Magician and the Sophist helped by trying to sew up the parts that were damaged. A piece of flesh on my shoulder wouldn't stay in place – it was all runny, like flesh from a several-days-old corpse.

'When I got up the next day, I found that many parts of my body were on the ground, and there was a strong smell of rot. None of my assistants was nearby – they'd gone up to the roof to escape the smell.

'I wrapped myself in a large piece of cloth and went looking for them. Fluids from various exposed parts of my body seeped into the cloth. I stood at a distance from them on the roof and asked, "What's happening? Is this the end?"

'The Magician looked at me anxiously. The others were smoking and peering through the gaps in the parapet at what was happening on the streets down below.

'"Whenever you kill someone, that account is closed," the Magician said. "In other words, the person who was seeking revenge has had his wish fulfilled, and the body part that came from him starts to melt. It looks like there's a time

142

factor. If you exact revenge for all the victims ahead of the deadline, then your body will hold together for a while and start to dissolve only later, but if you take too long, when you come to your last assignment you'll have only the body part of the last person to be avenged."

'"That's bullshit," said the Sophist. "He doesn't die and he doesn't fall apart – none of that lousy shit," he continued, throwing his cigarette on the ground. "You're just trying to frighten us. The saviour doesn't die."

'The Sophist turned to the eldest madman, who was more interested than the others in this idea. He soon raised his fist in the air and shook it. "Yes, the saviour doesn't die," he declaimed.

'The two of them continued to argue while the others watched what was happening below. Apparently two groups were about to clash in broad daylight. It was risky to stay on the roof and look through the openings in the parapet wall because you might be killed by a stray bullet. But curiosity got the better of everyone.

'I spread the piece of cloth on the roof and lay down, naked in the sun. Sticky fluids were oozing from my wounds and from the fissures where the stitches were coming apart. I needed a complete overhaul. In fact – and this was a conclusion that took me by surprise – I needed new spare parts.

'Down below, deafening bursts of gunfire broke out, and piercing screams. I felt I was roasting in the sun, so I stood up, wrapped myself in the cloth, and went over to the parapet. The battle was furious. One group was soon defeated and took flight, while the other managed to capture two members of the group that was running away. With their rifle butts they pushed them against a wall that was riddled with holes made by PK machine guns. One of the two captured men had serious wounds and was groaning; he might have been asking for help. The other one was silent and

143

unbowed, like a holy martyr, as if he knew there were spectators who would praise him for how bravely he had faced death. It didn't take long. The captors pushed the young men against the wall, shouted "Allahu Akbar!" two or three times, then opened fire. The men collapsed to the ground, and the gunmen clutched their rifles to their shoulders, like farmers with spades, and hurried off.

'I looked at my assistants. All looked horrified except for the Magician, who said: "Nice young men. What a waste!" Then he added, "Aren't they victims too?"

'"I don't know. Ask the Sophist," I replied.

'"They're all victims, as far as I can see," said the Magician.

'Over the next three hours, I lost my right thumb and three fingers from my left hand. My nose was disintegrating and large holes appeared on my body – my flesh was melting. I felt weak and had to fight off sleep. My six assistants were sitting in a room, on furniture taken from the abandoned houses, talking anxiously.

'According to the schedule that I have, my mission ends tonight. I'll get hold of the Venezuelan mercenary officer at a hotel in Karrada. I'll take lots of bullets before I get my hands around his neck, then I'll leave in a car belonging to one of the security agencies, arranged by the Enemy, and head to Abu Ghraib. There my mission will come to an end: I'll kill the al-Qaeda leader, then leave this horrible world of yours.

'As evening fell, I dozed off. When I opened my eyes, I found the three madmen bent over me. Splattered with blood, they were bathing me. We were in the bathroom of an apartment on the third floor. They had clearly been up to something.

'After heated discussion, my six assistants had come to a decision. The three madmen had left the building and crossed the dark street towards the building where the two young men had been executed. They dragged away the body of the man who had died bravely, leaving the body of the man who had pleaded for his life – we called him "the saint". In a room on the ground floor of our building, the body was prepared to provide spare parts for me. The parts I needed were cut off and put in a black plastic bag. Then the saint's body was carried off and thrown atop the rubble of a house that had been destroyed by American missiles.

'The eldest madman cut out the rotten parts of my body, and the other two madmen – the young one and the elder one – stitched in the new parts. Then they all carried me to the bathroom on the top floor, where they washed off the blood and the sticky plasma fluids and dried me. The Enemy gave me the uniform of a US special forces officer and some identity papers. Then the Sophist set about applying a thick layer of women's foundation cream to my face and gave me a mirror. I looked but didn't recognize myself. I moved my lips and realized the face was mine.

'"What happened?" I asked.

'"We've brought you back to life," said the Magician, a cigarette hanging from his lower lip and his arms spread along the back of a chair in the sitting room. He was the mastermind behind all this. He convinced my other assistants that the saint was a victim whose soul would seek revenge, so there was no harm in using his body for spare parts.

'Standing up, I felt a surge of vitality and new sensations, as if I had awoken from a deep sleep. Strange faces appeared around me, and I forgot what I had been planning to do in the morning. Putting on a Marines cap, I hurried out of the building and headed east, where the gang that had carried out the execution had last been seen. The saint's fingers pushed open doors, showing me the way. I found them sitting on the ground, drinking tea. The guard stationed at a nearby building didn't see me coming, so they were taken

145

by surprise – I had got close enough to grab their rifles or push aside their weapons and subdue them with punches and kicks. Bullets were fired, and others came in from nearby rooms. For all the shooting and screaming, the outcome was not in their favour. I was shot in the back many times but got my hands on their necks and soon broke one after the other. Half an hour later there was only one member of the group left, sitting terrified in the corner. I couldn't see his face clearly in the dim light of the rechargeable electric lamps, but I could see he was crying. I moved closer and saw that he was shaking, like a frightened sheep submitting to a butcher. He was well aware that it was no normal enemy that he and his group were up against tonight. It was the wrath of God. In the end, I caught a glimpse of his frightened eyes. Because he felt guilty he made my task easier, abandoning any attempt to resist even before I touched him.'

4

'I killed the Venezuelan mercenary in charge of the security company responsible for recruiting suicide bombers who had killed many civilians, including the guard at the Sadeer Novotel, Hasib Mohamed Jaafar. I killed the al-Qaeda leader who lived in Abu Ghraib and who was responsible for the massive truck bomb in Tayaran Square that killed many people, including the person whose nose Hadi picked up off the pavement and used to fix my face. I had spent several weeks making preparations, tracking and infiltrating hostile groups. It takes some time, but if you have a strong case, you can win the trust of the group that's opposed to the person you're targeting.

'My list of people to seek revenge on grew longer as my old body parts fell off and my assistants added parts from my new victims, until one night I realized that under these circumstances I would face an open-ended list of targets that would never end.

'Time was my enemy, because there was never enough of it to accomplish my mission, and I started hoping that the killing in the streets would stop, cutting off my supply of victims and allowing me to melt away.

'But the killing had only begun. At least that's how it seemed from the balconies in the building I was living in, as dead bodies littered the streets like rubbish.

'We strengthened our defences in the face of the increased killings. The three madmen got some light and medium weapons and set up PK machine guns on the roof, pointing in all four directions. They closed off the entrance to the building with concrete blocks and bags of soil from I don't know where. They worked long hours on it, for several days, and then I found they had recruits to help them with the work. Overnight the building had become a virtual military barracks: apart from all the weaponry, it now had troops who had volunteered to protect this miniature garrison.

'Each of my three madmen promoted his own idea of me to his clique, amassing followers who were fed up with what they saw around them and were seeking some kind of salvation.

'The young madman took over the whole ground floor with his followers, who had come from various parts of the capital. Like him, they believed I was Iraqi citizen number one. I found out later that he had given them numbers instead of names, so he was number two, and the others took numbers starting from three and rising as the number of his followers grew day by day.

'The elder madman and his followers took over some of the apartments on the first floor. Like him, they believed that I was the black hole and the Great Azrael, the Angel of

147

Death, who would swallow up the whole world under the protection of divine grace.

'The eldest madman took the other two apartments on the first floor for himself and his followers, who were fewer in number. He imposed on them his own holy book, in which he ordained that I was the image of God, incarnate on Earth, that he was the "gate" to this image, and that they were forbidden to see me. So when they ran into me in the corridors or on the stairs, they had to bow quickly and cover their faces with their hands in fear and dread.

'The Magician was uncomfortable with these developments and thought they would not end well, because we were now more visible.

'"You might not die if our building is shelled, but we'll be mincemeat," he told me. He looked to the Sophist for confirmation, but the Sophist remained silent. A few minutes later, when the Magician went out to the bathroom, the Sophist came over to me and said, "He's jealous. He wants to keep you under his control. Please don't take seriously what he says."

'The Sophist had no affection for the Magician, and I took what he said as an attempt to win my favour and take over the Magician's place. He wasn't happy with the absolute certainties that the Magician put forth, especially when it came to my itinerary and the routes I took, which were usually precise and safe.

'The Enemy wasn't always around. He would be away for long periods and then reappear. On his last visit he brought wireless equipment, mobile phones, and a security system involving cameras on the balconies and a monitoring screen.

'That was the last service the Enemy performed for me, and I never saw him again. He called me on the phone a few days later. He sounded anxious and said his cover had been blown. There was an internal inquiry under way in the department to track his latest movements, and the Americans had also sent for him. It seemed likely he would be accused of collaborating with terrorist groups or something like that.

'After that he vanished. When we called the number he had called us from, the phone was out of service.'

5

'I know that things haven't been going the way I would like. That's why I'm asking anyone who listens to this recording to help me by not obstructing my work until I finish it and leave this world of yours. I've already been here too long. I've had many predecessors who have turned up here, carried out their missions in tough times, and then left. I don't want to be any different from them.

'I was careful about the pieces of flesh that were used to repair my body. I made sure my assistants didn't bring any flesh that was illegitimate – in other words, the flesh of criminals – but who's to say how criminal someone is? That's a question the Magician raised one day.

'"Each of us has a measure of criminality," the Magician said, smoking a shisha pipe he had prepared for himself. "Someone who's been killed through no fault of his own might be innocent today, but he might have been a criminal ten years ago, when he threw his wife out onto the street, or put his ageing mother in an old people's home, or disconnected the water or electricity to a house with a sick child, who died as a result, and so on."

'As usual, the Sophist reacted negatively to what the Magician had said. Late one day I went to the roof to verify a report that the Americans had withdrawn from the area. I noticed that the Sophist was following me. Standing before

149

me, with a serious expression on his face, he said, "Please don't believe what the Magician says. He's speaking for himself. He killed someone ten years ago and threw out his wife and his mother and killed a baby. He's a criminal."

'I looked away, picked up the telescope that the Enemy had brought me on his last visit, and started to look to the far ends of the street, where the Americans had posted their Abrams tanks. The tanks were gone, the makeshift quarters, the observation posts on the tall buildings, and the checkpoints on the side streets. They had completely withdrawn, as I'd been told, and that was strange.

'I turned to the Sophist and said, "Don't let it worry you. Get the Magician out of your head. Didn't I take the revolver with me on my last mission, at your urging?"

"'Yes."

"'Then shut up and don't talk about this ever again."

'I went back to looking through the telescope, but my mind was elsewhere. I had serious suspicions that when they last patched me up they had used body parts from a criminal. Maybe without knowing it, they had used parts from a terrorist. Maybe that was why I wasn't in a good mood and felt confused and flustered. I looked out on the streets and the roofs until things began to look hazy, my vision clouded by a bright milky film. I put down the telescope and asked the Sophist to follow me downstairs.

'An hour later I had recovered my sight. I was worried the problem might be that my eyes had worn out and would need to be replaced. But I no longer trusted the parts my assistants brought me. The street was covered with bodies, and new bodies piled up every evening, almost all of them those of criminals who had been fighting each other.

'When I had a chance to talk to the Magician in private, he told me unequivocally that half my body was now made up of the body parts of criminals.

"'How did that happen?" I asked him, as he filled another shisha bowl and then took a deep breath through the tube to make the coals glow. He blew out the smoke and looked at me scornfully. "Was the body of the saint really holy?" he asked.

"'What do you mean?" I said.

"'If he bore arms, he was a criminal," he replied, taking another hit from his pipe. I then realized that the Sophist was outside the door, listening to our discussion. I was in the process of getting ready for a new mission that night and wasn't going to allow a repeat of the sterile argument they had had, so I stood up and asked the Sophist to help me prepare. The new mission involved a militia leader who lived in a working-class neighbourhood in the east of the city. Producing some clothes that looked like the militia's uniform, the Sophist sat me down on a chair in front of a dressing table and started applying make-up to suit my new identity. But he had not forgotten what he had heard the Magician saying to me, and he began his response as he ran his hands across my face.

"'He convinced you that now you're half criminal," he said, "that half your flesh comes from criminals. Tomorrow he'll tell you you're three-quarters criminal, and later you'll wake up to find you've become totally criminal. But you're not an ordinary criminal. You'll be the super-criminal, because you're made up of criminals, a bunch of criminals. Ha!"

'He didn't stop talking till I went out, leaving him fuming with rage that I didn't answer. Unfortunately, we're now enemies.

'Just a short time earlier, very important changes were taking place outside the building. Part of the Magician's prophecy had started to come true. The number of followers recruited by the three madmen had grown so much that the apartments they had taken over could no longer

151

accommodate them. Having so many people also brought logistical demands related to food, drink and bedding; I didn't know how they were getting hold of these things.

'After some shouting among the three madmen and their followers, they decided to expand into other buildings, leaving some guards on the ground floor of the building where I lived and moving into adjacent ones. That evening I was amazed how many young gunmen bowed down to me in the street. All of them believed I was the face of God on Earth, according to the teachings of the eldest madman, who wore an orange turban, had a long beard, and became the prophet of a religion that was new in both substance and imagery. It was very much the same with the elder madman, but his followers looked pale and were less noisy. The two groups accused each other of quackery and talking gibberish. As for the followers of the young madman, the Iraqi citizens, there were now more than one hundred and fifty of them, and they were thinking of taking part in the upcoming elections.

'That night I killed the militia leader and fifteen people who were defending him. On the advice of the Sophist, I used the revolver because the unconventional means of killing with which I started my campaign no longer worked. I left the militia leader's massive body lying in the courtyard of his house, his guts full of lead, while his mother, wife and sisters hovered around it in black clothes, beating their breasts and cheeks in grief and anguish.

'Using one of the militia leader's cars, I got back to Dora, and I heard the sound of gunfire as I approached our base. In the absence of the Americans and the Iraqi army, the militias were fighting to gain territory. I abandoned the car and made my way through gaps in the walls, following the route the Magician had given me.

'In the meantime my eyesight had turned cloudy again. I leaned against a wall, staying like that for some minutes, then wiped my eyes and felt my right eye had turned into something like dough or paste. I pulled at it gently, and it moved with my hand. Then the whole thing came out, like a dark lump, and I tossed it aside. I was worried the same thing might happen to my left eye and I would lose my sight completely. Sitting by the wall, I listened to the gunfire – it came from every direction. Eventually the light returned to my left eye. I peered up and down the street through a big gap that some shell had made in the wall, then noticed something black coming towards me in the distance. The outlines became clearer: it was a man. Some light fell on his face, and I could see him even more clearly. He was in his sixties, fat, with a paunch, wearing chinos and a short-sleeved shirt, and he was carrying some black bags. I later found out that one bag contained bread and the other fruit. It was odd for him to turn up here. Perhaps he had come the wrong way. Where had he come from, and where was he going?

'As I watched him, he turned down a side street. He was heading straight to the building where I lived. The gunfire seemed to be louder in that direction. Had the militias surrounded the barracks the three madmen had set up?

'I walked behind the man, keeping enough distance so he wouldn't notice me. I remembered what the Magician had said about everyone being a criminal to some extent and the Sophist's objections to this. I didn't forget for a moment that I was about to lose my eyesight, maybe even before I reached the area around the building.

'The fat man stopped every two or three paces, looking around in fear. He looked as if he had been crying or was about to cry. I wanted to get close to him and ask what had brought him this way, but I was distracted and everything in my head got mixed up. The man stopped again and listened to the bullets hitting the upper floors of the surrounding buildings. He was frozen to the spot, and I couldn't help stopping too, about twenty yards away from him. If he had looked back, he would have seen me. My left eye started to mist up again, and I felt it would run down my face like leavened dough. I raised my revolver and aimed at the innocent old man. He was definitely innocent, not one of those people that the three madmen had brought to replace my body parts and keep me going.

'I fired one round from my revolver, just as I began to lose all sensation in my eye. I heard nothing after that – the shelling by the rival groups had stopped, and there were no footsteps or crying or even the sound of breathing. Now blind, I took some cautious steps forward until my shoe hit something. Bending down, I felt around for the warm body of the frightened old man. The bullet had hit him right in the skull. He had been expecting death to come from the upper floors of the buildings or from the ends of the streets in front of him, but it had come from behind.

'I took out a little knife and did my work quickly. What would the Magician say now? These are eyes from the body of an innocent victim. The proportion of criminal parts in my body wouldn't increase. But what should I tell him? In retribution for this victim, who should I exact vengeance on?

'The Sophist would say I've realized the Magician's vision and turned into a criminal who kills innocent people. He'd say the Magician has pushed me in that direction with the help of the djinn he had enlisted to influence my thinking. The Magician would speak more calmly, explaining that I was responding to the impulses of my criminal body parts and that, in order to break away from this frightening path, I would have to get rid of all this flesh of ill repute. They would argue, and we wouldn't come to any conclusion, like the conflicting ideas in my head right now.

'I managed to install my new eyes and could see again. Seeing the body of the innocent old man, I had an idea and I clung to it – it looked like the truth I had been seeking. The old man was a sacrificial lamb that the Lord had placed in my path. He was the Innocent Man Who Will Die Tonight. So that was that. He had been going to die in a few minutes, or within half an hour at the most. The bullets from the fighters were bound to hit him, and he would have died right here. His body might have been mistaken for the body of one of the criminals and none of the madmen or their followers would have been able to find him.

'So all I had done was hasten his death. All the other innocent people who came down this desolate street would die too.

'My eyes needed stitching to hold them in place. My followers would do that when I got back to base, but until I got there I had to be careful not to look down. So I took the old man's glasses, which I found in the top pocket of his shirt, and put them on to hold my eyes back if they worked loose.

'I went into the lane that led to the wall of sandbags that the followers of the three madmen had built around the buildings they had taken over as their barracks. My head was swimming with conflicting thoughts, but I held firm to the idea that I had only hastened the old man's death. I was not a murderer: I had merely plucked the fruit of death before it fell to the ground.

'The sound of fighting had died down, but it turned out my assumption had been wrong. It wasn't the militias that had been fighting because the Americans and the Iraqi army had left the area. It was the followers of the three madmen who had sparked the hostilities that night. That was the last thing I had expected to happen, but the Magician had predicted that disagreements would break out when outsiders started joining my first six followers.

'I didn't have a chance to find out more from the Magician or talk to him about his prediction. He was lying on a pile of stones in front of the building where I live. There was a bullet hole in the middle of his forehead.

'I went to my apartment on the third floor; no one was there. The state of the furniture suggested a fight had taken place. When I looked out from the balcony, I saw the Magician's body right below me. He must have been thrown from the balcony after he was shot. My intuition told me that only the Sophist could have done this. But where was he?

'The next morning I went out to inspect the area. There were bodies everywhere – on the street, on the pavement, some propped up against the walls, others slumped over balconies or piled at the entrances to apartments or rooms. Only the young madman was around, and he seemed completely insane. I took him to my third-floor apartment and questioned him. Apparently those who had survived the massacre had fled, many never to return. The elder madman and the eldest madman had been killed. The Sophist had killed the Magician and then escaped.

'The young madman looked pale and spoke slowly, as though he might lose consciousness. When I looked at him with the innocent eyes I had taken from the old man, he looked like a total criminal. He had survived the festival of death because he was more murderous and more criminal than the others.'

'The battery's going to run out, sir.'

'Yes, I know.'

'It's the last battery we have. The batteries in the bag have all run out.'

'I know. I won't need any more batteries. I've finished recording.'

'The recording's finished? What will you do now?'

'Only one thing – this.'

'No, sir. No, master. I'm your slave and your servant. Why are you doing that? No, sir. I'm your slave, your – sla . . . ve.'

'Hello, hello, hello. Yes.

'Jeez, I'm RUNNING OUT OF TIME. You wasted so much time, damn it!'

CHAPTER ELEVEN

The Investigation

1

This was the second or third time Mahmoud had listened to the Whatsitsname's recordings. He couldn't get over the shock of the story or the soft, calm voice in which it had been recounted. He opened the laptop the editor had given him and copied the audio files from the Panasonic recorder. Then he saved a copy to his flash drive and put the flash drive in a pocket of the trousers lying on the chair next to him. Returning to his comfortable bed in his room on the second floor of the Dilshad Hotel, he succumbed to the faint hum coming from outside as the afternoon turned to evening and the August heat abated.

Dozing again, he may have been almost unconscious when the phone rang. He picked it up and heard the voice of Hammu, the fat man who worked around the clock at the reception desk.

'Sir, there are people asking for you, some visitors,' he said. Mahmoud got dressed and descended the green-carpeted staircase. He noticed his stomach was rumbling: he had had breakfast late and hadn't had lunch yet.

The visitors were four men in civilian clothes. He thought he recognized one of them: a young man in a striking pink shirt, with hair so short there would be nothing to grab. The young man pulled him to one side. 'Brigadier Majid wants to see you,' he said in a low voice.

'Why? Has something happened?' asked Mahmoud.

'I don't know. He says you're friends, and he wants to see you urgently.'

'Okay,' said Mahmoud, looking towards the reception desk, where plump Hammu was scrolling through the television channels with the remote, oblivious to what was happening around him. Mahmoud thought of calling Saidi to see what he knew but realized he had left his phone in his room, along with his identity card and money.

'I'll just run upstairs to get my ID and some cash,' he said.

'There's no need. We'll bring you back right away,' said the man with the crew cut, with a firmness and determination that made Mahmoud anxious. If he didn't cooperate, maybe the man would rough him up. He clapped his key with the heavy brass tag onto the reception counter. Hammu came to his senses.

'I'm off,' said Mahmoud. He spoke with a tremor, trying to convey his anxiety and imprint the moment in the receptionist's memory. But Hammu's face showed no emotion, as if Mahmoud didn't exist. If something bad happened to Mahmoud and Hammu was questioned, he might not remember anything.

With the four young men, Mahmoud got into a new GMC truck with tinted windows and went down the same streets that he and Saidi had taken on their ill-fated visit to Saidi's mysterious childhood friend. The CD player was playing 'The Orange', and the song summoned conflicting emotions in Mahmoud, who was growing more anxious and frightened. He had noticed the truck had government licence plates, but that wasn't enough to reassure him – because he knew of many abductions that had been carried out with government vehicles. Looking at the four men, he tried to work out their social origins. He knew that such things were very much in play these days, that in many cases they determined the course of events, as well as the fate of those who were abducted.

The CD player kept repeating 'The Orange', and one of the men tapped his fingers to the rhythm. Finally the truck reached the headquarters of the Tracking and Pursuit Department, which Mahmoud had visited earlier.

Mahmoud was brought into the office of Brigadier Majid, who was sitting in his grand chair with a fat, unlit cigar in his mouth and his ankles crossed on his large table. Mahmoud detected the distinctive smell of apples as the brigadier rose from his seat and, without taking the cigar from his mouth, welcomed him, inviting him to sit down. Then a muscular young man came in, put two cups of weak tea on the table between them, and left.

Brigadier Majid told Mahmoud that he had given up smoking years ago but that these days he missed cigars. He used to smoke cigars to excess until the doctors told him to stop. But life was going well.

'The smell of tobacco is better than the smell of smoke, isn't it?' the brigadier said.

Mahmoud agreed, aware that his emotions had changed in the half hour or so since he had left the Dilshad Hotel. The sound of 'The Orange' was still ringing in his ears, and there he was – looking at Brigadier Majid's face, which seemed friendly enough, smelling the scent of apple, and tasting the slightly bitter astringency of the weak tea before it slid down into his rumbling stomach.

The whole conversation in that office took Mahmoud by surprise. Brigadier Majid was no friend of his. His loyalty was to the government, and the fact that he was a childhood friend of Saidi's meant nothing. Mahmoud realized why Saidi had been making fun of Brigadier Majid. He knew the man and others like him well. The man would have no qualms about using brute force to serve those in power, whether Saddam Hussein, the Americans or the new government. Brigadier Majid had served or would serve them all.

The brigadier could have asked Mahmoud directly for the information he wanted, because Mahmoud was not a criminal and harboured no hostility to him or the government or the regime he represented. But he wanted to frighten Mahmoud, to intimidate him. He wanted to undermine Mahmoud's confidence so he would more readily give up the information he wanted. It was a vile method suited for use more on criminals than on the colleague of a childhood friend who had already drunk tea with you. Real, dark, sweet tea, not the mysterious tea at this meeting.

'It's not tea,' said Brigadier Majid. 'It's a herbal mixture, with ox-tongue leaves, sparrows' tongue leaves, pigs' tongue leaves, and several other tongue leaves. I call it the 'tongue loosener' because it makes the person who drinks it give up his secrets. You can see that I drank it with you, and that's because I felt embarrassed by the fact that we're friends, and I have to get over that in order to do my job and ask the essential questions.'

Mahmoud was speechless. What was the man talking about? Did he really think they were friends? What did he mean by ox-tongue leaves and giving up secrets? And what did he put in the weak tea, Mahmoud wondered?

2

Brigadier Majid did in fact give up some secrets. He had contacted his sources in the security services and obtained information about Mahmoud. He had easily got hold of the registration number of a complaint filed against Mahmoud about a year earlier in Balda Police Station in Amara. The plaintiff was a man of influence in the province.

Mahmoud was surprised to hear this. He felt this visit and the interrogation were becoming more mysterious. But Brigadier Majid didn't seem to know anything more that would flesh out the details of Mahmoud's secret, which was unknown to everyone other than his photographer friend, Hazem Abboud.

The complaint accused Mahmoud of inciting murder, with the means of incitement a story that Mahmoud had written in *Sada al-Ahwar*, the local newspaper where he had been working. That's all Brigadier Majid knew, and Mahmoud didn't want him to find out anything more. He would do his best to make sure the 'tongue loosener' he had drunk did not work.

Brigadier Majid brought up other incidents from a year ago that hadn't resulted in any legal proceedings against Mahmoud, but he didn't spend much time on these. He then swung round and took a copy of the latest issue of *al-Haqiqa* off a pile of files. He waved it at Mahmoud, pursing his lips as if to say, 'This is what we're really here to discuss. All the earlier stuff was interrogation nonsense to shake your confidence. Now you'll have to give me some answers.'

'What's this extraordinary story?' asked the brigadier.

'What about it?'

'Who's the guy telling this story?'

'It's a guy who sells junk in the area. It's fantasy. The editor liked it and told me to write it up.'

'Fantasy? Hmmm,' whispered the brigadier. He then started to browse through the magazine, while asking Mahmoud a series of questions. Mahmoud answered confidently and calmly. The brigadier didn't want to give away any secrets. He didn't want to tell Mahmoud that the Whatsitsname he had written about – the Frankenstein's monster in his article – was not fantasy but a real person, or that he had spent most of his time for the last several months trying to have him arrested, or that his personal life and his professional future were riding on this strange man, or that he was trying to dispel the aura of mystery with which the man surrounded himself, or that he had sworn to grab him with his own hands and expose him on television so the whole world could see he was nothing more than a useless, despicable, lowly person who had made himself into a myth by exploiting people's ignorance and fear and the chaos around them.

'Is this junk dealer in the area?' asked the brigadier.

'Yes, he lives on Lane 7 in Bataween. His house is in ruins. They call it the Jewish ruin; you can't miss it. You'll recognize it right away.'

'Yes, yes.'

Mahmoud kept talking casually. He could see the focus was shifting away from him and towards the mystery man. Hoping to win back the brigadier's friendship and restore his own confidence, he reached into his trouser pocket, took out the Panasonic recorder, and handed it to the brigadier.

'You'll find everything the Whatsitsname recorded on this,' he said.

The brigadier summoned the muscular young man who had brought their tea and told him to make a copy of the recordings. After ten minutes, the young man returned and handed the recorder back to the brigadier, who held it by the plaited cloth strap and swung it back and forth for a while, looking distracted and uninterested.

The brigadier said nothing more to answer the questions that were swirling inside Mahmoud's head. It was the brigadier who asked all the questions, so Mahmoud was none the wiser. Mahmoud began to lose interest in his interrogator's preoccupation with the Whatsitsname, and he wasn't even concerned about the fate of the junk dealer he had just implicated. He just wanted to get out of this fancy office. Even when the brigadier changed the subject to talk about other matters at the magazine, the general situation in the streets, and so on, it didn't seem to improve the dynamic between them, even though it seemed the brigadier was intent on repairing the damage he had done half an hour earlier.

The brigadier was an evil man, Mahmoud was thinking, and it would be impossible to trust him again. He hoped this meeting, which had soured his stomach, would be their last.

The brigadier stood up, took the dark shaft of the cigar off the table, stroked it with his fingers, and stuck it in his mouth. He went behind the vast desk, opened one of the drawers, took out a silver lighter, busied himself with lighting the cigar, and took a deep drag until the end of the cigar glowed red and thick smoke came out of his mouth. He took a few steps towards Mahmoud, who, concluding the meeting was over, rose too and noticed that he was taller than the brigadier. He noticed also that the brigadier's eyes, screwed up at the time because of the sting from the smoke, were light brown, which made him handsome and gave his face a bourgeois touch. Together, they walked towards the door.

'I was lucky when I was a smoker,' said the brigadier with a smoky sigh. 'Everything turned bad when I gave up smoking. Now I take a few puffs every so often, just to get my luck back.'

It was the kind of friendly exchange close friends might have. At least that's the feeling Brigadier Majid wanted to leave Mahmoud with, thinking as he was about what

Mahmoud might say about the meeting to Saidi, his child-hood friend.

They stood at the door, and the recorder stopped swinging back and forth. The brigadier gave it to Mahmoud. 'By the way,' he said. 'I was joking with you. There's no such thing as a tongue loosener. That was just weak tea in which we dissolve a chemical compound that prevents heart attacks. Because people sometimes have heart attacks when they're being questioned. We protect them with this drink and protect ourselves from being accused of killing suspects.'

They laughed like real friends, and Mahmoud went out to find the four young men waiting for him. On the way back through the pitch-black streets he thought about everything that had transpired between him and the brigadier. He was struck by the brigadier's final remark, in which he confirmed he was treating Mahmoud as a suspect. As for the story of the drink that prevented heart attacks, no doubt that was just another bad joke.

3

What stayed with Mahmoud from that interview with the brigadier were his anxieties about the incident at Balda Police Station in Amara and the complaint against him by the criminal Mahmoud called the Mantis because of his unusual height.

The Mantis's brother had led a small gang that terrorized the locals until he was arrested and detained. The news of his arrest was greeted with great joy by many, including Mahmoud, who then wrote a newspaper article about the need to enforce the law against this criminal. He philoso-phized a little in the article, saying there were three types of justice – legal justice, divine justice and street justice – and that however long it takes, criminals must face one of them.

Publishing the article won Mahmoud points for courage and for embodying the journalistic ideal of enlightenment in service of the public interest. He generally wasn't so reckless as to condemn criminals who were free, lest he find himself face-to-face with a pistol, but he was confident in the legal process so he gave himself free rein. Two or three days later, though, the criminal was released, and he drove around town in his pickup to celebrate his acquittal. Mahmoud was shocked. A day later two masked men on a motorbike, one at the handlebars and the other with a rifle, went to the criminal's house. As the criminal came out of the house, the man with the rifle aimed at his forehead. The criminal took one bullet and collapsed among his friends, while the masked men escaped on the motorbike.

Mahmoud was delighted with the news. He quickly wrote a new article, repeating his theory about the three types of justice and saying that this time it was street justice that had been served. He submitted the article, but the editor, a man with leftist roots who was well known in society, tore it up and summoned Mahmoud.

'This theory of yours is no use to me. I'm looking for advertisers. I want the paper to succeed; you want to play Tarzan,' said the editor.

Mahmoud was angry. He exchanged words with the editor and threatened to leave the paper, but the editor wouldn't back down. A few days later Mahmoud heard something that persuaded him to leave the paper and stay home for several months.

The Mantis had taken on the role of gang leader after the murder of his brother, and at a memorial service for the brother a member of the gang had given the Mantis a clipping of Mahmoud's article.

The criminal's family was looking desperately for any leads to the killers. It wouldn't do any harm, they reasoned, to accuse the journalist of incitement to murder, since he had openly called on people to take up arms against a good man who had helped protect the city from thieves when the police and army and other means of law enforcement had disappeared.

At first they didn't know who Mahmoud was, but it didn't take them long to find out his original tribal name and where he lived and who his brothers and uncles were. The case immediately became a dispute between clans, with demands for blood money for the dead man and the Mantis making several threats, but the dispute was later resolved to the satisfaction of Mahmoud and his family. In the presence of his brothers and uncles, Mahmoud swore he would never work again as a journalist in that province. But the dispute did not stop there, as some of the Mantis's friends continued to pass on threats from the Mantis, who kept Mahmoud's article in his pocket and sat in coffee shops brooding about the three forms of justice. He would take the article, now rather tattered, out of his pocket and read aloud excerpts about divine justice, legal justice and street justice. Since he thought that legal justice, in this case through tribal customs, had failed, he was going to enforce divine justice on Mahmoud by himself.

Some time later Mahmoud's friends told him that the Mantis was accusing him of being a Baathist and was saying that his father, an Arabic teacher, was an atheist. Mahmoud lay low at home, fearing what this madman might do, until his friend Farid Shawwaf called him to say there was a job at the newspaper *al-Hadaf* in Baghdad. When Mahmoud discussed the job with his brothers, they were convinced it was the ideal solution – because maybe Mahmoud leaving Maysan Province would help them solve the problem more calmly and persuade the Mantis to tone down his insults against Mahmoud's family.

Mahmoud now recalled all these details with great reluctance, because they weakened his self-confidence and reminded him that he had done stupid things. Whereas in Baghdad, at least until the annoying interrogation in Brigadier Majid's office, he felt confident and hopeful: he was gaining strength, especially with the support that Saidi was giving him and the doors he was opening for him.

Mahmoud went out to a nearby restaurant and had a magnificent breakfast: clotted cream with hot bread and strong, sweet tea. He added minutes to his phone with a new phone card and called his elder brother Abdullah. In recent months Mahmoud had been calling intermittently to check up on his mother's health, but he never mentioned the Mantis: he and his brothers seemed to have an unspoken agreement to avoid the subject. Mahmoud thought that the three forms of justice might have done their job and resolved the problem with the Mantis. It didn't make sense that such a criminal would still be free.

Mahmoud heard his brother's voice on the line, and they spoke for several minutes. Mahmoud told him he was going to transfer part of his salary to a money changer in the main market in Amara. After a short silence, Mahmoud dared to ask about the Mantis.

'What's he up to? What's become of him?'

'That guy has all the luck,' his brother answered.

'What do you mean?'

'He's looking good these days. He's started wearing a suit and tie. He's a senior official in the provincial headquarters.'

'How can that be? You mean he hasn't been killed or jailed? And the crimes he committed?'

'Crimes? No one can say anything about him now. It's a travesty, and it came out of the blue.'

'But he's forgotten the story of his brother, hasn't he?'

'What are you talking about, bro? He wants to erect a statue of him.'

'I miss Mother. I want to come home. It wouldn't be a problem, would it?'

'Don't come. Don't show your face. Stay where you are, for God's sake, unless you want the three forms of justice applied to you. Now the Mantis often talks about them, even on the radio. He's stolen your idea.'

4

Saidi smiled as he listened to Mahmoud recount what had happened to him the previous day in Brigadier Majid's office. When he got to the part about the weak tea, Saidi burst out laughing. He took it lightly as usual: there wasn't a disaster in the world that could change his mood. There he was, as well dressed as ever, clean-shaven and scented with expensive perfume, sitting behind his massive desk as if he were about to appear on a television programme.

Farid Shawwaf came in with the first proofs of the magazine's political news section, which he was responsible for. He put them in front of Saidi, who asked him to show them to Mahmoud. Farid sensed the change that had come over his old friend Mahmoud, and yet he didn't want to submit to him as he would to a real editor-in-chief. Or he was trying to head off any chance of that happening. He spread the pages in front of Mahmoud and waited for him to comment. Mahmoud said the layout was good. He said this with difficulty, because he, too, didn't want to seem condescending. Farid went out, and some other young men came in, then the old caretaker entered with two cups of Nescafé. A certain silence reigned in Saidi's office after they all had left. Saidi stood up, went to the window, pulled aside the curtain, and looked out onto the street. He turned to Mahmoud and said, 'Brigadier Majid is one of the people you'll have to get used to dealing with.'

Mahmoud said nothing but waited for further explanation because he didn't plan to see Brigadier Majid and would try as far as possible to make sure that kind of meeting didn't happen again.

'There are people like him in our world,' said Saidi, 'and we have to learn how to deal with them tactfully, how to get along with them, how to accept that they exist.'

Saidi went back to looking out from behind the curtains, as if he was expecting someone. He stayed like that for some moments, then came and sat on the sofa opposite Mahmoud. He picked up his cup of Nescafé and started to drink, enjoying its bitterness. Then he looked at Mahmoud and made a dramatic revelation: 'In fact, Brigadier Majid doesn't pursue weird crimes. He's employed by the Americans' Coalition Provisional Authority to lead an assassination squad.'

'Assassination squad?'

'Yes, for a year or more he's been carrying out the policy of the American ambassador to create an equilibrium of violence on the streets between the Sunni and Shiite militias, so there'll be a balance later at the negotiating table to make new political arrangements in Iraq. The American army is unable or unwilling to stop the violence, so at least a balance or an equivalence of violence has to be created. Without it, there won't be a successful political process.'

'Why don't you tell your political friends about this?' asked Mahmoud.

'They all know, but no one has definitive proof. Or they look at the Tracking and Pursuit Department that Brigadier Majid heads as if they're looking at a text – each party interprets it according to its own interests.'

'Could Brigadier Majid really be so brutal? He seems like a pleasant man.'

'Just a minute ago you were calling him cruel and evil. How come he's suddenly pleasant?'

'What I mean is he doesn't seem like a criminal in the way you've just described him, as the head of an assassination squad. That's hard to believe.'

'Anyway, the best way to protect yourself from evil is to keep close to it. I humour him so he doesn't stand in the way of my political ambitions, and so he doesn't put a bullet in the back of my head, fired by one of those fat guys with shaved heads, in response to an order from the Americans.'

'My God, it's serious business.'

'As long as he's our friend, there's nothing to fear from him. Didn't you say he was laughing with you and talking about smoking? Don't worry about him. He's a nice guy.'

'A while back I said he's a nice guy and you got upset.'

'Yeah. Never mind. Nice, pleasant, funny. That tea story!'

Saidi kept laughing, and Mahmoud smiled, but inside Mahmoud felt a growing sense of unease and fear. An unknown enemy loomed large. It was an enemy he thought he had left in Amara, but now it was active in Baghdad. Although he trusted Saidi, he couldn't believe everything he said. Maybe Saidi wanted to frighten him or tease him, or place him in hypothetical situations in order to get him thinking, to create a kind of challenge to bring out his hidden talents or achieve some other clever, calculated outcome.

A few minutes later the caretaker knocked on the door and told the editor he had a visitor. A dark, slim young woman with dyed hair came in, wearing jeans and lots of accessories. Her exotic perfume filled the room. It wasn't Nawal al-Wazir; she was more flamboyant than Nawal, livelier and younger. She shook hands with Saidi, and they exchanged kisses on both cheeks. Saidi didn't bother to introduce her to Mahmoud, but she shook Mahmoud's hand anyway and enthusiastically kissed him, too, on both cheeks. Saidi and the woman had an appointment, so Saidi picked up his leather briefcase, and they prepared to leave together. Saidi looked at Mahmoud and reminded him of what to do with the magazine. 'Be a hero, my friend, okay?' he said with a smile and a wave goodbye.

5

A week later Saidi travelled to Beirut, maybe with the thin dark woman or some other thin woman, leaving Mahmoud swamped, not just with editing forty-five pages of the magazine but also with an endless succession of administrative details – signing receipts, giving the staff their pay, and meeting people who suddenly turned up at nine o'clock in the morning looking for Saidi to ask for a job or for some other reason. He took the calls that came in on the mobile phone connected to the charger – announcing themselves with numbers and abbreviated names in English and sometimes just two or three letters, such as 'TY', who was Taleb Yahya, the manager of Ansam Printing, which printed the magazine and which Saidi had once thought of buying. 'See' was a woman who gave Saidi the title of Haji; Mahmoud didn't know what kind of relationship she had with Saidi. There were many 'doctors' – Dr Adnan, Dr Saber, Dr Fawzi – all of them officials in parliament or the office managers of parliamentarians or spokesmen for political groups. 'SM' was an easy abbreviation: that was Sorour Majid, the brigadier, who called from time to time. Mahmoud guessed there was another level to the relationship between the two men that Saidi hadn't spoken about yet. They had common business or financial interests, and all the talk of astrologers and fortune-tellers, and then the story of the assassination squads, was just camouflage.

But none of these things affected the way Mahmoud saw Saidi. He always found excuses for him. He admired him. Saidi was a real superman, albeit without supernatural powers but with his own human talents. Mahmoud made excuses for the mysterious aspects of Saidi's personality because no one knew whether Saidi's mystique stemmed from a need to protect himself or whether it was derived from myths others had created about him.

Like Saidi, Mahmoud wasn't immune to the seductions of illusion. He had assumed many of the traits of the man who inspired and mentored him. He had put on weight. He shaved every day. He wore suits and ties and coloured shirts, though he and his friends Farid Shawwaf and Adnan al-Anwar used to make fun of such men, associating suits with politicians and civil servants, as well as with the militiamen in natty suits who would jump out of their vehicles in the middle of the street to drag people out of their shops or cars and beat them up or abduct them. But everything changes, and those who don't wear suits don't appreciate the advantages.

Farid Shawwaf made fun of the transformation of his old friend and thought that Mahmoud had started to cross to the other side. When Mahmoud laughed off such talk, Farid admonished, 'You're getting more and more like them. You're trying to be one of them. Anyone who puts on a crown, even if only as an experiment, will end up looking for a kingdom.'

Mahmoud now very much resembled Saidi. One day, sitting behind Saidi's desk and talking to his colleagues, he noticed he was even holding a cigar the same way Saidi did, as if it were a thick pen. He also peppered his speech with 'my dear' and 'my friend' just like Saidi.

But he wasn't really like Saidi, said a voice in his head, not very much like him at all. Saidi had a fortune, though no one knew how big it was, and multiple sources of income, and this magazine was just a front, whereas Mahmoud was dependent on his salary, without which everything would fall in on his head.

Before the end of the workday, the mobile phone that Saidi kept in his office rang. Mahmoud picked it up and saw 666 on the screen, and the image of Nawal came into focus in front of him.

'Hello,' he said.

Silence.

'Don't be childish,' he continued. 'I know who you are, and Baher's away in Beirut. Speak.'

CHAPTER TWELVE

In Lane 7

1

Abu Anmar stood on the pavement and looked across the street at the Rasoul Real Estate office. A sense of gloom came over him: Faraj the real estate agent had put up a new sign; he was doing well for himself. Meanwhile, Abu Anmar couldn't understand why his hotel business was in constant decline. He hadn't had a real guest in a month or more, other than his two permanent guests. Even Hazem Abboud came only now and then to take pictures of the balconies that were collapsing and the coats of paint that were flaking off the walls. He might sit down to have a glass of tea with Abu Anmar, but since the summer he had practically stopped spending the night at the hotel.

On Hazem's last visit, Abu Anmar told him with some enthusiasm that he was working on renovating the hotel. Hazem noticed that many of the rooms no longer had any furniture. Abu Anmar didn't tell him how hard he had had to negotiate with Hadi the junk dealer. If he had had any alternative, Abu Anmar would have kicked him out the door rather than submit to his tiresome bargaining. What Hazem didn't know was that Abu Anmar couldn't replace the carpet in the lobby or the shabby wooden table at which he usually sat. He couldn't replace a single broken window or repair the leaks or blockages in the pipes and the sewerage. He couldn't even buy a bottle of air freshener to cover up the smell of rot and mould. He was getting rid of the hotel furniture in order to stay alive, to eat.

Abu Anmar didn't know what he would do, but he was prepared to be adventurous and take a risk if necessary. He had to stand on his own two feet and not let anyone see him as a laughing stock, especially that bastard with the moustache and the hennaed beard who was sitting at his polished desk behind the clean front window of his air-conditioned office, looking out at him morning and evening from the other side of the street.

2

Since the Whatsitsname had stopped visiting, Hadi had gradually gone back to being his usual self. Some people felt he was more like his old self than ever, even to the point of excess, as if he were trying to make up for having stayed out of the public eye in recent months.

At his old space by the big front window of Aziz's coffee shop, Hadi told a new story about meeting the Iraqi president on a street in Jadriya the night before. An armour-plated black Mercedes stopped, and the driver got out and rushed to the other side to open the door for the president, who was extremely fat. The president put his right foot on the pavement, but his body stayed slumped in the back seat. Hadi ignored the car and kept walking with his canvas sack of empty soft drink cans.

'Hadi, Hadi!' called the president.

'Yes, Mr President.'

'Can't you stop telling your stories? Stop talking about us. There's nothing we can do, and you're going to start a revolution against us.'

'What can I say, Mr President? Do your job properly, and I won't tell stories about you.'

'Why don't you come along with me? Come, let's make a deal. They've made us a good dinner in the Green Zone.'

'No, Mr President, I'm not hungry. But if there's arak, I'll come. Do you drink arak, Mr President?'

'Shame on you – I drink distilled water. You should quit telling your stories, Hadi.'

The president laughed and shut the car door, and then the car drove off down the street and disappeared.

Most people just laughed at these little scenes with which Hadi embellished his stories. Once someone had shown him a copy of *al-Haqiqa* magazine with a picture of a disfigured Robert De Niro on the cover. In it was Hadi's story about the Whatsitsname, with details that had never been part of the story. Hadi's name didn't appear in the story, but Aziz the Egyptian and some of the regulars at the coffee shop knew Mahmoud al-Sawadi, who had written the story, and knew that Hadi was his source. Turning the pages without any reaction on his dry, wrinkled face, Hadi said the journalist had made up parts of the story.

Hadi felt exploited. Mahmoud had promised he would act in the Whatsitsname's interests and treat him fairly. Two days later Hadi received his last visit from the Whatsitsname, who came to his house at night to tell him about the civil war between his followers and to say that the Americans had again sealed off the area where he had been living and had tried to arrest him several times with help from a special missions unit of Iraqi intelligence, forcing him to not stay in one place for more than a day. As for the story the journalist had written about him, it hadn't done him much good: it had portrayed him as a figment of Hadi's sick imagination.

The Whatsitsname was looking for believers who would facilitate his work and wouldn't use their belief in him for their own purposes, as the three madmen and their followers had done. He didn't want to be turned into just an urban legend, as the journalist had portrayed him. Hadi promised the Whatsitsname that he would pass this on to the journalist when he saw him, but the Whatsitsname said it didn't matter any longer.

'There's no harm in warning him so he doesn't offend me again. I'm now taking revenge on people who insult me, not just on those who did violence to those whose body parts I'm made of,' the Whatsitsname said.

Hadi never again saw his creation after that. He knew the big criminal the Americans and the Iraqi police were looking for, and who was always mentioned on television, was the Whatsitsname. He and the Whatsitsname were linked only in his mind and maybe in the mind of Mahmoud al-Sawadi, but eventually Brigadier Majid, pacing anxiously around his spacious office with a fat cigar in his mouth, lost in thought about the best way to track down the One Who Has No Name – as that fortune-teller with the pointy beard called him – eventually he made the connection.

3

Faraj was sitting behind his desk in the real estate office, carefully monitoring the door of the Orouba Hotel across the street. He knew all Abu Anmar's routines by heart, and knew the financial straits he was in.

Abu Anmar emerged through the hotel door, swung his vast frame around to close the door behind him, then slowly descended the three steps to the pavement. He adjusted his headcloth on his shoulders and walked off, twirling his string of big shiny prayer beads around his fat hand like a propeller. Before he passed the Akhawain laundry next door, a hand touched him on the shoulder. He turned to find Faraj with his thick red beard, smiling at him.

The narrow gap between him and his rival unnerved Abu Anmar. For the first time he noticed two large moles on Faraj's face, one at the inner end of his left eyebrow, apparently inflamed, and the other right above his thin moustache.

'Go and finish your errands, and then drop in and have a cup of tea with me,' Faraj said.

'Inshallah,' replied Abu Anmar, twirling his beads faster and giving a quick nod of his head. Abu Anmar quickened his pace, and Faraj went back to his office, rubbing his chin; he seemed energetic and relaxed. That morning he had slapped a thin young man with unkempt hair and a goatee beard, sending him spinning before collapsing to the ground. The young man was a member of the Association for the Protection of Historical Houses. He had gone to Elishva's house, and she had welcomed him in and given him a glass of tea, according to Umm Salim. Someone had come running to tell Faraj, who hurried to the lane to find the man sticking his head out of Elishva's house and taking out his camera to snap photos of the *mashrabiya* balconies of Umm Salim's house. Abu Salim, Umm Salim's husband, put his head out of the window on the second floor and stared in amazement at the young man, who took another picture, as if Abu Salim's appearance enhanced the traditional ambiance of the old house. He felt someone approaching, and turned and saw Faraj's angry face. Then came the resounding slap.

Faraj's assistants picked up the young man and gave him a shove. He hurried off and looked behind him to see them waving him away, while some of them held Faraj back to keep him from running after the poor young man.

Faraj dusted off his clothes and straightened his skullcap. He turned and saw Elishva looking through the gaping doorway. Her face was pale and tired, more like that of a ghost than of an ordinary woman. Faraj raised his hand and waved it in front of her face.

'Won't you drop dead already and give me a break? You're as tough as old boots, for God's sake!' he said.

Faraj went back to his office, and the slap he'd planted on that poor thin young man continued to echo down the lane. Less than an hour later Abu Anmar returned to his hotel with some black shopping bags. Faraj shouted to one of his young workers and sent him to the hotel to remind Abu Anmar of their appointment.

It would be Abu Anmar's first and last time in Faraj's office. He hadn't known it was so grand and spacious. His emotions swung between envy at the wealth of his rival and surrender to the sensory effects of the office's opulence.

The young servant put a glass of tea in front of Abu Anmar and another in front of Faraj, and amid the clatter of spoons Faraj got straight to the point.

'Abu Anmar, you're very dear to me. You're a professional and you understand business. I'd like us to work together, you and I.'

'Okay. What did you have in mind.'

'Good, good. I've noticed what a terrible state your hotel is in. It's going to waste.'

'I'm hoping to have it renovated,' said Abu Anmar.

'What with, Abu Anmar? Where will you get the money?'

'God is generous.'

'Yes, God is generous. No need to be embarrassed, my

brother Abu Anmar. I know very well that you don't have a penny. I'm your brother – don't be shy with me. I mean, I'd like us to be partners, you and I. I'll take on the cost of renovating the hotel and furnishing it, and we'll be partners, half and half. What do you say?'

4

'Where are you from?' asked Hadi.

'We're from the traffic department,' the two officers in pink politely replied.

Hadi was sitting on his bed in the middle of the courtyard as the sun set in the west. The officers, along with some assistants, sent by Brigadier Majid, had raided Hadi's house.

'But I haven't committed any traffic offences for two years,' said Hadi. 'And besides, I don't have a car.'

'Are you making fun of us, sir?' replied one of the officers, who had a thick bandage around his neck. Hadi had no way of knowing that it was this officer whom the Whatsitsname had tried to throttle on that terrible night of the chase. And now he was apparently trying to work out whether Hadi was the same height and had the same physique as the monster who had almost killed him. Taking hold of Hadi's arms, he thought this scrawny old man wouldn't be agile enough to run or put up much of a fight, but he wasn't quite certain.

'Playing the hero and resisting the Americans, are you?'

'I'm a junk dealer. Look around you.'

Hadi pointed at ten wooden wardrobes lined up against the wall.

'Yes, of course. You could always open a bureau for terrorist services, car bombings, and assassinations with silencers.'

'Silencers?'

'Go ahead, pretend to be innocent.'

They left Hadi and went off to search his room. A powerful stench hit them in the face. His things were in piles, and there was a small mound of Heineken beer cans in the corner. There were shoes; jugs made of copper, aluminium and plastic; wooden tables with broken legs; clothes; pigeon and chicken feathers; bedcovers and faded blankets; a stove; two gas cylinders; a plastic barrel full of kerosene; and a cupboard littered with onions, garlic, empty milk cans and tins of fish and beans. They quickly left, then surrounded Hadi's bed again and resumed their questions about the crimes he was committing in the streets of Baghdad.

A plaster statue of the Virgin Mary, her arms spread in a gesture of peace and with faded touches of colour on her long dress, had caught the officers' interest.

'Are you Christian?' asked one of them.

'No, I'm Muslim.'

'So what's this statue of the Virgin Mary for?'

'I don't know. There was a copy of the Throne Verse on top of it. The inscription fell apart and the statue appeared.'

'My God, you're a story. What are you going to do with her?' the officer with the bandage around his neck asked threateningly. And then the guys from the traffic department began to question Hadi about crimes he knew nothing about, asking him about a corpse or Whatsitsname in a fictional story he had made up to please the people sitting around him, to make himself more popular among the local people, so they would like him and sympathize with him.

'Are you completely sane?' Hadi asked in a sudden display of courage, frustrated by the interrogation. 'What corpse? What Whatsitsname? What are you talking about? Now you're making up a horror film to attack me with, all because of a made-up story, some coffee-shop talk.'

'Hey, don't get fresh with us or else I'll give you a good pummelling,' threatened the man with the bandage. The other pink officer held his arm to calm him down and took charge of the interrogation. They continued to pace around Hadi's bed, asking him questions even after people's faces had become difficult to make out in the dark. The voices became harsher, and hands Hadi couldn't identify pushed him onto the bed several times. Then one of them gave Hadi a sharp thump on the face, and he fell to the ground, hitting his head on one of the few intact floor tiles among the loose and broken ones. The interrogation had taken a new turn – one that was commonplace in all Iraqi police stations. Hadi had heard many stories about it from other people. Two assistants lifted Hadi's arms, and the pink officer with the bandage started punching Hadi in the stomach like a madman. This went on for two full minutes.

The punches didn't stop until Hadi threw up the beans and vegetables he had eaten at noon and the two cans of Heineken he had drunk an hour before the officers had burst in on him. The foul-smelling mixture soiled the clothes of the officer, who jumped back, cursing and swearing. The two goons who had been holding Hadi's arms let go of him and left him to fall to the ground to continue vomiting.

An hour later, in darkness punctuated by the glow of his colleagues' cigarettes, the calmer of the two officers concluded that the junk dealer was just an old liar, degenerate and half crazy. He might be protecting a real criminal, but the officer felt that taking him to the police station would just complicate the case they were investigating. He decided to leave this old drunk where he was and never to visit him again but to have a few people monitor him to see who visited him and who he met. He should feel at ease and not be afraid he was being watched.

The officers' assistants switched on some powerful electric

lamps, lighting the place up. Hadi was lying on his back on the courtyard floor. He didn't seem able to get up.

The officers searched the place again. In a glass coffee jar on the dining table, behind the piles of onions, they found the small amount of cash Hadi had made from selling Abu Anmar's furniture in the Harj market. The calmer of the two officers put the money in his trouser pocket, then picked up some other things at random. He took a table made of metal and wood, and others picked up pieces of furniture and various antiques: a broken chandelier, a wooden wall clock with a pendulum behind a glass window. One of the assistants, after daring to venture deep into Hadi's room, found a set of plates in a cardboard box – with pictures of King Ghazi and King Faisal II, and of Abd al-Karim Qasim, Baghdad Central Station, and other historical sites and nature scenes. He picked up the cardboard box, took it out to his friends, and opened it up with a sense of triumph.

They behaved like thieves. The calm officer, wanting to add to Hadi's confusion about who they were, gave Hadi a warning.

'That statue of the Virgin is *haram*,' he said. 'Do you understand? We want you to smash it right now.'

He aimed the powerful lamp into Hadi's face and saw his lips move. He moved closer and repeated his order. With difficulty Hadi moved his lips again.

'I can't. I can't,' he said.

'Why can't you? You mean you don't want to?'

'Look at me. A curse on your fathers. I can't stand up.'

The angry officer kicked Hadi in the stomach, winding him completely. One of the assistants went into the room and hit the statue in the wall niche several times with the butt of his pistol, knocking the Virgin's head off; the rest of the statue remained in place. The man pointed the beam of his flashlight at the statue to see the effects of his work. He felt a tremor of fear when he saw the woman peacefully spreading her arms but without a head.

The official mission didn't stop at this point. Before they left, the officer with the bandage wanted to apply a final test to Hadi, the same test he had used with the eleven ugly men they had detained in Bataween earlier that day.

The assistants stripped Hadi naked, then examined him in the lamplight to see if there was any stitching on his body or any sign of wounds. The angry officer took out a small sharp knife the length of a finger and cut into Hadi's arms, then his hips and thighs. Hadi cried out. The officer stopped and waited to see the blood. Hadi writhed on the ground as his blood spilled, black and sticky, onto the courtyard floor. It came out in small bursts, then stopped and congealed. It was black blood. The angry officer probed him with his fingers. His colleague didn't move, overcome by a sense of disgust. Why were they doing this? They were collecting information. Why were they stabbing someone for information?

Amid the waves of pain, a voice in Hadi's head told him that things would proceed as in an American action movie. His superhero would suddenly appear on the roof in the form of a dark hulk, then come down and at the speed of lightning fell his enemies with powerful punches, saving his friend and creator, his ageing father. But that didn't happen. One of the assistants picked up a walkie-talkie and in a low voice summoned the driver. Two minutes later everyone left Hadi's house, taking with them the things they had stolen. The officer with the bandage was upset, feeling they hadn't accomplished what they had come for. Before he reached the door, he turned as if he wanted to go back to beating Hadi, but his colleague pulled him away.

'You worm, you'll be seeing stars again if you're not care-ful,' he shouted, looking into the darkness where Hadi's body was sprawled.

5

Abu Anmar was shocked by Faraj's offer. He hadn't expected anything like it. But as he walked the short distance between the door of the Rasoul Real Estate office and that of his hotel, the truth became clearer in his mind: Faraj had come up with the cleverest, most cunning way possible to finish off Abu Anmar forever.

He had made him an excellent offer. They would be partners, Abu Anmar with the bricks and mortar, the walls and the roof, and Faraj with everything else. Faraj's share would be more than Abu Anmar's, but Abu Anmar would be in charge of managing and supervising the hotel. The most irritating thing was that Faraj wanted to change the name from the Orouba Hotel to the Grand Prophet Hotel.

The men argued for a full hour, and in the end Abu Anmar rejected the offer and went back to his hotel with heavy steps. Despite the heat, he closed the glass door firmly, as if he wanted to drive the image of Faraj's office far out of sight.

As he sat on his chair behind the reception desk, he set about drinking, calmly and slowly, and flicked through the thick book that contained prophecies of the end of the world. His mind was wandering, retrieving a stream of images from deep in his memory – of his youth and his glory days. He thought about the time when, as a trader travelling between Baghdad and Qalat Sukkar, a town on the banks of the Gharraf Canal in the south, he formed a partnership with the original owner of the hotel, and how, after his partner died, he ended up buying up the whole hotel. He felt he was standing on the edge of a complete cycle of his life, as he sat there looking at the reflection of his face in the closed door of the hotel.

His reflection in the glass door swung away, and the door opened. It was his old friend Hazem Abboud, panting, his face sweaty and a cloth bag hanging heavily from his left shoulder.

Hazem had gone through hell to find a taxi to bring him here. He had been threatened by an armed group where he lived and thought it would be best to spend the night away from home, and maybe other nights too, until he had a clearer picture.

Hazem noticed that the hotel seemed almost empty of furniture. Abu Anmar told him about everything he had done in the last few weeks, concluding with the offer that Faraj had made that afternoon. Hazem bowed his head a moment, then told him he could always take out a mortgage on the hotel or get a loan from the government with the hotel as security, in order to have it refurbished.

'That would mean debts, and who could guarantee the hotel would do well enough to repay them? I would end up falling into a big hole, and then the government would take over the hotel. Things are getting worse and worse.'

'Then accept Faraj's offer.'

'No, impossible. I will not work under this criminal. I will not let him humiliate me at my age. I was the king in this area when he was renting houses to whores and pimps. I was king.'

Abu Anmar leaned down to take a massive photo album from the big drawer in his wooden desk. There were black-and-white pictures of Abu Anmar in a suit and tie, looking thin and young. In one he was standing next to a basketball team from Maysan Province, in another sitting next to some short-haired girls who were in a church choir from Mosul. There were pictures of celebrities and people who had once been famous but who nobody but Abu Anmar seemed to know.

'So, what will you do? Will you just go on like this till your savings run out?' asked Hazem.

'No,' said Abu Anmar, draining the dregs of his drink, filling another glass calmly and slowly, and putting it on the small wooden table in front of his friend. 'I won't accept that bastard's offer, but I'll make a counterproposal. I'll sell him the whole hotel.'

CHAPTER THIRTEEN

The Jewish Ruin

1

Elishva was sitting as usual in the parlour with her shedding cat. Through the thick lenses of her glasses she was contemplating the picture of the saint, the yellow light of the oil lamp dancing on the picture's ripples, while her ears picked up cries and groans of pain coming from the house next door. The sounds continued for a quarter of an hour.

She should have gone to the service to commemorate Saint Shamouni and her seven children on their feast day, but she preferred to stay at home. After Faraj had slapped that poor young man, Umm Salim came to see her and said that Faraj was evil and might do anything. He might forge the title deed to her house and throw her into the street. Besides, no one had even seen the title deed – perhaps Elishva didn't even have it.

Why was Umm Salim telling her this? Had she turned against her? But she had made her a tempting offer: Elishva could move into a room in Umm Salim's house, and then one of Umm Salim's children could convert Elishva's house into lodgings and rent out the rooms, and the rent money would go to Elishva. Faraj and others who had designs on the old woman would feel she was protected.

But that might be a way for Umm Salim to get hold of her house, she thought. Perhaps greed was at work inside the fat old woman and she was just another wolf in sheep's clothing, or maybe she was working for Faraj.

She didn't respond to Umm Salim's proposal. Umm Salim assumed the feeble-minded old woman needed time to think. But she wasn't thinking about Umm Salim's proposal. That thin young man who wanted to buy her house on behalf of the state? He hadn't understood that she wasn't going to sell her house. She wouldn't feel proud living in a house that belonged to the state when it had once been her house, and the money she would make from selling it would be more than she needed.

She shut her eyes awhile, and her head felt heavy. Nabu dozed off on her lap, and maybe she too was about to fall asleep on the sofa when she heard a noise in the courtyard and the sound of heavy footsteps. She turned towards the door: standing there was the spectre of her son, Daniel.

2

Hadi felt he was dying. But a strong pair of arms picked him up from the broken tiles covered in his sticky blood. He opened his eyes but couldn't see anything – it was completely dark. The arms lowered him gently onto the foam mattress in the middle of the courtyard. A damp cloth ran over his body, then two dark hands helped him put on his shirt and trousers.

'Don't worry, you're not going to die, but you deserved this thrashing,' the stranger said before disappearing. A few minutes later, Hadi heard a commotion. He felt a torpor in his limbs and seemed about to fall asleep when flashlights shone on his face.

'What do you want from me? What do you want from me?' he shouted, thinking the interrogators had come back, perhaps to finish him off this time.

'What have they done to him?' one of them said. They started to turn his body over and inspect his wounds.

Abu Salim had noticed the people when they first went into Hadi's house but couldn't tell what was happening inside. He watched from the balcony till he saw the interrogators come out with some stuff in their hands, then get into the truck and drive off fast. One of them waved out of the truck window a table lamp with a shade made of coloured glass and hit it against the wall. Abu Salim went into action, calling some of his children and shouting for some of the young men who lived nearby. They burst into Hadi's house, and when Hadi came round from his delirium, Abu Salim's youngest son ran home to get bandages, disinfectant, medical gauze and medicine, because he sold such things in a stall in the Shorja market and had considerable knowledge of first aid. He told Hadi that the wounds on his thighs needed stitching, and he wasn't good at that, but he could bandage them up till the morning, and the next day he should go to a nurse or a dispensary to have them stitched, and he shouldn't move too much during the night so his condition didn't deteriorate. They treated him with great decency and compassion, and also tried to find out what had happened, but when they pressed him with questions, Hadi started to swear: he wasn't prepared to go through two interrogations in one evening.

A feeble breeze blew down from above into the hollow where Hadi lived between two-storey houses with high walls. The drugs that Abu Salim had given him had had an effect, and he regretted his harsh words, but the questions kept coming: Would the interrogators come back? Why did they suddenly stop before getting the answers they wanted? Why did they cut him like that? Who had pointed them in his direction? Was it the journalist? Or one of the customers at Aziz's coffee shop?

He didn't yet know that his savings from the hard work he had done over the past week had disappeared, or that the statue of the Virgin Mary had had its head smashed, or that the valuable plates and his most precious possessions had been taken. All that would become clear on the afternoon of the next day. For the moment he felt that everything he had been through had had the effect of a powerful slap, maybe from a heavenly hand, to open his eyes to the error of his ways and to the abyss into which he was sliding.

He would make a fresh start for himself. He would hold out till his wounds healed completely and then go to the Sabunji hammam in Sheikh Omar. He would plant himself like a statue under the hot steam for three hours, then shave his head and face and buy smart new clothes and leave this damned Jewish ruin and rent a large, airy room in Faraj's new lodgings, then think about renting a shop to buy, sell and repair used things, because he was good at that. He would find a wife who would put up with him and restrict his drinking to one session a week. He would do all these things and keep doing them if he could sleep peacefully that night and if he could wake up alive and well in the morning.

3

The Whatsitsname didn't think the savage beating and the knife cuts would be enough to kill Hadi, but it looked like the kind of punishment he deserved for his many sins and mistakes. That's what the Whatsitsname was thinking as he came down into the courtyard to put his creator on the bed and help him put his clothes on. When he heard the neighbours approaching, he quickly climbed up the stones towards Elishva's house.

He found Elishva sitting in the parlour, staring blankly at the picture of Saint George the Martyr. She saw him in the doorway, and not a single muscle in her face twitched. She looked at him as if he had been living there for some time and had just come back from the bathroom.

He felt lonely. He hadn't spoken to anyone in weeks. He had only two acquaintances left: the junk dealer and the mad old woman. He could have finished off the pink officers and their three assistants without batting an eyelid, but that would have created a bigger problem for the junk dealer, who would be accused of killing them. In order to help Hadi resume his normal life, he had better not show his face to him again.

The Whatsitsname was now at a loss for what to do. He knew his mission was essentially to kill, to kill new people every day, but he no longer had a clear idea who should be killed or why. The flesh of the innocents, of which he was initially composed, had been replaced by new flesh, that of his own victims and criminals. He thought if he took too long avenging the victims in whose name he was acting, the body parts he had taken from them would decompose in situ. It would be the end of him, and he would be free of this world.

But he wasn't sure this was the right choice either. He had to stay alive until he worked out what his next steps should be. And because he was an exceptional killer who wouldn't die by traditional means, he thought he should exploit this distinctive talent in the service of the innocent – in the service of truth and justice. Until he was sure of his next steps, he would concentrate on ensuring his own survival. He would salvage the spare parts he needed from the bodies of those who deserved to be killed. It wasn't the ideal option, but it was the best one possible for now.

The Whatsitsname explained some of his worries to the old woman. She was listening and stroking the back of her old sleeping cat. She didn't seem capable of understanding such a complicated subject, but she was someone who would listen, and that's what the Whatsitsname needed at the moment.

He told her he sometimes ran into some of his followers who were on the run after surviving the minor civil war they had fought at the barracks in the shell of the building in Dora. The way they treated him depended on which of the three madmen they had followed, and they didn't seem to have lost much of their faith in him.

One night he saw Citizen 341 walking down the street in the Waziriya district. He bowed to the Whatsitsname and kissed his hand. The man said he had no idea what had happened to the other numbers – who had been killed and who had survived the terrible bullet fest that night. Also, although he still believed and had a deep desire to reorganize, he had no idea who Citizen 342 was, or Citizen 340, or where they would resume counting if they gained new supporters and believers, or which numbers were now vacant and how many citizens there really were now.

Another night he had some serious putrefaction problems and ran into a follower who believed he was the saviour. The man took him to his house in the Fadhil district, avoiding the neighbours and prying eyes. When they were in the courtyard, this believer went into the kitchen and came back with a large knife. He told the Whatsitsname he could kill him and take the parts he needed. The offer took the Whatsitsname by surprise. After thinking for a few minutes, he decided it was a good idea, especially as the alternatives would cause much more commotion and he might have to kill off many people before he managed to replace the worn-out parts with fresh new ones.

He cut the man's arteries at the wrists, so he died slowly and went into a coma before he gave up the ghost. He didn't want to stab him in the stomach or cut his throat because that would seem violent, and this believer, or anyone else in the same situation, wouldn't be able to control himself and the animal instincts of his body. He might scream or maybe decide on impulse to fight back against the death that was coursing through his body.

Elishva kept listening to what she thought was the spectre of her son who had disappeared two decades ago, without giving any sign that she understood what he was saying.

It was getting late for the old woman, and she had a feeling her visitor might go on talking till the morning. If there was anything of her son in him, he ought to understand that she was holding out against death, and she wouldn't give advice that promoted any kind of death.

'Why don't you relax, my boy?' she said, wanting to put an end to his long ramble. 'Shall I make up a bed for you in the courtyard?' He felt she was reminding him of the role she had played in shaping his identity. He also felt that in other circumstances he would really like to accept her offer, to lie down on a low cotton mattress and look at the square patch of sky, counting the stars till he fell asleep. But that was a life that wasn't his.

She took off her glasses, rubbed her eyes, took a deep breath and let out a long sigh. When she opened her eyes again, her talkative visitor was nowhere to be found. She looked at the picture of the saint hanging in front of her, his lance raised and the dragon crouching beneath him. She wondered why he hadn't killed the dragon years ago. Why was he stuck in that posture, ready to strike, she wondered? Everything remains half completed, exactly like now: she wasn't exactly a living being, but not a dead one either.

'You're tormenting me,' she said, picking up the sleeping cat and putting it beside her on the sofa. The cat opened his eyes, gave a long yawn, and stretched.

'You haven't killed this dragon, have you, you warrior?' she said, then waited patiently for his answer. She stood up, still staring into the handsome face of the silent saint.

'Everything will come to an end, Elishva. Why the hurry?' said the saint, his lips not moving in the slightest. Nothing in the picture moved, and yet she could hear his voice clearly.

4

Hadi lay awake, looking up at the square of blue sky above and the birds darting past. He closed his eyes a while, then opened them again and caught sight of the silhouette of an American helicopter flying past, making a thunderous whacking noise. He wanted to get up, but he didn't think he had the strength. Then suddenly his whole body convulsed at the sound of a powerful blast and the ground shaking beneath him.

It was a car bomb in the Sadriya district, several miles from Bataween in the heart of the old capital. But Hadi didn't find out anything about the explosion till late in the day. He sat on his bed, his body throbbing with pain, and then he heard a movement at the front door of the house. It was Aziz the Egyptian with two young men from the neighbourhood. Aziz swore as he shoved the temperamental door closed, then gave Hadi a broad smile and approached with a bowl of clotted cream, some bread and a Thermos of tea.

'Thank God you're safe,' said Aziz, patting his friend on the shoulder. Less than an hour later, the young man who worked with Hadi showed up. He had an appointment to deal with the rest of the stuff from the old hotel and was taken aback to see Hadi tied up in bandages.

After breakfast, Aziz encouraged Hadi to inspect his house. Hadi was shocked to discover that his savings and some valuables were missing. At first he suspected the people who had dressed his injuries, but then his suspicions shifted to the interrogators. Seeing the damaged statue of the Virgin, Aziz looked upset.

'That's the mother of Jesus. Why would anyone do that?' he asked, touching the broken pieces of plaster, then brushing his hand as if he didn't want to get involved in any accidental sabotage.

Hadi felt sick when he remembered all the money he had made from selling the furniture from the Orouba Hotel that had now gone missing. An hour later he came to his senses. He told his assistant to go buy some polish, nails, sandpaper, wood filler, and other things for preserving and maintaining old furniture. They would work on the battered old wardrobes, then take them to market and sell them as soon as possible.

When everyone was gone, Hadi noticed the plaster icon of the Virgin. He used to wonder whether it might be possible to get it free in one piece and sell it to a church. He pulled out smashed parts of the icon, then looked at the hole that the statue had left in the wall, and brushed aside the dust to reveal a dark wooden plank two feet high and a foot wide. He wiped it again and uncovered an engraving in the shape of a tree. In fact, it was a large candelabra with writing above and below in what Hadi soon realized was Hebrew. When he was younger he had seen similar things on the walls of some of the houses in Bataween, and he immediately thought this,

197

too, was something he could sell. When this occurred to him, he felt a pang of fear, thinking of the interrogators. He remembered his resolutions of the previous night and made up his mind to change everything.

Hadi heard something at the door – his assistant must have come back from the market. He dragged a folded rug from the corner of the room and propped it up against the wall in front of the statue niche and the wooden plank, hiding them completely.

5

Nader Shamouni, the deacon, had trouble reaching Elishva's house. The Americans had blocked the road at Tayaran Square because of a car bomb close to the Gilani gas station and another explosion in the Sadriya market that had killed dozens of shoppers and shopkeepers. Nader wanted to get out of his car, but a policeman warned him that he couldn't park there. He thought about calling Father Josiah to tell him he couldn't complete his mission, but wiser counsel told him it might be like this every day. He should complete his mission whatever it took, especially as he wasn't going to have problems like this often in the days to come: he had decided to leave Baghdad with his family. He had told Father Josiah a long time ago but kept postponing the move, realizing he would be leaving his home, his neighbours, and his life in Baghdad to move to Ankawa at the behest of his daughters and relatives who had been living there for several years. When the move was still tentative, Nader discovered one morning that the keyhole on his front door had been filled with some kind of glue. He tried to remove the glue but wound up having to replace the lock. Before a week had passed, he discovered that the new lock had been filled with the same sticky substance. Someone was harassing them, he told his family – probably just some kid – and he decided not to repair the lock and to make do with bolting the door from the inside.

But he found the lock on the door leading from the kitchen to the garden had also been filled with this sticky substance. Angry and tense, he called a quick family meeting. At first he suspected his daughters and his wife, but soon dismissed that idea. Someone must have climbed the fence and come in when they were asleep.

Many similar incidents had taken place over the past three years, and given the deteriorating security situation in Baghdad, there was no authority that could be trusted to help him. The father of one family in the congregation had recently been abducted. The family persuaded the kidnappers to free him only by paying a large ransom. Nader called his brothers and relatives in Ankawa and told them of his decision.

'It's a temporary measure. We'll leave home till things calm down in the capital,' he said. He didn't foresee the possibility that never coming back would become a very real option.

Nader parked his small Volga at the end of the lane and walked to Elishva's house. He wouldn't see her again, he reckoned, and that was reason enough to make his last meeting with her friendlier. He had known her and her late husband and her children for decades and could see that the old woman was tired – she had new lines on her face and around her eyes behind the big glasses she wore. Maybe he noticed all this because he hadn't sat so close to her for a long time: she hadn't been to church in about a month.

Elishva's daughters, Hilda and Matilda, kept calling Father Josiah, and he kept assuring them that their mother was healthy and safe, but they asked to hear her voice – they knew she was angry, and they wanted to make up with her. Nader told her all this and said that the priest was asking her to come see him next Sunday after Mass. Elishva just scowled.

'Matilda's going to come to Iraq for you,' Nader continued. 'She said she'd come to see you and then take you back with her.'

'She won't do it. She's a coward.'

'She will do it. She was crying during her conversation with Father Josiah.'

'I'm not going anywhere. I won't leave my house.'

'But what use is the house, Umm Daniel? What use is it when you're alone, like someone sitting in a tent in the desert?'

'My family are here and my neighbours. My life is in this house.'

'I know, but don't you miss your daughters?'

'They're fine. Why are they asking me to leave my house?'

'Well, you know, life's getting hard here. What use is the house if life is hard? Fear, death, anxiety, criminals in the street, everyone watching as you walk past. Even when you're asleep, it's nightmares and jumping in fright all the time. The whole country's starting to look like the Jewish ruin next door.'

'"Fear not those who kill the body but are not able to kill the soul."'

'Yes,' replied Nader, who had no ready reply to the biblical reference. Without intending to, he started to share his own personal worries.

'You must come on Sunday, for my sake, Umm Daniel. If you like, I'll come and pick you up. Would that be okay?'

She agreed.

In the three days before Sunday, Nader was consumed with preparations. He had listed his house with a real estate agent and sold much of his furniture, storing the rest on the upper floor. He was so busy that he didn't even attend Mass on Sunday. On Monday morning he left the house keys with a friend, asked him to arrange for the things in the storeroom to be sent to Erbil by truck, and set off with his family in his small Volga, bound for the north.

He either forgot about or deliberately ignored the old lady. From the way she looked, he thought, she might not last another year, and he would never see her again. For her part, Elishva didn't think she would see the deacon with the Turkish moustache ever again either, but both of them were wrong.

CHAPTER FOURTEEN

Tracking and Pursuit

1

Brigadier Majid was in his office watching Farid Shawwaf speak on television about Criminal X, as the journalists were now calling the One Who Has No Name. The television channels were covering the criminal almost every day, showing Identikit drawings of his face, with a caption stating the reward for anyone who provided information leading to his arrest. If he could arrest this nameless criminal, the brigadier thought, it would be the crowning glory of several years' efforts. The criminal was a television star, and when the brigadier caught him, he too would immediately become a celebrity.

'They're offering money they know very well they'll never have to pay out,' Brigadier Majid told one of his junior officers. He felt instantly that this was the kind of sentence the well-dressed man on television might have said – the man who always wore suits the brigadier coveted but knew he would never wear as long as he was stuck in his office at the Tracking and Pursuit Department.

He took a small mirror out of his desk drawer and studied the black rings under his eyes and the way his face sagged.

He wiped his face with the palm of his hand – something he did habitually but only when he was alone in the office. For the last three years his work had been proceeding without great surprises. With his eccentric assistants, he drafted predictions about explosions on the streets of Baghdad, picked up rumours and analysed them, provided confidential advice to politicians who were forming alliances for the coming elections or thinking about entering into business partnerships. He would get upset when his rank and military career were ignored and someone from government headquarters would call him after midnight to ask how to interpret some dream. He spent much of his time on such nonsense.

In the golden age when life was easy, before the criminal without a name appeared, he had sometimes been taken by surprise by a visit from a prominent politician. Their names were all the same to him, and they would ask him many questions, as if he was the one who could read the tea leaves and foretell the future, but he knew there was only one question that brought them all the way to his office:

'When and how will I die?' It usually came at the end of an exhausting list of questions, to give the impression that it was just one of many.

'Should I order an armour-plated car, or don't I need one?' one of the politicians once asked him. His parliamentary bloc had been assigned only three armour-plated cars, the politician explained; should he fight to obtain one?

Anyone else in his place would have exploited these politicians to promote himself, to try to obtain a more senior position and escape being trapped in the Tracking and Pursuit Department, but Brigadier Majid wanted to demonstrate his worth through real effort, not by telling the fortunes of politicians but by arresting criminals. All this changed, though, with the appearance of the dangerous criminal.

Farid Shawwaf had disappeared from the television screen and the news had come on, when one of the officers took the brigadier by surprise with a terrifying idea that Majid had never thought of before.

'If bullets really don't kill him and he knows we're trying to track him down, what if he followed us, found our head-quarters, and then came here to wipe us all out?'

2

The senior astrologer was pondering the same question as he turned over the playing cards in the room he shared with the junior astrologer. He shuffled them again, like a skilled poker player, then drew a single card and held it right in front of his eyes. He stared at it as if he could see in it a deep chasm or a door that opened onto a whole world only he could see.

He knew that one day he would come face-to-face with the criminal and would recognize him. But for the moment, the face was vague and refused to take shape. He stroked his long white pointed beard and closed his eyes. The criminal was running over the roofs of the buildings in a poor part of Baghdad, but there was no point in telling Brigadier Majid about it because the criminal never stayed where he was, and he moved at an extraordinary speed that no human could match.

The junior astrologer was watching his master's studied movements carefully. The senior astrologer was annoyed that his young disciple seemed so relaxed.

'He could very well burst in on us now and kill us both,' said the senior astrologer.

'If that's what's going to happen in the end, then what's

the point of doing anything? What can we do to stop him? Are we gods?'

'If you can foresee what's going to happen, then that's a gift from God, and He's telling you that you can change fate for the better. I'm the god showing you what will happen because what happens depends on what you do. If you don't do anything, then what you foresee will come about. If you act, you can take advantage of God's permission to change what's going to happen.'

'Yes, you always say that,' replied the junior astrologer, hinting that the conversation was over and he no longer wanted to listen to any more lectures from his master, who didn't seem able to teach him anything new.

The junior astrologer stood up and stretched. He picked up his bag of sand from the table, stuffed it in his pocket, and went off to bed.

3

There were still fine grains of red sand on the edge of the wooden table where the senior astrologer was sitting. He stood up and wiped the table with his hand, then wiped his fingers on his flowing robe. He decided to go out for a smoke, despite the cold. He needed air.

As soon as the senior astrologer left the room, slamming the door behind him, the junior astrologer sat up straight in bed. There was a mission he wanted to carry out that night.

He got up and sat down at the table, ruling out the possibility that his master would suddenly change his mind and come back. He took a bag of red sand out of his pocket, poured it all onto the table, and started to play with it. He made it into a large ring, then took another handful of sand in his fist and carefully poured a thin line of sand inside the ring. It was stupid child's play, Brigadier Majid once told himself when he saw the junior astrologer playing with his bags of sand. But the sand was from a special place in the Empty Quarter of Arabia, and it had magical powers appreciated only by those who knew how to exploit them. Brigadier Majid misjudged the importance of the young astrologer's work.

The senior astrologer felt the cold of the night seeping into his bones. He tossed his cigarette butt and decided to go back to his room to sleep. At the same time, his young disciple was about to finish his secret experiment. He was trying to make contact with the spirit of the One Who Has No Name. While his superior was interested in knowing what the criminal's face looked like, the junior astrologer was interested in his soul. Over the past weeks he had managed to contact the family of Hasib Mohamed Jaafar, the guard who was killed at the Sadeer Novotel and whose soul settled in the body that Hadi had assembled in his shed.

The junior astrologer succeeded that night in making a connection with the spirit of the monster. There were mobile phone vibrations between him and the monster, through which he transferred something into the monster's brain that made him stop moving for a minute. If the senior astrologer had been there, he would have seen in his playing cards that the monster really did stop. He was leaning against the wall of a tall building on a dark street lined with car repair shops and looking at the wall of an abandoned secondary school somewhere in the southern suburbs of Baghdad. The junior astrologer now felt he was superior to his superior.

When the senior astrologer came back into the room, he shut the door behind him, then looked at his disciple's bed and saw his disciple was sleeping with his face to the wall, just as he had left him. He walked past the wooden table and noticed grains of sand on it. He was sure he had wiped it clean an hour before.

4

The Whatsitsname stopped suddenly in the middle of a side street and turned to look back in the direction he had come from. There were few cars driving along the main road. As if emerging from a long daydream, he realized he didn't remember how his feet had brought him there. Neither did he know where he was heading or where he would spend the night. The few people who crossed his path when he moved around at night either ran away from him or were old disciples who would spring to his assistance.

In his mind he still had a long list of the people he was supposed to kill, and as fast as the list shrank it was replenished with new names, making avenging these lives an endless task. Or maybe he would wake up one day to discover that there was no one left to kill, because the criminals and the victims were entangled in a way that was more complicated than ever before.

'There are no innocents who are completely innocent or criminals who are completely criminal.' This sentence drilled its way into his head like a bullet out of the blue. He stood in the middle of the street and looked up at the sky, waiting for the final moment when he would disintegrate into his original components. This was the realization that would undermine his mission – because every criminal he had killed was also a victim. The victim proportion in some of them might even be higher than the criminal proportion, so he might inadvertently be made up of the most innocent parts of the criminals' bodies.

'There are no innocents who are completely innocent or criminals who are completely criminal.' The sentence drilled its way into his head once again, and he stood there, clearly visible in the headlights of a car that had turned onto the side street. The driver stopped for long enough to recognize what he was seeing in the middle of the street, then turned slowly and went back the way he had come.

5

The senior astrologer went into Brigadier Majid's office with some of his colleagues – but not his young subaltern – while the brigadier was having breakfast on the sofa opposite his vast desk. He handed the brigadier a pink envelope, in line with the usual procedures.

'At eleven o'clock this morning a car bomb is going to explode outside the Ministry of Finance,' said the senior astrologer before the brigadier could even open the envelope, which contained the same information. Brigadier Majid put a piece of bread with clotted cream in his mouth, then stood up. He called a number on his mobile phone and waited till someone answered, then asked to be transferred to a more senior officer. He relayed the substance of the prediction, then sat back down at his table and resumed his breakfast.

Two years earlier, when the senior astrologer would come in with information like this, the brigadier would treat it as an emergency. He would get in touch with the security commanders, and he would be devastated when he heard on the news that the explosion had taken place despite his warning.

'Idiots. When they identify the car bomb, they prefer to run away rather than dismantle it,' he would always say. But now he was calmer, especially when he saw that there were other crimes and security incidents taking place and that his own team was failing to detect them.

'We mitigate the effects, but we can't stop them all. If they want to establish complete security, let them put us in charge of the country,' he sometimes said, with exaggerated confidence in himself and in the competence of the team of magicians and astrologers who worked under him. But he was deluded.

The senior astrologer waved his hand, and the other astrologers left the room. When they had shut the door behind them, the old astrologer sat down in front of the brigadier, who was calmly sipping a glass of tea.

The senior astrologer anxiously appealed to the brigadier. 'Do you remember, sir, when we started seeing the spectre of the One Who Has No Name?'

'That would have been in the springtime, towards the end of April.'

'Have you ever thought about how this monstrous criminal was made?'

'I don't know. Why do you ask? If it weren't for all the rumours and my trust in what you say, I wouldn't believe such a creature exists. Where are we living, and in what age? Ogres and succubi, in this day and age? They aren't just manifestations of people's fears,' said the brigadier irritably.

'No, sir. He exists. You're entitled not to believe me, but when we get our hands on him, you'll see.'

'Did you come just to tell me this, or is there something else you're hiding?'

'Yes, I think we played a role in creating this creature, in one way or another. Things were proceeding as usual before he appeared. I think some of our staff helped create him,' said the astrologer. The brigadier held his glass of tea in mid-air. He didn't drink from it or put it down.

'What do you mean?'

'Someone inspired the creation of this creature to stop crimes before they happen. What's the point of predicting where a crime is going to happen when you can wipe out the criminal before he becomes one.'

'What do you mean?' the brigadier asked again, the tea glass still poised in mid-air. He was annoyed and confused. He wouldn't believe what his favourite astrologer said because he hadn't offered any proof, even if he did sell the government and the Americans information extracted from playing cards, and with sand, mirrors, rosaries made of beans, and so on. But the brigadier wouldn't buy stories like this so easily.

CHAPTER FIFTEEN

A Lost Soul

1

Mahmoud dreamed he was holding her hand, his fingers intertwined with hers. They strolled lazily past the Sheraton Hotel and towards Abu Nuwas Street, their hands doing the talking, passing messages between their souls like an electric wire.

There were no sounds in the background – no car horns, no police cars or Hummers. The world around them was more cheerful, less dreary and depressing, and the future didn't seem completely unknown. There was an assurance of something better, making things seem less oppressive or, like the Midas touch, turning them into gold.

'Have you ever seen a golden piece of shit?' he asked. 'Do you think it would be beautiful or just another piece of shit?'

He didn't know why he had asked this. But when he looked at her, he found that she was just a tree with cracked bark, another eucalyptus tree on Abu Nuwas Street. He noticed a bitter taste in his throat and could smell the tyres of the passing cars. In his hand was a handkerchief soaked in his own sweat. He was squeezing it tight for no obvious reason.

211

He woke up sweating and felt deeply depressed. He had slept a long time. He didn't want to get out of bed. He went back to sleep, to the reassuring images in his dream. It was noon by the time he was standing under a cold shower. He called Raghayib, the woman who arranged women for him, and waited in his room. He watched television, smoked, watched the cars and passersby on Saadoun Street from his hotel window. He stayed that way till sunset, when Zeina showed up.

It was hot and humid outside. Although the sun had set, heat still radiated from the street, so the first thing Zeina did after entering Mahmoud's room was stand naked under the shower for a quarter of an hour. Her hair, which she held together with a pink clip, was soaked. Her make-up was now gone, and she didn't care what Mahmoud thought when she came out of the shower stripped of everything, her skin cold and wet, and with an unalloyed sense of relaxation.

Just like the previous time, she told him her name was Zeina, but Mahmoud said her name was Nawal al-Wazir. She laughed and said that the name Nawal was old-fashioned, older than the traditional greeting *Assalam aleekum*. Then she laughed again and lay down on the bed, spreading her legs and giving him a view of where she had shaved her pubic hair. He said to himself that using *Assalam aleekum* to represent antiquity was itself old-fashioned, but it sounded nice when she said it. All he wanted to do was to put his arms around her and run his hands along her clean, naked body. 'This is the moment you've been waiting for, my boy,' he said to himself. 'After tonight, life won't be anything like it used to be.'

He heard Zeina asking him to turn out the light. He took off his clothes and threw himself beside her on the bed. The light from the television cast moving flashes of light around the room. She asked him to turn off the television too, but as on the previous occasion, he wanted her to dance to a song from the Gulf.

'Dance, Nawal,' he said.

She laughed and pulled him towards her.

'Still Nawal?' she said.

He took hold of her plump arms and pulled her closer, forgetting about his request that she dance. His heart was beating like a drum. When he wrapped his arms around her, she used her free hand to grab the remote control lying on the pillow and turn off the television. It wasn't pitch black – there were faint lights coming through the balcony window – but when he looked at her, he didn't see anything, just lines of light that traced the outline of a woman who could have been any woman in the world. And yet he still saw her as one particular woman, Nawal al-Wazir, the woman he loved. There she was in his arms, even if she said her name was Zeina.

He covered her dark body with kisses, and she laughed, which he didn't like. He dived deep into her, the pleasure coursing through him with a rising tempo, but then she started to moan uncomfortably, faking pleasure. She wasn't with him but was looking forward to him climaxing quickly so she could be done with him.

'Shut up,' he scolded her, and she stopped. Then he clamped his hand over her mouth as he pressed against her from behind. When he had finished, she left the bed grumbling. She sat down naked on the chair next to the balcony window and started smoking. Mahmoud could see her face in profile in the diffused light. She was furious, but she was still beautiful. A minute later he shouted at her, and she replied angrily, 'Who's this Nawal you're going on about? I tell you my name's Zeina, God damn it, and then you call me Nawal?'

2

Mahmoud took a cigarette out of his packet and began to smoke, while Zeina sat next to the balcony window. He went over what had happened to him in the last twenty-four hours.

In the morning he had headed to Aziz's coffee shop, wanting to relive something of the old atmosphere and forget the monotony of the magazine. He gave Aziz a friendly greeting and expected to see Hadi the junk dealer there.

'Is he at home?' asked Mahmoud.

'Don't go to his place, sir. Leave him alone, for God's sake,' Aziz said in a serious tone that Mahmoud hadn't heard from him before. When the coffee shop emptied out somewhat, Aziz came and sat next to him. Mahmoud asked about the Whatsitsname, whether he was really the criminal people were talking about. Aziz said it was all a 'made-up story' and then told him about Nahem Abdaki, the close friend, partner and companion that Hadi had lost in an explosion at the beginning of the year. Hadi had lived through many disasters, but after a while he turned everything into amusing stories.

'The Whatsitsname that Hadi talks about is in fact Nahem Abdaki, may he rest in peace,' he added.

'How could it be him?' asked Mahmoud. Aziz explained that after the explosion, Hadi had gone to the mortuary to collect the body because Nahem didn't have any family other than his wife and young daughter. Hadi was shocked to see that the bodies of explosion victims were all mixed up together and to hear the mortuary worker tell him to put a body together and carry it off – take this leg and this arm and so on.

Hadi collected what he thought was Nahem's body, then went to the Mohamed Sakran Cemetery with Nahem's widow and some neighbours. But Hadi was changed after that. He didn't speak for two weeks, after which he went back to laughing and telling stories, and when he told the Whatsitsname story at Aziz's coffee shop, Aziz and some of those sitting there knew that Hadi had written Nahem out of it and put the Whatsitsname in his place.

'Okay, but the recordings? I gave him a recorder, and he recorded conversations between him and the Whatsitsname.'

'Hadi's a big bullshitter. He probably got one of his friends to record it. He has lots of friends we don't know.'

'I don't buy it. What he says in the recordings is powerful stuff. I mean, it's from someone intelligent. Big stories with depth.'

'I really don't know. But Hadi's a mischievous devil; he could come up with anything.'

Mahmoud believed Aziz, although there were gaps in his story, questions without answers. On his way back he stopped at the end of Lane 7 and looked from a distance at the ramshackle front wall of 'the Jewish ruin', where Hadi lived. He thought about ignoring Aziz's wishes and knocking on the door to get the story directly from Hadi, but he was worried Hadi might in fact be smarter than he was, as Aziz was sure he was, and might drag him back into the maelstrom of his outlandish story. For now Mahmoud didn't have the energy for this.

3

Ali Baher al-Saidi had been away for several days when a group of men with thick grey moustaches and prominent paunches turned up at the premises of *al-Haqiqa* magazine to make enquiries about him. Mahmoud received them warily. They asked for Saidi's telephone number in Beirut, and

Mahmoud said he didn't have it. They asked about Saidi's house, his relatives, his companies, and so on. Mahmoud denied knowing anything. When they had given up all hope of obtaining any useful information, they left, disgruntled.

In the afternoon Mahmoud, racked with anxiety, tried to call Ali Baher al-Saidi, but he didn't pick up. Mahmoud tried calling a second and third time, and finally Saidi picked up. As usual he was relaxed. Mahmoud told him about the visitors, and Saidi praised the way he had dealt with them. He asked Mahmoud to deal firmly with others like them but didn't explain who those others might be or why they were asking questions. He asked Mahmoud to call his private secretary and ask her to come to the magazine to keep such visitors at bay.

'She knows how to answer them, and it's not your job,' he said. 'You just concentrate on the magazine.'

Saidi got off the phone quickly, leaving Mahmoud puzzled. He was too embarrassed to call him back and ask him more questions.

Mahmoud called Saidi's secretary the next day, and she told him she had resigned. Her fiancé wouldn't agree to her working at a place full of men, saying it was dangerous on the streets. Mahmoud didn't know how to answer and preferred not to argue.

He was right in the firing line, a situation he wasn't used to. He woke up at eight o'clock in the morning, washed, shaved, put on smart clothes to emulate Saidi. Taking out a small notebook, he looked at his priorities for the day. He called Sultan, Saidi's personal driver, to take him on reporting assignments. From that point on, his phone never stopped ringing. The magazine staff – all except for Farid Shawwaf – looked up to him as the 'big boss' and a carbon copy of Saidi himself. Maybe they saw him relaxed and happy, as Saidi always appeared to be. But in fact he was anxious and afraid of surprises. He was even more afraid of failing in Saidi's eyes. He couldn't wait to move out of the limelight and go back to being a number two who receives orders from the boss.

Mahmoud was very busy when Nawal al-Wazir called on Saidi's phone. He saw the number 666 and picked up, but no one answered. He could hear a sigh at the other end of the line, or imagined he did, before the caller hung up.

Two days later the old caretaker, Abu Jouni, came in and dropped a bombshell: Nawal al-Wazir was in the office. She had come in a white Suzuki so small it looked like a toy. She took off her wraparound sunglasses and sat on the red leather sofa, radiating vitality and good health and smiling at Mahmoud, whose heart beat violently. She looked many times more beautiful than she had two months before.

'So that joker friend of yours has left you tied up here while he goes gallivanting around, has he?' she said.

'He's gone to a conference in Beirut on the media and human rights.'

'Yes, you told me, yes. Now you'll see how he tricks you.'

She put out her cigarette in the ashtray before it was finished, then continued: 'He's gone there to play around. There is no conference.'

'Really? I wouldn't know.'

'You're a nice guy, Mahmoud. As soon as I saw you with Saidi, I said, "They're like chalk and cheese, these two." And that friend of yours is a real bullshitter.'

'Is he my friend or your friend?' Mahmoud dared to ask. He saw her smile, then chuckle.

'Yes, *my* friend,' she said. 'But don't get carried away. He was just helping me on a film. He gave me its plot in the first place.'

She looked at her watch, opened her strange oval-shaped handbag, and took out a small key, then looked at Mahmoud and said, 'Do you mind?' She went up to Saidi's vast desk and leaned over to the bottom drawer, the one that was always closed. Mahmoud didn't know what was in it and didn't have a key for it, but Nawal was opening it. She took out some files and a small box that might be for a watch or an expensive fountain pen, and then a paper box of the kind used by the shops that develop and print photographs at Bab al-Sharqi. She gathered everything in a thick plastic bag with an ad for Gitanes cigarettes on it, then lifted it and shook it to judge the weight.

'Don't worry,' she said. 'He knows. He gave me the key. These are my things. The script for the film and some other stuff.'

'And why are you taking them? I mean, what's happened?'

'Everything's over, and I advise you to be careful. You remind me of my brother who moved to Sweden ten years ago, and my late husband, may he rest in peace.'

'So what should I do?' asked Mahmoud. 'Why should I be careful?'

She turned towards the door, then looked back at Mahmoud. She gave a long sigh and said, 'We can't talk here.'

He thought she was suggesting they leave the magazine offices and go somewhere else to talk, but for some reason he begged off, saying he was busy and promising to call her to set a time to meet and talk.

In fact, he was suspicious and wanted time to digest what she had said. He escorted her to the front door, and was dazzled by the colour of her brand-new Suzuki. She didn't seem to be a beggar or a prostitute; she was a respectable woman. Perhaps Mahmoud had made a mistake and should have gone with her wherever she wanted. Hadn't he dreamed of seeing her? Hadn't he imagined her face and her figure in his elaborate sexual fantasies? He had even chosen a woman to sleep with because she looked like Nawal.

Before she drove off, Mahmoud stood in her car's path like an idiot. It could have hit him. She came to a sudden halt, and Mahmoud raised his hand to signal that she should wait for him. He hurried back into the office, grabbed his leather bag, had a word with Abu Jouni, and then ran out. He opened the car door and sat next to her. As she drove off, he felt a stiffening in his crotch but tried to look composed. He was content just to be next to her, as if the dream that was so depressing to wake up from had started to come true.

Before they emerged onto the main street, they came across Sultan in his four-wheel drive, trying to turn into the lane. Nawal made way for him, and as he drove past, he tried to make out the faces behind the windshield. Noticing Mahmoud, he didn't approve, acknowledging them with just two quick honks of his car horn, the same way truck drivers greet each other.

4

Nawal said Saidi was evil, the evillest man she had ever known. She had met him through friends and had read a book of his that was published in London called *The Conditions for Democracy in Rentier States*. He had convinced her that he could finance her first full-length film by introducing her to organizations with links to the American Embassy in Baghdad that were willing to subsidize films from the Islamic world produced by women. They had agreed on the concept, and then he had written the screenplay. He told her it would be about the evil we all have inside us, how it resides deep within us, even when we want to put an end to it in the outside world, because we are all criminals to some extent, and the darkness inside us is the blackest variety known to man.

He said we have all been helping to create the evil creature that is now killing us off.

Nawal said that Saidi had tried to be intimate with her several times. He wanted from her what most men want. When she came to a dead end with him, she suspended the project and kept out of sight until today, when she came to retrieve her things from Saidi's desk before he came back. When she had a good look at Mahmoud, she felt there might be some hope for the film after all, that it could be made with help from a competent, ambitious young man such as him.

'I've read what you've written for the magazine. Amazing. You're going to be a great writer, Mahmoud.' Mahmoud's eyes sparkled with pride, as if he were receiving the prophecy of a trusted fortune-teller. But he wanted more from Nawal. He had learned some effective tricks from Saidi. The accusation his friends made, that he had become just like Saidi, didn't bother him at all. But in order to make the likeness complete, Mahmoud had to pass one more test. He had to have Nawal al-Wazir in the same way Saidi had had her. Or perhaps Saidi hadn't really had her, as she insisted, in which case Mahmoud would outdo Saidi, would leave him in the dust.

'I agree,' he said. 'I'll finish off the screenplay for you, but just for you.'

She smiled, as if he had paid her a compliment, then she took a sip of juice and looked out at the afternoon sky from the sixth-floor cafeteria of an expensive hotel on Arasat Street. Mahmoud had no idea how he had plucked up his courage, but he reached out and put his hand on hers. Maybe he thought he was still in the dream he'd had the night before, but whatever the case, he no longer felt so inhibited and thought it unlikely she would react violently.

His intuition was sound: Nawal didn't react. She continued looking out at the light coming in through the big window and sipped her mango juice quietly, then turned to him and said, 'You seem unwell, Mahmoud. Let's just talk about the screenplay, please.'

Mahmoud didn't remove his hand. He squeezed hers a little, and she felt compelled to pull her hand back slowly.

'What's up, Mahmoud? I've been talking to you for an hour about Saidi and his games. You don't seem to have understood.'

'No, I understand. I'm sorry. But I think about you.'

'Why do you think about me? You've got young women at the magazine. Women your own age. Think about them.'

Something didn't make sense to Mahmoud. Why couldn't Nawal have said all of this at the magazine? What would have happened if the staff had heard her speaking badly of Saidi? Mahmoud sometimes heard his colleagues at the magazine making fun of Saidi and his exaggerated fashion sense. And then the idea of writing the screenplay didn't seem like such a good idea. Nawal hadn't spoken about film till now, and she sounded like a businesswoman or the bored wife of a businessman, not a film director. She looked like she spent more time sitting in front of the mirror than behind a camera.

She was looking for a man to sleep with, thought Mahmoud, and when Saidi stayed away so long, she cast her net wider. She wanted a taste of this dark young man. That's what Mahmoud told himself as he leaned back in his chair, keeping a polite distance between himself and Nawal.

5

Mahmoud had been sitting in a bar in the Zawya district for longer than he could remember. The sky outside had darkened, and he had drunk himself into a state of confusion as he went over in his mind how miserably his meeting with Nawal had ended. They had agreed to meet again so he could give her a preliminary summary of the screenplay, then they left the restaurant and got into the elevator to go downstairs. As soon as the door closed and they were alone, Mahmoud turned to Nawal, put his arms around her, and kissed her on her red lips. She submitted to him as he pressed his lips against hers and held her soft body tight in his arms. He had waited so long for this. When the elevator had reached the ground floor, Nawal pushed Mahmoud away with her hands and exited as soon as the door opened. Mahmoud tried to keep up with her. At the door of her car she said, 'That wasn't a nice thing to do. If I loved you, I would be more than generous. Try to respect me.'

He wanted to apologize, but she shut the door in his face and drove off.

He mulled over her parting words in his drunken head, trying to get to the bottom of what she meant. Why hadn't she rebuffed him more forcefully? She had lit a fire in him, then abandoned him.

When he left the bar, he found it hard to walk steadily. He realized the curfew would start in less than an hour. Who would drive him to Bataween at this time of night?

Seeing few cars on the main street, he resorted to the emergency option before long and called Sultan.

After a nerve-racking half hour, Sultan's car pulled up. When Mahmoud got in, he realized that Sultan, too, was drunk. He showered him with apologies for having called so late but was more relieved than he would have imagined to have grim-faced Sultan beside him.

Out of the blue, Sultan started speaking in a tone Mahmoud hadn't heard from him before – like a big brother, not like a driver to his boss.

'If you don't mind me saying, sir, I saw you today with that

Nawal.' Before Mahmoud could respond, Sultan continued. 'Forgive me if I'm intruding, but I have this opportunity to talk to you now and might not have it tomorrow or any other day.'

'Why not?'

'I'm going away tomorrow.'

'Going away?'

'Yes. But I wanted to tell you, sir. You see, that woman Nawal is not cool. I hope you don't believe anything she says. She was Mr Ali's girlfriend. He used to have fun with her. I mean, she stuck to him like flypaper, and then she wanted to marry him, and Mr Ali doesn't have time for stuff like that. I mean, you know . . .'

'Yes.'

'Anyway, it's because of her that they brought this case against him. She started running after Mr Ali, and then she started threatening him if he didn't marry her. She's a rude, loose woman, and she has connections in the Green Zone and relatives in parliament who caused trouble for the boss. You thought he'd gone to Beirut for a conference? No, he's avoiding that whore Nawal.'

'Okay, and when's he coming back? You mean there's a possibility he won't come back at all?'

'No, he'll come back. He's mobilizing his friends to block the case, but they advised him to leave Baghdad for a while.'

'Okay, and why are you going away tomorrow?'

'I have to take the boss's sisters and mother to Amman. His mother's very ill and needs treatment, and Mr Ali's now waiting for us in Amman.'

Mahmoud got out in front of the Dilshad Hotel and thanked Sultan profusely. Before going into the hotel, he took out his phone and dialled Saidi's number in Beirut. He got an automatic message saying the number he had dialled was out of service.

CHAPTER SIXTEEN

Daniel

1

At dawn the next day, Sultan was driving Saidi's mother and his two unmarried sisters from Baghdad to Amman. But the car never reached Amman. Other drivers on the same route said armed gangs were hijacking cars and, depending on the passengers' religion, massacring some in the nearby orchards. Saidi tried to call Sultan several times, but no one answered.

A day earlier someone else had left Baghdad, in this case with no plans to come back. This was Abu Anmar, the owner of the Orouba Hotel. He turned the ignition key of the new GMC truck he had bought with the money from his deal with Faraj, then adjusted his headdress and headband and looked at his face in the rear-view mirror: he felt he was on top of the world. He had transferred the rest of the money to his nephews in his hometown, Qalat Sukkar, in the south, where he was now headed, having washed his hands of Baghdad, a city he no longer recognized. After twenty-three years, the city had abandoned him, becoming a place of murder and gratuitous violence.

Ten minutes after Abu Anmar had left, Faraj removed the Orouba Hotel sign. He threw it on the ground and trod on it, then called on one of his young workers to take it to the sign writer and have him remove the name Orouba, or 'Arabness', and rewrite it with the name Grand Prophet Hotel. He was confident he would succeed where Abu Anmar had failed.

It was a good season for business, as far as Faraj was concerned. He had made two major deals within the month and felt he was closing in on others. The dire state of the country offered opportunities only to the bold and adventurous, and Faraj was not short of a sense of adventure. Gangs were on the rampage in the streets of Baghdad, and people were abandoning their homes or shops for fear of being kidnapped or killed. Faraj was seizing these opportunities. Overnight he had become a major landlord with a growing staff. Some people accused him of leading a criminal gang, but except for some slaps and kicks that he dispensed liberally to those who had the misfortune of standing in his way, he hadn't killed or robbed anyone, not openly at least.

Four young men who worked with Faraj went to the hotel, opened the door wide, and set about finishing what Abu Anmar had started – clearing the hotel of all its old contents.

With a china bowl in one hand and his black prayer beads in the other, Faraj watched his workers with a sense of satisfaction. He was about to go to the bakery to buy some bread and clotted cream for his family's breakfast when a massive explosion deafened his ears and the china bowl slipped out of his hand. It was the largest explosion that had ever taken place in Bataween.

2

Faraj didn't die in that explosion. It wasn't his time yet. He had more to learn. For one thing, he had come to accept that Elishva really did have secret powers.

A week before the explosion Faraj had made another successful deal. With Elishva. She had finally given in and accepted his offer to buy her old house – because Daniel had finally come back. It was the twenty-ninth anniversary of the installation of His Holiness Mar Dinkha IV as patriarch of the Assyrian Church of the East. Elishva had gone to celebrate the occasion in the Church of Saint Qardagh in the Camp al-Gilani district. She felt spiritually fulfilled and was proud of herself for crossing Tayaran Square, going through the pop-up fruit and vegetable market and the busy car park at the end of Sheikh Omar Street, and then walking back the same way without feeling any fatigue or any of the usual pain in her legs. She was thinking of spraying the courtyard with water and sweeping it now that she had some energy. Then she heard a light knocking on the front door.

The residents of Lane 7, especially Umm Salim, her taciturn husband and her children, and some inquisitive young men who lived nearby, had been watching Elishva in recent months, trying to catch sight of her son. Elishva had been chatting about his return and about what the two of them had been up to, but no one had seen anything conclusive. They ended up saying that thieves who knew Elishva was senile were taking advantage of her to make off with some of her valuable possessions. But then the old woman's son really did appear. He had black hair parted down the middle and long on the sides, as in the traditional images of Christ. He had a pale white complexion and was slim, with the body of a twenty-year-old. He wore a white shirt with a high collar, torn jeans, white sports shoes, and a red leather bag of the kind that young conscripts had in the early 1980s. He looked sad and romantic, like a dejected lover. He walked with slow, hesitant steps, looking around as he went, like a stranger or someone who had left long ago and had just returned. He seemed to be looking for traces of distant memories of the place he came from. Behind him came the old deacon, Nader Shamouni, dawdling to give the stranger a chance to see the place and relate to it without interference.

So had the old woman really been telling the truth? Had her son really survived the slaughter of the 1980s? Over the last three years the local people had heard many stories that were no more believable. Dead people had emerged from the dungeons of the security services and non-existent people appeared out of nowhere outside the doors of their relatives' humble houses. There were people who had returned from long journeys with new names and new identities, women who had spent their childhoods in prison cells and had learned, before anything else in life, the rules and conventions for dealing with the warders. There were people who had survived many deaths in the time of the dictatorship only to find themselves face-to-face with a pointless death in the age of 'democracy' – when, for example, a motorbike ran into them in the middle of the road. Believers lost their faith when those who had shared their beliefs and their struggles betrayed them and their principles. Non-believers had become believers when they saw the 'merits' and benefits of faith. The strange things that had come to light in the past three years were too many to count. So that Daniel Tadros Moshe, the lanky guitarist, had come back to his old mother's house wasn't so hard to believe.

When the two men arrived at the old wooden door of Elishva's house, the thin young man knocked, looking around between each rap on the door, aware that inquisitive strangers might be watching him closely. The door opened, and Elishva appeared – tiny, with a black scarf on her head and thick glasses on her nose. She looked up, then inched forward with laboured steps until she stood in the lane in front of the young stranger, examining him in the full light of day. It was definitely him – the very same young man with the slight grey smile that was in the old picture in her sitting room. He had the same look, the same clothes and face, the same smile that spread across his face when his dark eyes met the old lady's. So Saint George the Martyr had carried out his promise after all, bringing Elishva's son back to her just as he looked that morning when he left the house reluctantly and in sadness, his heavy boots pounding the pavement till he disappeared from sight at the turn onto the main street.

Elishva looked around her and saw Umm Salim standing at the door of her house. She saw other onlookers – women and children and young men at the other end of the lane, towards Bataween's main street, and in the upper windows of the *mashrabiya* balconies. She wanted to be sure that everyone was a witness to her miracle. Here was her beloved son, come back to embrace her.

He leaned down tentatively, and she wrapped her arms around him, pulling her son towards her with a strength she did not possess.

'This is Daniel, Elishva,' said Nader Shamouni, though this was as clear as daylight to the old woman. She held him in her arms for two minutes or more. Then she noticed that Umm Salim and some of the other neighbours had come forward, surrounding her in growing numbers. Umm Salim actually touched Daniel's arm to make sure he was not a phantom. Daniel slipped out of the old woman's arms, looked into her face with a smile, and addressed her. He had to make sure she was still in her right mind and knew what was happening around her.

'How are you?' he asked in Assyrian, giving an even broader

smile. She scanned his face and ran her veiny hands down his arms, then pulled him gently into the house, saying, 'I'm fine. I'm fine.'

Inside the house, in the sitting room, Nader Shamouni spoke firmly, trying to put an end to the old woman's fantasies. He told her he didn't have much time, that he had to go back to his family in Ankawa, that Father Josiah was awaiting his answer, so she had to make up her mind. Her daughters, Matilda and Hilda, were now in Ankawa, having come from Australia with some of their children for one purpose – to take the old lady back to Australia with them.

'This is Daniel, your grandson, Elishva,' said the deacon. 'Hilda's eldest son. She used to send you pictures of him in the mail. Don't you recognize him?'

Phone calls between Matilda and Father Josiah had helped to pinpoint the strategy: that there was a strong similarity between Daniel her grandson and Daniel her dead son, strong enough to confuse the old woman. Matilda, Hilda and her son Daniel had flown to Iraq and stayed in Nader Shamouni's house in Ankawa. The next day the deacon and Daniel had gone to Baghdad. The young man, who spoke Assyrian and English but wasn't fluent in Arabic, was nervous about the mission. He was motivated by a sense of family duty rather than by any personal nostalgia or strong feeling towards his grandmother, of whom he remembered little since he had left with his family at a very young age.

The whole plan depended on one element: the old woman being moved by the sight of her grandson and going along with his suggestions. Daniel told his grandmother she had to come with him. She had to sell the house and get rid of all her stuff. She had to live with him. He said the last sentence in a sincere tone. As he talked to her, he felt the influence of the place slowly seep into him. A mysterious sadness came over him when he looked up at the grey pictures hanging on the walls. He felt he recognized the house and had faint memories of the times he and his mother used to come and visit his grandmother and grandfather more than a decade earlier.

Nader left them to go over these memories together and went off to the Garage al-Amana district to run some errands. Elishva and her grandson chatted till night. The more they talked, the more Daniel had the impression that he and this frail old woman really did have shared memories, and the more the grandmother was convinced of the illusion that her grandson and her departed son were one and the same person. When Elishva stood in the kitchen, to make dinner by the light of the oil lamp, and caught sight of her pale, wrinkled face in the windowpane, she knew she had travelled far in time and no longer had a son in his twenties who was frightened of going to war. But she was exposed to feelings she hadn't experienced for a long time – smelling and touching her son's arms and stroking his hair and having him put his head on her lap. These were valuable things that mattered in her life, not just fantasies in her head, and she was willing to do anything to preserve them.

She washed a large china basin, although it was already clean, and put it in an aluminum tray to receive the tomato omelette from the frying pan. She saw her cat, Nabu, come into the small kitchen, drawn by the smell of food, and at that moment she decided to accept the request of the son who was her grandson. She would do anything to make sure she could continue to caress his skin and his hair and smell his childlike smell, which she had never forgotten.

3

Daniel turned on his mobile phone and called his mother in Ankawa. He told her in clear English, 'Now's the time to act, not to tell the truth. Speak to the old lady, but humour her. Agree with everything she says.'

He gave the phone to the old lady, and the women chatted amiably for a quarter of an hour. Elishva was happy and was seeing the world with new eyes. She made Daniel kneel in front of the picture of Saint George and offer him thanks because he had fulfilled his promise to her. As she folded her hands in silence in front of the picture, she waited for the saint to say a few words to convince her son that a miracle really had taken place, but the saint held his tongue.

The light from the oil lamp faded. Elishva tried to stand up to fill it with oil. Daniel went to help her but discovered that the barrel was empty. The oil had run out without the old lady noticing. Elishva took this as another sign that her time in Baghdad was running out.

Selling the house and the old furniture wasn't easy. Elishva was thinking of those young men who had visited her several times and asked to buy the house to save it from demolition and convert it into a cultural centre or something, but they had stopped coming ages ago. So there was only Faraj, the real estate man.

Faraj was aware of the strange news that Elishva's son had reappeared. Maybe the son had been a prisoner of war in Iran and had just come back. Maybe he had lost his memory, as in those foreign films. But the guys who worked with him assured him that the old woman's son was still young, whereas he should have been in his forties by now.

'Perhaps they put him in a freezer for twenty years, and now they've thawed him out and brought him back to his mother,' said Hammoudy, Faraj's youngest son. His father gave him an unexpected slap on his cheek, which silenced everyone.

As usual, Faraj was inclined to anticipate the worst and prepared himself psychologically to face it. Then, twenty-four hours after Daniel had arrived, the young man turned up in Faraj's office with Nader Shamouni, offering to sell him Elishva's house.

4

Faraj asked to come to the house to examine the structure before agreeing on a final price. In the meantime Elishva had summoned Hadi from next door and told him she wanted to sell all the furniture. Hadi was stunned into silence for about thirty seconds. He waited for the old lady to finish what she was saying, but she had summed everything up in one sentence. He had been certain that this Assyrian woman hated him deeply, so what had suddenly changed?

He inspected the contents of the house with her. There was plenty of furniture and furnishings – beds made of iron and brass, ornate knickknacks and unusual wooden tables. Everything was antique, except for the stove and some of the appliances. Doing some quick calculations, Hadi worked out that he didn't have enough cash to buy all these things, but he could borrow from some friends because this was a unique opportunity.

Hadi wanted the old lady to give him a price for taking everything in one lot, whereas she wanted to haggle over every single item. After an hour of discussion, he managed to persuade her to accept his offer, and then he left the house to collect the money he needed from his friends.

The old woman's only condition was that he wasn't

to remove the furniture while she was there. She didn't want to see her house disappear before her eyes but wanted to remember it as it had always been, tidy and clean and smelling of the people who had lived in it and passed through it.

The night before her departure, the old lady stayed up late in the parlour. She sat on the sofa facing the picture of Saint George and spoke to him at length, the light from the decorative glass sconces in the corners of the room creating a sacramental ambience. The saint said nothing. He had performed his miracle and his role was over – that's how the old woman finally understood it. One thing occurred to her. She had packed up everything that carried the family's memories, even her children's baby clothes. The only thing left was her favourite picture of her favourite saint, but she felt she couldn't take it in its heavy wooden frame.

She got up and, watched by Nabu the cat, stood on the sofa against the wall where the picture was hanging, lifted the picture to free the thick string from the hooks, then took it away, leaving a pale square and some cobwebs on the wall. She put the picture face down on the floor and set about bending the little clips that held the back to the picture frame. When she took out the picture, it was thin and bent easily in her hand. It had lost some of its former grandeur, but now she could see the saint's face up close – his fine eyebrows and glistening red lower lip. She thought of rolling the picture into a tube and adding it to her other treasured possessions, but then she had another idea. She went into her room and fetched some large sewing scissors, then went back and knelt next to the picture. She pushed Nabu away when he tried to jump onto her lap, and started to cut into the picture, making a long straight line across until the tips of the scissor blades were close to the saint's head. Then she cut in a circle, making a kind of halo around his beautiful face. When the circle was complete, she removed the face.

233

This was the part she liked. She threw a glance at the rest of the picture and felt a pang in her heart. With a hole where the face had been, the picture now felt hostile towards her. She left it where it was and, followed by Nabu, took the face to her bedroom.

5

To mark Elishva's departure, Umm Salim staged a major weeping and wailing performance in the lane. She started early in the day, and many of her neighbours saw her white arms for the first time when she raised them in the air in lamentation as Elishva and her grandson drove off down the lane. When she raised them, her wide sleeves fell back, revealing the dazzling whiteness of her fine round arms, a complexion more likely to be seen on a young woman than on one her age. Some wondered aloud why Umm Salim had worn such loose sleeves if she wasn't pleased with herself and how white her arms were.

Before closing the front door, Elishva called after Nabu, but the cat escaped up the stairs. She shouted after him again, and the cat looked towards her and gave an undulating meow, as if to say he wasn't a coward like her and wasn't going to leave the house, then he disappeared at the turn on the stairs. Elishva locked up the house and handed the key to a young man who worked for Faraj.

Umm Salim predicted that disaster would befall the lane because of Elishva's departure. She noticed Hadi the junk dealer and some young men moving furniture from the old lady's house to his house and was reminded of April 2003, when people looted the houses of officials from the old regime. She shouted at Hadi and his helpers, thinking they were robbing the old woman's house, and didn't stop swearing until her friends managed to get her into her house and close the door behind her.

Hadi moved all of Elishva's furniture to his house, leaving behind just some rubbish, including a portrait of Saint George with the face cut out. When Hadi saw the picture, he was frightened, thinking it might be magic or some strange ritual act.

The door to Hadi's house stayed open, with people coming and going to see what there was to buy. By midday Hadi had sold half the stuff to people living in the area and felt he would make a good profit. He looked up at the wall between his house and the old lady's and saw the mangy cat looking down at him in silence, as still as a statue. For a moment he felt the cat was looking at him with the old lady's eyes. He picked up a small piece of brick and threw it at the cat but missed, and the cat didn't budge from its position.

By the end of the day Hadi was quite exhausted. As he fought to keep his eyes open, a lively apparition was making its way along the walls of the houses. It leaped onto the dilapidated wall of Hadi's house and then over to the roof of Elishva's house. It went down the stairs and found Nabu in the inner courtyard. The cat let out a drawn-out howl.

The creature, on the run from the security agencies and wanted by many parties, went down on its knees and examined the remains of the picture of Saint George. He lifted it up and saw the hole where the head was missing, then folded the picture carefully several times until it was about the size of a school exercise book. He looked around at the room and felt pangs of sadness. He would never again see the old lady who had contributed to his birth and given him the name of her missing son. He felt closer to her than to other people and felt that he had helped to keep the memory of her son alive. Now that she was gone, he had lost one of his reasons for existing. She had left him without realizing that she was leaving one of the last threads that linked her with her late son.

The creature sat down and leaned back against the wall. Nabu came by and rubbed up against his boots, leaving some of his shedding hairs, then curled up in a ball at his feet, drawn to him by his warmth.

They stayed like that till morning.

CHAPTER SEVENTEEN

The Explosion

1

At half past five in the morning, while the Whatsitsname was fast asleep with Nabu the cat on the floor of Elishva's old parlour, Brigadier Sorour Majid was having disturbing dreams in his office at the Tracking and Pursuit Department. The senior astrologer strode down the corridors, woke up the guard sleeping outside Brigadier Majid's office, and knocked loudly on the door.

Brigadier Majid woke up with a start. When he saw the senior astrologer standing in front of him, he guessed it was an urgent matter that couldn't be put off till sunrise. The senior astrologer put a pink piece of paper in front of him, and before the brigadier had a chance to read it, the old astrologer said, 'He's here. In this house in Bataween. You have to act immediately, before he wakes up.'

Brigadier Majid summoned the vehicles and got dressed in haste. Finally he would arrest this criminal, silencing his detractors. They might make him interior minister or defence minister or director of intelligence, he said to himself. He climbed into the four-wheel-drive truck with tinted windows.

Two small cars set off with him at high speed through the streets of Baghdad, which was almost deserted at that hour. The old astrologer was in the back seat with Brigadier Majid. He wanted to see the face of this dangerous criminal before it was disfigured by punches and slaps from Brigadier Majid's assistants. He had never before had any trouble conjuring up people's faces, but the features of the One Who Has No Name had always eluded him. That's what made him more mysterious and more dangerous than all the others. He thought about this until they reached Saadoun Street, where there was a major commotion – police cars and American military vehicles lined up against the pavement by the Orfali Mosque and the photography shops, and more police cars at the roundabout near the Liberty Monument. When they reached Tayaran Square, they were sure that Bataween was being sealed off.

'What's going on?' Brigadier Majid shouted. He got out of the vehicle and spoke with some officers, showing them his identity card, but they wouldn't let him through. There was a search under way for a suspected car bomber in a white, late-model Opel, which was parked close to Elishva's house.

The senior astrologer didn't get out of the four-wheel drive. His appearance would arouse suspicion – his strange clothes, his tall conical hat with a tassel, his long hair, his thick beard carefully combed, its pointed ends held together by a hair clip. In the best of times they would have laughed at him or thought he was an actor in a children's theatre. He looked out from the car's open window.

The suicide bomber was sitting in the lane in the white Opel, completely surrounded. That's what Abu Salim could see from his window in the wooden *mashrabiya* balcony. He should go downstairs to warn the rest of the family to get out of the house, or at least move into one of the back rooms. The house was bound to collapse if the suicide bomber blew himself up.

But Abu Salim didn't do anything. He had woken up from his doze to the sound of megaphones ordering the suicide bomber to get out of the car with his hands up. He had gone up one floor, looked out the window, and was surprised to see the car right under his balcony, but he still saw no need to act. He didn't even notice he was barefoot.

In the meantime Abu Anmar had managed to leave the area in his new truck before they imposed the security cordon. Faraj the real estate agent had come out of his house and stood looking across the street at the hotel he had just bought. He was planning to go to the bakery just down the lane, to buy bread and a bowl of clotted cream, when the bomb went off.

2

Hadi saw the dark wooden panel of the Jewish carving fly through the air and the wooden candelabra break loose from it and shatter. Or maybe he imagined it during his long hospital stay.

Everything in his house was thrown into chaos in the fraction of a second it took for the full force of the explosion to strike. Not only was the driver wearing a suicide belt but the car itself was also rigged with explosives. The explosion rocked the whole neighbourhood – cracks would later be found in the Liberty Monument – but the most serious impact was on the old houses in Lane 7, some of which had been built in the 1930s.

Elishva's house collapsed. So did Hadi's. Elishva's things and some other wooden furniture caught fire in Hadi's courtyard, and the fire spread to Hadi's bed. The fact that Hadi had survived was seen as a miracle, reminding everyone of the lies he had been telling for years about how he had survived falling down mountains and flying through the air after explosions. He had indeed defied death this time.

The blast threw Faraj many feet in the air, resulting in a serious injury and some bruising on his face. The facade of Umm Salim's house was destroyed, while the walls inside were cracked. Fortunately, most of the family was asleep inside and survived. As for Abu Salim, he crashed to the ground with his balcony, suffering leg and arm fractures and wounds and scratches, but he didn't die. He was taken to the nearby Kindi Hospital, where he raved at the journalists who came to take pictures of the injured and to listen to their accounts of the incident. He was like a broken record, going on and on about everything he had seen from his balcony over the years – the people coming and going at the six houses within his view, the whores who went in and out of the printing press next to Elishva's house, the thieves who climbed over the walls. A week later he had a special visitor: a well-dressed man in his forties, with a digital recorder, who sat on the chair nearby, greeted him in a friendly manner, and asked him to speak. Abu Salim asked him who he was, and he said, 'I'm the writer.'

'Writer of what?'

'I write short stories.'

'What would you like me to tell you?'

'Tell me everything.'

3

The senior astrologer saw from behind the partially open window of the four-wheel drive how Brigadier Majid got past the guards who had closed off Lane 7. This made him anxious. He opened the door and got out, his long, thick beard swinging from side to side as he hurried along. When he reached the guards, he called out to the brigadier.

'What are you doing, sir? Do you want to die?'

'I have to arrest this criminal myself,' said the brigadier.

'You'll be killed, sir. Come back – I implore you. Come on. Let me read the cards.'

The brigadier saw the senior astrologer crouch on the ground and then sit cross-legged, as he did in the offices of the Tracking and Pursuit Department. He took a large pack of playing cards from his pocket and started shuffling them like a professional. Then he threw them on the pavement, set some of them aside, and removed others. He picked up one card and looked at it closely, as if he had discovered something. The brigadier crouched down next to him. The guards standing at the end of the street didn't know what was going on but were intrigued and took their eyes off the suicide bomber's car for a few moments.

The astrologer pulled out a new card, looked at it intently, and said, 'The One Who Has No Name is not in the house.'

'What do you mean? So why did you bring us here? Where is he?'

'He was here until a quarter of an hour ago. He went over the roofs. I don't know exactly where he went. Maybe he hasn't left Bataween yet. But he has left the house – that's for sure.'

'But I want to be certain,' said the brigadier. He stood up and turned towards the lane and the white Opel.

'It will cost you your life,' said the old astrologer, quickly gathering his cards and putting them back in the pocket of his long gown.

'There's something else,' said the astrologer, expecting Brigadier Majid to turn towards him. 'This car bomb – in a way we're responsible for it.'

241

The brigadier turned round at that and walked up to the old astrologer. 'How so?' he asked.

'We have to go back to the department immediately. It's one of my assistants – the junior astrologer. He moved the car to this place with the intention of killing the Criminal Who Has No Name, but now the criminal has escaped, and the suicide bomber doesn't know why he was sent here.'

'What do you mean? What kind of nonsense is that?'

'We must go back now,' the astrologer insisted, walking back towards the four-wheel drive. Then the car bomb exploded.

Brigadier Majid and the astrologer were engulfed in a thick cloud of dust. They jumped into the car and went back to the office, where the brigadier summoned his whole team and opened an inquiry into the incident. He discovered that the suicide bomber had originally intended to go to the police academy and blow himself up in the middle of a gathering of new officers, but something made him drive to the backstreets of Bataween instead. The astrologers broke out into an uproar, ignoring the brigadier as they exchanged insults. Within an hour the brigadier realized the inquiry he had opened wouldn't do any good – it might even put him and his department in the firing line from other branches of the government – so he closed it down and temporarily suspended the activities of the astrologers.

Two weeks later a committee of senior officers in military and general intelligence came to question him in the presence of an American liaison officer. While he had been dreaming of being promoted to director of intelligence, he now found himself facing the possibility of early retirement.

4

Mahmoud was asleep in his room when a powerful tremor in the distance shook the hotel. He opened his eyes for a few seconds, then went back to sleep. Around half past eight he heard about the horrific incident from a young man who worked at the hotel.

'There's now water from damaged sewage and drinking-water pipes spilling into Saadoun Street and the Bab al-Sharqi tunnel. They say dozens of houses have been flattened. There's a crater in the middle of Lane 7, a huge crater, and some people say they saw a stone wall at the bottom of it.'

Mahmoud thought of the Orouba Hotel, which was near the site of the explosion. Maybe something had happened to his photographer friend, Hazem Abboud, or to Abu Anmar and others he knew in the area. He called Hazem, who told him he was not in Baghdad but was embedded with the US Army, taking pictures of combat operations for an American news agency. He said Abu Anmar had left Baghdad, having sold the hotel and gone back to his family in Qalat Sukkar.

This came as a surprise to Mahmoud, but it was a relief that no one he knew had died, he told himself, and went out into the street and hailed a taxi to the office.

On the short trip he ran through the situation at the maga-zine. The deadline for the next edition was fast approaching. He hadn't paid the salaries of some of the staff. Saidi hadn't sent him anything. The accountant with the grim face hadn't answered Mahmoud's calls in two days. Saidi had to come back to relieve him of this anxiety. When he saw him, he would tell him he wanted to go back to his old job as just a sub-editor.

When he reached the offices, he saw some government vehicles parked in the lane. Maybe they were checking the National Bank of Iraq nearby. But when he went through the front door, which was wide open, he was sure they had come to see him. Armed guards in plain clothes stopped him and asked for his identity card. When they found out he was the editor of the magazine, they let him in. The old caretaker looked at him in bafflement but didn't say anything, just continued to wipe the tables and move around as though it were an ordinary day. Everyone seemed to have fled the magazine, or else they knew something he didn't know and preferred not to be involved.

When Mahmoud went into Saidi's office, he saw four men with moustaches, dressed in suits. They were about the same age as Saidi. When he introduced himself, they asked him to sit, then told him they were shutting down the magazine and confiscating all its assets.

'What's happened?' he asked.

Mahmoud felt his stomach starting to twist. One of the men looked at him intently, raised a finger in his face, and said, 'Your friend has stolen thirteen million dollars of US aid money.'

'Thirteen million dollars?! How did he steal it? He's a well-known writer, a well-known person.'

'Ask *him* how. And now give us the keys to this safe.'

Mahmoud gave them the key, and the strange men acted fast, confiscating everything – but Saidi never left any money at the magazine. They had turned the offices upside down, moving the furniture around and even pulling up the carpet in the conference room, looking for places where Saidi might have hidden his stolen money.

'How could Saidi do this? Has he really done this to me?' Mahmoud asked himself. It all seemed like a big misunderstanding, and that these men would apologize, give him back the keys, and ask him to forgive them.

The man with the biggest moustache, who seemed to be in charge of the group, came up to Mahmoud.

'Call your boss, and if he answers, give me the phone.'

Mahmoud hurriedly called Saidi, though he was well aware that there would be no answer. He called him again from another phone, but the result was the same.

'The number is out of service,' Mahmoud said apologetically. The man with the thick moustache looked at him in disbelief.

Everything was over in forty-five minutes. Abu Jouni put his wet mop over his shoulder and just left the building, not even looking at Mahmoud as he walked past. Mahmoud didn't know what he was going to do. He had been waiting for his back salary to pay off his debts to the hotel. He called the accountant on his mobile phone and then his friends and colleagues at the magazine. Some numbers just kept ringing; some people answered to say they were sorry but couldn't do anything. In the end the man with the thick moustache turned to Mahmoud, patted him on the shoulder, and said, 'Let's go, my friend. You're coming with us for questioning.'

'Questioning?'

'Yes, did you think it would be easy?'

Mahmoud got into one of their vehicles. He knew, from the way Saidi joked with his friend Brigadier Majid, that being questioned by the Iraqi security agencies would be 'physically painful', as Saidi described it. He was in shock. Everything had collapsed. He had lost his sense of self, and in order to save himself he decided he wouldn't hide anything, because he was innocent. Thirteen million dollars! He struggled to take it all in, as the government vehicle tore off down the road towards an unknown destination.

5

The interrogation of Brigadier Majid seemed endless. The panel, composed of Iraqi intelligence officers and liaison officers from the US military police, decided to wait for more material evidence before making a formal accusation against the brigadier and his office. In the meantime, through his friends who were senior officers, the brigadier managed to postpone his interrogation and defer further humiliation for a while.

He called in the senior astrologer, the junior astrologer, and the other lower-level astrologers for a quick meeting. He had discovered that a secret struggle had been under way for some time among his staff and was now rebounding on him personally, threatening to get him fired and maybe put on trial.

'You're all fired,' he told them, and waited for their expressions of disbelief. But instead they stood up and didn't say a word. 'Why don't you say something?' he shouted at the senior astrologer.

'I already knew,' he replied. 'It's all because of my stupid assistant. He's my enemy, and he's destroyed me. This has nothing to do with you, sir. It's not your fault.'

Brigadier Majid was puzzled. Of course they had consulted their cards and mirrors and prayer beads made of beans before coming to the meeting, so they knew about his decision. But he had expected them to fight back or ask for forgiveness or say they would try to help him fix the situation, not just to abandon him. He didn't have it in him to go back on his decision – they would see him as weak. The department had collapsed from within, and now he was all on his own.

The senior astrologer went back to his room. He calmly packed his bag, then went into the bathroom and rubbed his beard with soap and water to get rid of the hair gel. He took out a small pair of scissors, cut off half his beard, and trimmed it to suit the appearance of a religious man. That was to be his new image.

He took off his flamboyant clothes and threw them into a large rubbish bin in the bathroom, then put on a white cotton shirt with thin vertical blue stripes, dark cotton trousers and summer shoes. He picked up his bag and was about to leave the department for his home in the Zaafaraniya district, south of the capital, when he noticed fine grains of red sand on the floor, on his bed, and everywhere. He noticed the junior astrologer coming in, and he thought, What gall. He wanted to shout in his face, 'You've destroyed everything, you idiot,' and maybe for a moment he thought of pouncing on him and strangling him with his ageing hands, but that was no use now. He could keep an eye on him and do things to him by his own methods, even kill him on the spot, although he had never done that with anyone else.

The junior astrologer was also changing his clothes, but he was putting on pyjamas. He looked at his master, in his new guise, with a certain disdain, as if he wanted to remember this moment well – the moment when the senior astrologer fell off his perch and became just an ordinary person.

They didn't exchange a word, only glances, and then the senior astrologer left the department, angry and bitter, throwing his small bag over his shoulder.

Getting into a taxi, the senior astrologer told the old driver the address, and they agreed on a price. The astrologer tossed his bag into the back seat and stretched out in the front. He looked like a cleric disguised in civilian clothes. A few minutes later he noticed they were driving down a street with no other cars and no pedestrians. The taxi slowed down, and the driver cleared his throat and said, 'I think I'm lost.'

The driver turned back the way he had come, but then

discovered that the Americans had blocked the road. One of the soldiers was pointing a powerful flashlight at drivers and asking them to go down a side street. At the end of the street the driver found he didn't know which direction to take. He pulled up against the kerb and said, 'Forgive me, brother. My house is behind these buildings. Don't worry about the fare, just get out here, please, and find yourself another taxi. This street is safe.'

The astrologer protested, but the driver refused to relent. Once the astrologer got out, the driver drove off in haste, leaving the astrologer waiting, with his bag, in the street for another taxi.

After two minutes, the astrologer decided to head to a street with more traffic. He proceeded down a side street, then realized it was long and unlit. He knew, or thought he knew, what was going to happen that night, so he didn't see any reason to be frightened. Feeling exhausted, he remembered he hadn't had lunch, and now it was past dinnertime. And apart from all that, he was a frail old man – even his small bag seemed heavy. He continued down the dark side street, and through his round glasses he could see the vague shape of a man standing in the middle of the street.

The astrologer's throat was dry, so he swallowed some saliva, then stopped two yards from the man in the street. Should he speak to him? Why not walk past and keep walking till the end of the street? He wasn't so naive as to do that. He knew, or had an inkling, that the meeting he had long awaited was about to come about, and he didn't want to show any sign of fear or weakness. He was too old for that, and his dignity wouldn't allow him to beg for mercy from his executioner.

'This is the long wall of two girls' schools – a primary school and a secondary school,' said the stranger, whose face was shrouded in darkness. 'And these are shops and car repair garages with offices on top that they lock up an hour before sunset. There's no one else on this street right now. A car might come by, or maybe one won't.'

'Do you think I'm frightened or that I want to call for help?' said the old astrologer, lowering his bag softly onto the surface of the road. He might need both hands while talking to the apparition of the dangerous criminal he had waited to see for so long. That was why he had gone to Lane 7 in Bataween. He didn't know how long the conversation would last, but he wanted to see the man's face before the final moment came. Why had he failed to work out what he looked like, and why was the man now standing in such a position that the distant streetlights did not light up his face?

'You should know, before you do anything, that this was all planned by my disciple. He failed to kill you that day with the car bomb, and now he's using you to kill me. It's a battle between me and him, and he's using you against me,' said the astrologer.

'Are you saying you saved me that morning?'

'No. I won't lie to you. I wanted to arrest you – so I could at least see your face. I want to know what you look like.'

'And I want the playing cards you were using to search for me. And I want those hands of yours as well.'

'I threw the cards in with the rubbish. I'm not looking for you any longer. I've retired.'

'Yes, the cards don't matter. What's important are the hands that dealt them.'

'I'd like to see your face, if I may.'

'What's the point of that? It changes. I don't have a permanent face.'

'Let me see.'

'Yes,' said the Criminal Who Has No Name, turning on the astrologer and grabbing hold of his hands. He squeezed them tight, and the astrologer felt his strength ebbing away.

He fell to his knees, and the criminal kept pushing him down and squeezing his hands.

'This isn't your battle. You don't understand. This isn't your battle,' the astrologer said, his voice shaky. Then, as he stared straight at the criminal's dark face, the headlights of a distant car lit it up for him. By the light of the car he finally saw it. Even he, with his cards and magic tricks, hadn't believed he would get to see it. Some voice from his past told him that everything he had lived through was nonsense and lies, and that he was so immersed in these lies that he had come to believe them.

This face he had just seen for the first and last time was also from his past. He recognized it, but whose was it?

During his slow death throes on the desolate street, he would be wholly convinced that it was a composite face, made up of faces from his distant past. It was the face of his own personal past, which he had thought had no face or features. And now it had appeared to him clearly, caught for a moment in the headlights of a passing car.

The driver of the car had seen something suspicious half-way down the street and changed his mind about turning onto it. What he failed to see from a distance was someone taking an axe to the arms of a man laid out on the asphalt.

CHAPTER EIGHTEEN

The Writer

1

I met Mahmoud Riyadh al-Sawadi in the Baghdadi Café. The place was crowded with intellectuals, writers, actors, directors and artists. The long metal benches outside, on the pavement, couldn't fit everyone, especially after sunset, when the scorching summer heat relented.

I was sipping my tea, when I saw him selling his Rolex and his laptop. He looked as if he hadn't showered or changed his clothes in days.

From his pocket he took a small gadget attached to a long silver cord that you could hang around your neck. I figured out that it was a digital recorder. He was talking to his friends about the device, and some of them started laughing. One of his friends pointed to the metal chairs near the table where I was sitting. He came over, and our eyes met.

He said it was a Panasonic digital recorder and that he wanted four hundred dollars for it – one hundred for the recorder itself and three hundred for the story that was recorded on it. It was the strangest story that had ever come his way, he said, and a writer like me could use it to write a great novel.

Even before he spoke I had made up my mind to buy the recorder, not because I needed it, but as a kind of charity. I was even more resolved when I heard he had large debts and needed to pay them off before going back to his family in Maysan Province. But I didn't expect to buy a story or pay four hundred dollars. I couldn't pay such an amount on short notice.

I was curious about him. He wasn't disturbed, someone with psychological problems, or a swindler. He was intelligent and well spoken. But he was in a difficult position. I felt he deserved help, so I said, 'I'll pay three hundred dollars. That's all I can afford. Two hundred dollars now, and the third hundred I'll have to borrow from the owner of the hotel where I'm staying.'

'But I want it now. I want four hundred dollars or else I won't be able to pay the layout woman.'

'The what woman?'

'The woman who does the layouts at the magazine. She's still trying to collect her salary.'

He spoke at length about what had happened at the magazine. The staff had found out he was living at the Dilshad Hotel, and they had made a scene at reception, demanding their salaries.

I paid for the tea and walked with him to a nearby restaurant. I ordered takeaway, and we went to the Fanar Hotel on Abu Nuwas Street, where I was staying. Together we drank two glasses of the whisky I keep in my room and ate our dinner.

'Why don't you just skip town?' I asked him. 'Aren't you going back to Maysan? Just go. You're not responsible for the problem.'

'I can't,' he said. 'I feel sorry for them, and I earned masses of money at the magazine. In salary and allowances, I mean. I feel responsible. I don't want them to speak badly of me and put me in the same category as Saidi and his accountant.'

It was a strange attitude, with a large dose of idealism. But it won my admiration. During dinner I put on my headphones to listen to a little of what was on the recorder, which Mahmoud said amounted to more than ten hours. I was really excited.

I gave him the four hundred dollars, and we agreed to meet the next day. I wanted to drive him back to his hotel, but he said he could walk. Part of me knew he would never show up again. He played his part well and in the end extracted the amount that he wanted from me. He fooled me. But don't we always do that? Today he deceived me and tomorrow I will deceive someone else, also with good intentions, and so on.

I was busy writing a novel called *The Uncertain and Last Journey* and didn't want to abandon it to pursue the incomplete story told in the recordings. But then one morning I received an email from someone who called himself the 'second assistant' and who said he knew me through friends we had in common and that he trusted me but at the same time didn't want to reveal his identity to me, in order to protect both of us.

This 'second assistant' sent me numerous documents over several days, saying he thought they should be made public. They were about the activities of a government agency called the Tracking and Pursuit Department, and it was very exciting when I found that the documents referred to aspects of the story that Mahmoud had told me.

With my bottle of Black Label on the plastic table on the balcony, I sat down and drank slowly and with pleasure. I forgot about my novel and breathed in the smell of the trees that the moist night breeze carried from the river, and listened again, through the speaker on the digital recorder, to Mahmoud al-Sawadi's confessions and the tales of the Criminal Who Has No Name.

2

On his first day in detention, Mahmoud al-Sawadi was inter-
rogated for many hours. They didn't manage to get much
out of him.

'I'm just a member of staff. Saidi pays me a salary,'
Mahmoud said repeatedly, and they felt like he was telling
the truth. They didn't beat him, as he had expected – they
didn't harm him in any way. He spent the night with other
detainees, and early in the morning he was summoned
to sign a statement. They gave him back his wallet, his
mobile phone and his other belongings, then took him
to the door, saying he must cooperate and inform the
authorities of any new information he came across about
Saidi.

All this was only the first stage of Mahmoud's misfortunes.
He had lost an excellent job. He had been waiting to be paid
at the end of the month so he could settle his debts with
the hotel. And now he couldn't take a job as a mere editor at
another magazine or newspaper, having become accustomed
to the power and influence of being editor-in-chief, not to
mention the lifestyle he had grown used to because of Saidi.
He had put too much trust in Saidi.

Mahmoud sold his best clothes and shoes to the second-
hand clothes dealers at Bab al-Sharqi and agreed to sell the
rest of his stuff to some friends. Before selling his phone to
one of his friends, he made three last calls. The first was to
his elder brother Abdullah, to tell him he would be coming
back to Maysan.

'Why are you coming back? Aren't you happy in Baghdad?'
asked Abdullah.

'No. I miss you. Baghdad's heading for civil war. I'm worried I might die from a car bomb one morning.'

'But your work is there. Try to be careful.'

'The people who die every day are usually careful,' said Mahmoud.

'I don't understand, Mahmoud. You know your friend is now a senior official in the province. He might remember you and make trouble for you.'

'He won't remember me. He's too important now to bother with me. My article's ancient history.'

'As you say, brother,' said Abdullah. 'You know we miss you.'

'Good, I'll come back. Don't call me on this phone – I'm about to sell it. When I get home, I'll tell you what happened here.'

'Come home safe now.'

His second call was to his friend Hazem Abboud, who told him he wouldn't be back in Baghdad until the next week. He was busy taking pictures with the US military unit and might email Mahmoud some pictures for the magazine.

'What magazine?' said Mahmoud. 'There is no more magazine. I wanted to see you before I go back to Maysan.'

Hazem was taken by surprise. They chatted for three minutes, but when it became clear that Mahmoud wouldn't get to see his friend, Mahmoud looked for another number to call. The number 666 appeared on the screen, and he pressed the Call button and put the phone to his ear. A soft female voice answered: 'The number you have dialled is not valid or is out of service. Please . . .'

He wanted to hear her voice and see her before he left Baghdad. He didn't believe what Saidi or Sultan had said – they were lying and trying to tarnish her image. He knew he had a chance with her. If he heard her voice now, instead of that automated voice, he would find a good excuse to stay in Baghdad, even if he had to live in the Orouba Hotel again, with its stuffy, humid rooms, and if he had to work at any newspaper or magazine, whatever the pay. She was the only person who could give him hope and make him act a little mad – madness and hope that he greatly needed right now.

He called her number again, and again he got the automated message. He felt very bitter, as if night were descending on him, a night that would never end. He opened the back of his phone and lifted up the battery so he could take out the SIM card. He put the battery back in place and snapped on the back of the phone. Then he went to give the phone to his friend who had bought it. He put the SIM card in his pocket, then took out the digital recorder to try to sell it.

Mahmoud had told me all the details over two days, and I had listened to the recordings on the digital device. I was struck by the fact that the voice on the recordings, attributed to the man Mahmoud called Frankenstein, was deep, like that of a well-known broadcaster. I had suspicions that the whole story was made up, but a week later, in one of the wards at the Kindi Hospital, I heard the voice again, when I sat down next to the bed of an old man called Abu Salim. He told me further interesting details relevant to the story of this Frankenstein. I couldn't be absolutely sure the voices belonged to the same person, but the story completely engrossed me, and I started looking for other sources to corroborate it.

Mahmoud sold all his possessions and paid off the staff of *al-Haqiqa* magazine. He packed a small bag, the one he had originally brought with him from Maysan, and settled his account at the Dilshad Hotel.

The country was about to succumb to further waves of violence. It made sense to move away, and that's what many of Mahmoud's friends would do. Farid Shawwaf was going back to his little village near Ishaqi, north of Baghdad; he was going to renounce, at least temporarily, the glory of satellite television and smart suits. Zaid Murshid was going to Hilla. Adnan al-Anwar would go to Najaf, where his family and uncles lived. Because of his work as a press photographer embedded with US military units, Hazem Abboud wouldn't be able to go back to Baghdad's Sadr City, and he wouldn't find the Orouba Hotel still standing, or Abu Anmar; he would end up sharing a room in another cheap hotel with a photographer friend.

3

Abu Salim left the Kindi Hospital on crutches. His children came to discharge him. They didn't take him to their house on Lane 7 but rather to the home of the husband of one of Abu Salim's daughters, until they could rebuild the front part of the house.

The NGOs and archaeological authorities had asked for work to be suspended on filling in the crater that the explosion had left, because of the wall that had appeared in the middle of the pool of water from the burst sewage and drinking-water pipes. Some claimed it was part of the wall of Abbasid Baghdad and was the most important discovery in Islamic archaeology in Baghdad for many decades. Others ventured to speak, rather boldly, about the 'advantages of terrorism', which had enabled this important discovery. But the Baghdad city authorities ignored all this and took everyone by surprise by filling the large hole with soil. The spokesman for the city authorities said, 'We do not take half measures. We're going to preserve these remains for future generations, and they can judge for themselves how to deal with them. If they decide to demolish the whole Bataween district, that's their business, but for now we have to repave the street.'

Abu Salim may have left the hospital, but someone else

from Lane 7 had to stay rather longer – Hadi the junk dealer. The bandages on his hands and face had been removed, but he wasn't strong enough to get out of bed. He lay there, wondering what had happened to him and to his house, which had probably collapsed and become a real ruin. But was it really his house? By the time he left the hospital he might find that Faraj the real estate agent had levelled it, rebuilt it and registered it in his name.

But first he had to get well; he could sort out his other problems later. That's what Hadi kept telling himself, to calm himself down, although he couldn't bear having to lie down like that all the time and made desperate attempts to sit up and get out of bed.

One evening, needing to pee, he tried to get out of bed once again. The patients nearby were asleep, and the nurses on duty were elsewhere. He heaved himself upright and moved his feet, which were wrapped in bandages. Then he slowly put them down on the floor, touching the cold tiles with the tips of his toes. Within a few minutes, he had managed to stand. He started to move forward, supporting himself against his neighbours' beds. Then he put his hands on the wall and started walking slowly towards the bathroom.

Once he got there, he noticed his reflection in the mirror above the sink. The fire had completely disfigured him. He had realized this days earlier, when he came out of the coma and saw the pattern on the skin after the bandages had been removed, but he had expected his face to be in better condition. He was a horrible creature, and even if he made a full recovery he would never look the same as before. In shock, he wiped his hand along the surface of the mirror to make sure it was really a mirror and then leaned in to examine his disfigurement. He wanted to cry, but all he could do was stare. As he looked closer, he detected something deeper: this wasn't the face of Hadi the junk dealer; it was the face of someone he had convinced himself was merely a figment of his fertile imagination. It was the face of the Whatsitsname.

Hadi let out a horrible scream, startling the patients sleeping in the ward. His leg was in a plaster cast, and he slipped on the bathroom tiles and fell backwards, banging his head on the edge of the toilet seat and losing consciousness.

4

'My face changes all the time,' the Whatsitsname told the old astrologer that night. 'Nothing in me lasts long, other than my desire to keep going. I kill in order to keep going.' This was his only justification. He didn't want to perish without understanding why he was dying and where he would go after death, so he clung to life, maybe even more than others, more than those who gave him their lives and parts of their bodies – just like that, out of fear. They hadn't fought for their lives, so he deserved life more than they did. Even if they knew they couldn't prevail against him, they should at least have fought back. It wasn't honourable to surrender in battle, and what a battle! It was a battle to defend their lives, the only battle worth fighting in this life.

Fear of the Whatsitsname continued to spread. In Sadr City they spoke of him as a Wahhabi, in Adamiya as a Shiite extremist. The Iraqi government described him as an agent of foreign powers, while the spokesman for the US State Department said he was an ingenious man whose aim was to undermine the American project in Iraq.

But what project might that be? As far as Brigadier Majid was concerned, the monster itself was their project. It was the Americans who were behind this monster.

People in coffee shops spoke of seeing him during the day and vied to describe how horrible he looked. He sits with us in restaurants, goes into clothing shops, or gets on buses with us, they said. He's everywhere and has an amazing speed, jumping from roof to roof and wall to wall in the middle of the night, they added. No one knew who his next victim would be, and despite all the assurances from the government, people grew more convinced with every passing day that he would never die. They were well aware of the stories of bullets passing through him. They knew he didn't bleed and didn't let anyone catch a glimpse of his face. The definitive image of him was whatever lurked in people's heads, fed by fear and despair. It was an image that had as many forms as there were people to conjure it.

Although I had been immersed in this story for a long time, even I started to feel afraid.

5

Brigadier Sorour Majid was forced to retire. That was the last I heard. But apparently he didn't take it lying down: he sought a new job through his connections and finally succeeded in getting back into government service, not in the Tracking and Pursuit Department, which had been disbanded, but in some remote place outside the capital, as just a security officer in the local police headquarters. Yet again, he obtained an exemption from the de-Baathification decrees.

I spent many months visiting Bataween to fill in the other parts of the story. I sat in the coffee shop of Aziz the Egyptian, who said he had visited Hadi in the hospital three times. The first time, Hadi had been in a coma. The second time, Hadi spoke to him from behind layers of bandages. The third time, the doctors told him that Hadi had left without anyone noticing.

I didn't manage to speak to Faraj the real estate agent. He spent most of his time at home, and one of his sons had taken on the responsibility of running the office. Umm Salim prevented me from meeting her husband again, after my interesting first meeting with him at the Kindi Hospital. But I did get in touch with Father Josiah. I visited him in church and heard from him parts of the story of Elishva, her lost son, her daughters in Australia, and Nader Shamouni the deacon.

In messages from Maysan, Mahmoud al-Sawadi gave me the latest on his dealings with Ali Baher al-Saidi, who was on the run from justice. When I saw a picture of Saidi in an old issue of *al-Haqiqa* magazine, I remembered I had seen him before – at a conference for intellectuals at the National Theatre some years earlier. He was a brilliant and eloquent man. At the time I felt hopeful that men like Saidi would break into the political arena, rather than leave it to semi-educated people and illiterates.

The 'second assistant' continued to send me emails with documents from the Tracking and Pursuit Department, especially ones related to the inquiries that were still under way. The last document he sent me was about the junior astrologer's confession that he was responsible for killing his superior on a Baghdad street by controlling the Criminal Who Has No Name by remote suggestion and making the criminal cut off the old astrologer's hands to fit them onto his own body. But the junior astrologer strongly denied he was responsible for creating the criminal in the first place. He had succeeded only in exploiting it. He had wanted to eliminate the criminal, but his superior had intervened. That was the essential reason for the disagreement between them.

I was anxious as I wrote the story, fearing the door of my hotel room might suddenly open and I would be arrested. In the end, that's what happened. I had an incomplete seventeen-chapter version of the story in my hands when I was arrested and sent for questioning in front of a panel of Iraqi and American officers. My novel was confiscated, and they asked me many questions. They were polite and pleasant. They gave me water and a glass of tea and allowed me to smoke. They didn't harass me at all. They asked me about the documents I'd received, what I had done with them, and who this second assistant was. If he was the second, that presupposed there was a first, and the two of them must be assistants to someone. Were they my assistants? Was I running some network? What domestic or foreign connections did I have? What were my political convictions?

I was thrown into detention for a few days while their experts read the incomplete text of my novel. Then one morning they summoned me. They didn't say much. I found a written pledge on the interrogator's table. They asked me to sign it without reading it. I was worried and wanted to object, but I was afraid they would send me back to the cell. I signed the pledge in silence. They returned my personal belongings but not my copy of the novel. Apparently I was not allowed to rewrite it.

They set me free without even taking a close look at the identity card I had shown them. It was a fake, one of several I have to make it easier to get past the checkpoints that the warring sectarian militias in Baghdad sometimes set up.

The interrogation panel wasn't serious, I thought as I headed back to the hotel. It seemed like a formality. I sat in front of my computer and resumed writing. I kept at it for several days, until I received another email from the second assistant – the last message I would receive from him. It included a copy of the final report from the committee of inquiry.

I read it quickly, and was terrified. They were moving towards rearresting me. I had a feeling they would treat me differently this time.

I hurriedly gathered up my stuff, paid my hotel bill, and escaped to my house. On the way I remembered my fake identity card. I took it out of my pocket and threw it out of the taxi window. I assumed that, as in the case of the Frankenstein they had been trying to arrest, the people pursuing me would never see me again.

CHAPTER NINETEEN

The Criminal

1

Abdullah burst into his brother Mahmoud's room. 'The Mantis has been killed,' he announced. Mahmoud was half asleep on his bed, resting his eyes from the constant reading he had been doing since coming back to the house in Jidayda in Maysan. He discovered he had many books he had bought but had never read and others he wanted to reread, and he had had enough of the hustle and bustle of the outside world and needed a period of peace and tranquillity. Plus his mother was worried the Mantis might carry out the promise he had made about a year earlier to kill Mahmoud if he ever came across him in the streets of Amara, and he didn't want to make his mother anxious or cause trouble for anyone.

This went on for about two and a half months, but now his time in preventive detention was over: a group of men had ambushed the Mantis on the highway while he was travelling in a motorcade from Wasit Province. They fired a hail of bullets, killing him, the driver and some of his aides, before taking flight.

Mahmoud thought back to his theory about the three

kinds of justice, but he wasn't convinced it was valid. It was anarchy out there; there was no logic behind what was happening. He took a deep breath and gave a long sigh. What mattered now was that he had broken free of a worry that had been weighing heavily on him.

At last he left the house, with no particular destination in mind. His mother didn't even look up. When he reached the main street, he remembered he hadn't checked his email in ages.

He boarded a bus and headed for the market. He ran into some friends, who couldn't figure out why he was so cheerful. Then he headed to the Internet café, where he sat in front of a computer and opened his email. There were one hundred and eighty messages, most of them junk mail, but he noticed one message from his friend Hazem Abboud. He opened it and found ten photographs. They had been taken in various places, in the countryside and in villages, old sites and ancient buildings. In the accompanying note, Hazem explained his situation – that he would probably be able to get a green card because of his work with the US military and wouldn't be able to go back home for fear of assassination by the militias. Mahmoud felt Hazem was exaggerating and wanted to justify his long-standing wish to emigrate to the United States.

There was an email offering Mahmoud a position as Maysan correspondent for a major Baghdad newspaper. Then he found one from a name he didn't recognize; he opened it and was surprised to see that it was from Nawal al-Wazir, telling him she had tried to call him several times without success, and sending him her new phone numbers.

'You must call me, Mahmoud,' she wrote. He wanted to call her immediately, but the next message he opened made him forget everything else. It was from Ali Baher al-Saidi. He had clearly spent much time and effort drafting it. Mahmoud found it completely engrossing.

2

Dear Mahmoud,

How are you?

I've called you dozens of times but it seems your phone is permanently switched off. I've been worried about you, my friend. I heard from some friends about the interrogation you went through. That hurt me. They are real bastards. I fear they may have deeply distorted the way you see me and I may not be able to undo the damage, but you are very dear to me. I swear by the life of my mother, who was killed by terrorists in Ramadi on the highway to Jordan, and by the lives of my dear sisters, that I didn't steal a single penny from this lousy government or the American occupiers. It was a conspiracy against me, and I'm now on the run from their broken judicial system. They wanted to drive me out of the country because they knew I had an honest plan for the country and that the moment of confrontation was coming between the sincere patriots and those who work for foreign interests. They wanted to eat me for lunch before I could eat them for dinner.

You're not obliged to believe what I say. But tell me honestly, did I ever lie to you? Didn't I promote you personally, to give you the chance you deserved? Did I mistreat you or anyone else? Wasn't I helpful and cooperative with everyone? Think back a little and try to remember.

You may wonder why I'm spending this time and effort writing to you and why I'm so eager to persuade you of my point of view. I'm not interested in all the

things that have been said about me, or the smears in
the press, or the way they've portrayed me as an international criminal, or the arrest warrant they've asked
Interpol to issue. I can deal with those things. I have
a strong heart, and I have the energy to fight those
bastards. I'll beat them one day, you'll see. But I can't
bear the idea that you might think ill of me, especially
you. It matters because I see myself in you. We're very
much alike, even if you can't see the resemblance. I
think we are similar and you are someone pure and
noble, and what you think of me is more important
than anything else.

You'll remember Brigadier Majid and the time we
went to see him. After lunch, he told me what the
senior astrologer working with him had told him. We
didn't go there to buy a printing press or to interview
him or anything else. I couldn't tell you the truth at the
time, in case you got the wrong idea. I preferred to
keep it to myself, but now I feel compelled to disclose
it: the visit was for something specific – so his astrologers could tell your future. The future of Mahmoud
al-Sawadi. And I was really stunned and surprised by
what I heard. The senior astrologer said 'this young
man', meaning you, had a brilliant future. He would rise
to become one of the most important people in Iraq,
but he needed training. He needed a challenge in order
to learn how to handle it. I don't know how you'll take
this now, but in precisely fifteen years, Mahmoud, you
will become prime minister of Iraq. Yes, you will be
Prime Minister Mahmoud al-Sawadi. And I, ever since
I heard this and believed it, have made you my project,
and I have given myself a specific role in this project.
I will be John the Baptist, and you will be Christ. I will
help the weak sapling become a mighty tree.

267

I shall be back in Baghdad soon, Mahmoud. I will disprove all the charges against me, and you will see people go on trial because of the malicious accusations they've made against me. I'll get in touch with you from there so we can start again and work together.

Be sure to remember the senior astrologer's prediction, or try to forget it. It makes no difference, because what is inevitable will come true one day.

3

It was a bombshell. It reminded Mahmoud of the way Saidi spoke, of how persuasive he was. Mahmoud couldn't help having a whole range of feelings towards Saidi, who had given him plenty of help and exposed him to new experiences. He had become more mature and knowledgeable because of him. He was intrigued by the talk of the astrologers and the new explanation that Saidi offered for their visit to the Tracking and Pursuit Department. So Mahmoud had been at the centre of events when he thought he was on the periphery.

Mahmoud put his hands on the keyboard, eager to answer Saidi's email. He was on the verge of apologizing for thinking ill of him, but he soon remembered a slew of uncomfortable facts. He remembered how, under interrogation, he had almost to beg to defend himself against the accusation that he had helped to steal thirteen million dollars. He thought back to many times Saidi had contradicted himself. Sitting in the Internet café, he tried to form a clear, reliable picture of Saidi's convictions and principles, but he couldn't.

Mahmoud tapped lightly on the keys, but he didn't write anything. He was overcome with confusing emotions, and he noticed he was grinding his teeth. After everything Mahmoud had been through, Saidi had managed to trick him and win him over to his cause. He had scored a goal yet again.

'Fuck you,' Mahmoud typed quickly in English. He made the words big and red. He was about to press Send but stopped himself. He hesitated for about ten seconds, then deleted the two words. He combined Saidi's message and Hazem Abboud's into one and sent it to the writer. He signed out of his email account and left the café.

Later Mahmoud would send the writer another message, explaining why he decided against answering Saidi's email. He went out into the street and kept walking. He lit a cigarette and looked up at the ominous clouds. It was like those days he had spent in Baghdad a year earlier, when he had met Ali Baher al-Saidi, Nawal al-Wazir, and the others.

He walked towards the market, thinking, 'What if Saidi was telling the truth?' But he sensed it was all fantasies and lies. Saidi was preparing to dump another disaster on the head of gullible Mahmoud. But what if one per cent of his story were true? Isn't life a blend of things that are plausible and others that are hard to believe? Isn't it possible that Saidi reaching out to Mahmoud was one of those hard-to-believe things?

That's why Mahmoud didn't send a hostile response to Saidi's message, or any other kind of response. He left things in a grey area, like the sky that day, trying to use Saidi's own style against him, leaving him uncertain.

4

On 21 February 2006, the supreme security commanders in Baghdad announced they had finally arrested the dangerous criminal that official reports called Criminal X, and that the public called the Whatsitsname, along with many other names.

They projected a large picture of him on a big screen and announced his name: Hadi Hassani Aidros, a resident of Bataween and commonly known as Hadi al-Attag, the junk dealer.

The defendant had confessed to all the crimes he was accused of, including leading a murder gang, dismembering his victims, and planting them in back streets around Baghdad in order to spread alarm and fear. He had planned the explosion at the Sadeer Novotel by means of a rubbish truck packed with explosives and driven by a suicide bomber who was one of his followers. He had murdered a number of foreign security contractors and was responsible for the horrific explosion in Bataween, which resulted in deaths, destroyed houses, and did inestimable damage to Iraq's architectural heritage. On top of that, the criminal was implicated in acts of sectarian violence and in murders for hire on behalf of gangs and sectarian groups.

Aziz the Egyptian saw the picture of his close friend on television and didn't recognize him. That wasn't Hadi the junk dealer. That's what most of the people in the coffee shop said too. But when they broadcast recordings of the criminal's confessions, the voice was very similar to Hadi's. How could he be a murderer?

Seeing Hadi's disfigured face on television, while sitting with his family at home, Mahmoud al-Sawadi thought this was just another massive mistake. They wanted to close the case in any way possible. It was inconceivable that this elderly man was a dangerous criminal. He had sat with him for hours: he was just a drunkard with an unstable personal life and a powerful imagination, but his story about the Whatsitsname still posed many questions for Mahmoud. Hadi was permanently scatterbrained. He didn't have any of

the eloquence or composure apparent in the digital recordings of the Whatsitsname's strange long monologues. It was
impossible that Hadi was the Whatsitsname.

5

When people heard the news, the sky over Baghdad crack-
led with gunfire. Everyone was in a state of hysterical joy,
especially in Bataween. Nobody could believe that this
frightening criminal had been living among them, but what
the government said must be true.

Umm Salim came out and danced in the street, rattling her
golden bracelets on her white arms. Her husband looked on
shyly through the crack in the door, his hands pressed into
the pockets of his pyjama top. Veronica, the old Armenian
woman, came out to throw chewing gum and sweets on
the heads of the children in the lane, and despite the black
clouds that were gathering, people continued to dance in the
streets and on the roofs of buildings for more than an hour.
They were tasting a kind of joy they had forgotten in the
decades of disasters that had befallen the country. Everyone
was happy, even Faraj the real estate agent, who had been
sunk in pessimism and despair since the massive explosion
in Lane 7. Aziz saw the spontaneous celebrations but still
wasn't convinced that Hadi was the criminal. It was impossible. But he went to dance outside the coffee shop anyway.

Reduced to a state of childlike elation, no one could see, or
even tried to see, those timid eyes looking out from behind
the balconies and windows of the abandoned Orouba Hotel.

Since Faraj had taken down the sign outside, the hotel
hadn't had a name. It was no longer the Orouba Hotel, and
it hadn't yet become the Grand Prophet Hotel, as Faraj

had been planning to call it. He had lost a large part of his fortune on the two properties, one of which had been totally destroyed, the other seriously damaged. To repair it he would have had to spend a fortune, so he left it as it was – deserted, a ruin. He didn't give it another thought. Cats made their homes there, and young men might use it as a venue for hasty love trysts. Rowdier events might have taken place there, but nobody knew exactly. Nabu the cat roamed around the hotel. The spectre of an unknown man also lingered there, standing for the past hour at the glassless window of a third-floor room, silently watching the people celebrate, smoking and looking every now and then at the dark clouds overhead.

Nabu climbed the stairs, up the carpet that had been ripped long ago. The old cat jumped over the legs of broken chairs, then went up to the figure standing by the window. It wound itself around his left leg, then looked out and meowed softly. The man threw his cigarette out the window and listened as a local music troupe appeared on the street below, followed by a large throng of children cheering and clapping. Thunder shook the sky, and it began to pour. People ran home, and the music and celebrations stopped. Only the sound of the rain remained.

The man crouched down to pet the old cat, which had lost even more of its hair. They were now close friends.

Baghdad
2008–12

Oneworld, Many Voices

**Bringing you exceptional writing
from around the world**

The Unit by Ninni Holmqvist (Swedish)
Translated by Marlaine Delargy

Twice Born by Margaret Mazzantini (Italian)
Translated by Ann Gagliardi

Things We Left Unsaid by Zoya Pirzad (Persian)
Translated by Franklin Lewis

The Space Between Us by Zoya Pirzad (Persian)
Translated by Amy Motlagh

The Hen Who Dreamed She Could Fly by Sun-mi Hwang
(Korean) Translated by Chi-Young Kim

The Hilltop by Assaf Gavron (Hebrew)
Translated by Steven Cohen

Morning Sea by Margaret Mazzantini (Italian)
Translated by Ann Gagliardi

A Perfect Crime by A Yi (Chinese)
Translated by Anna Holmwood

The Meursault Investigation by Kamel Daoud (French)
Translated by John Cullen

Minus Me by Ingelin Røssland (YA) (Norwegian)
Translated by Deborah Dawkin

Laurus by Eugene Vodolazkin (Russian)
Translated by Lisa C. Hayden

Masha Regina by Vadim Levental (Russian)
Translated by Lisa C. Hayden

French Concession by Xiao Bai (Chinese)
Translated by Chenxin Jiang

The Sky Over Lima by Juan Gómez Bárcena (Spanish)
Translated by Andrea Rosenberg

A Very Special Year by Thomas Montasser (German)
Translated by Jamie Bulloch

Umami by Laia Jufresa (Spanish)
Translated by Sophie Hughes

The Hermit by Thomas Rydahl (Danish)
Translated by K.E. Semmel

The Peculiar Life of a Lonely Postman by Denis Thériault
(French) Translated by Liedewy Hawke

Three Envelopes by Nir Hezroni (Hebrew)
Translated by Steven Cohen

Fever Dream by Samanta Schweblin (Spanish)
Translated by Megan McDowell

The Postman's Fiancée by Denis Thériault (French)
Translated by John Cullen

The Invisible Life of Euridice Gusmao by Martha Batalha
(Brazilian Portuguese) Translated by Eric M. B. Becker

The Temptation to Be Happy by Lorenzo Marone
(Italian) Translated by Shaun Whiteside

Sweet Bean Paste by Durian Sukegawa (Japanese)
Translated by Alison Watts

They Know Not What They Do by Jussi Valtonen (Finnish)
Translated by Kristian London

The Tiger and the Acrobat by Susanna Tamaro (Italian)
Translated by Nicoleugenia Prezzavento and Vicki Satlow

The Woman at 1,000 Degrees by Hallgrímur Helgason
(Icelandic) Translated by Brian FitzGibbon

Frankenstein in Baghdad by Ahmed Saadawi (Arabic)
Translated by Jonathan Wright

Back Up by Paul Colize (French)
Translated by Louise Rogers Lalaurie

Damnation by Peter Beck (German)
Translated by Jamie Bulloch

Oneiron by Laura Lindstedt (Finnish)
Translated by Owen Witesman

The Boy Who Belonged to the Sea by Denis Thériault
(French) Translated by Liedewy Hawke

The Baghdad Clock by Shahad Al Rawi (Arabic)
Translated by Luke Leafgren

The Aviator by Eugene Vodolazkin (Russian)
Translated by Lisa C. Hayden

Lala by Jacek Dehnel (Polish)
Translated by Antonia Lloyd-Jones

Bogotá 39: New Voices from Latin America
(Spanish and Portuguese) Short story anthology

Last Instructions by Nir Hezroni (Hebrew)
Translated by Steven Cohen

The Day I Found You by Pedro Chagas Freitas (Portuguese)
Translated by Daniel Hahn

Solovyov and Larionov by Eugene Vodolazkin (Russian)
Translated by Lisa C. Hayden

In/Half by Jasmin B. Frelih (Slovenian)
Translated by Jason Blake

Ahmed Saadawi is an Iraqi novelist, poet, screenwriter and documentary filmmaker. In 2010 he was selected for Beirut39, as one of the thirty-nine best Arab authors under the age of forty, and in 2014 he became the first Iraqi to win the prestigious International Prize for Arabic Fiction. This prize was awarded to *Frankenstein in Baghdad*, which also won Le Grand Prix de L'Imaginaire in 2017. He lives in Baghdad.

Jonathan Wright studied Arabic at Oxford University. He is the translator of Hassan Blasim's *The Corpse Exhibition*, which won the Independent Foreign Fiction Prize in 2014. He lives in London.